His Majesty's
Well-Beloved

Baroness Emmuska Orczy

His Majesty's Well-Beloved

Copyright © 2020 Bibliotech Press
All rights reserved

ISBN: 978-1-64799-109-8

CHAPTER

CHAPTER I

HOW IT ALL BEGAN

1

From Mr. John Honeywood, clerk to Mr. Theophilus Baggs, attorney-at-law, to Mistress Mary Saunderson, of the Duke's Theatre in Lincoln's Inn Fields.

1662. October the 10th at 85, Chancery Lane in the City of London. Honoured Mistress,—

May it please you that I, an humble Clerk and Scrivener, do venture to address so talented a Lady; but there is that upon my Conscience which compels me to write these lines. The Goodness and Charity of Mistress Saunderson are well known, and 'tis not as a Suppliant that I crave pardon for my Presumption, but rather as one whose fidelity and loyalty have oft been tried and never been found wanting. 'Tis said, most gracious Mistress, that your fancy hath been touched by the tenderness and devotion of a Man who is as dear to me as if he were mine own Brother, but that You hesitate to bestow upon him that for which he craves more than for anything in the world, your Hand and Heart. And this because of many Rumours which have sullied his fair Name. Mr. Betterton, Madam, hath many enemies. How could this be otherwise seeing that so vast a measure of Success hath attended his career, and that the King's most gracious Majesty doth honour him with Friendship and Regard to the exclusion of others who are envious of so great a fame? Those Enemies now, Madam, seeing that your Heart hath been touched with the man's grace and bearing, rather than with his undying Renown, have set themselves the task of blackening Mr. Betterton's character before your eyes, thus causing you mayhap grievous Sorrow and Disappointment. But this I do swear by all that I hold most sacred, that Mr. Betterton hath never committed a mean Act in his life nor done aught to forfeit your Regard. Caustic of wit he is, but neither a Braggart nor a Bully; he hath been credited with many good Fortunes, but so hath every Gentleman in the Kingdom, and there is no discredit attached to a man for subjugating the Hearts of those that are both frail and fair. My Lady Castlemaine hath bestowed many favours on Mr. Betterton, so hath the Countess of Shrewsbury, and there are others, at least the Gossips do aver it. But on my Soul and Honour, he hath never ceased to love You, until the day when a certain great Lady came across his path for his misfortune and his undying Regret. And even so, Madam, though appearances are against him, I own, let me assure You that the swerving of his Allegiance to You was not only transitory but it was never one of the Heart—it was a mere aberration of the senses. He may never forget the Lady—he certainly will never forget her Cruelty—but he no longer loves Her, never did love Her as he loves You, with his Heart and Mind, with Tenderness and Devotion. The other was only a Dream—a fitful fancy: his Love for You is as immortal as his Fame. Therefore, gracious Mistress, I, the humble Friend of so great a Man, have ventured to set forth for your perusal that which he himself would be too proud to put before you—namely, his Justification. As for the rest, what I am about to relate is the true Historie of Mr. Betterton's Romance, the only one which might give you cause for sorrow, yet none for uneasiness, because that Romance is now a thing of the past, like unto a Flower that is faded and without fragrance, even though it still lies pressed between the pages of a great man's Book of Life. Everything else is mere Episode. But this which I have here set down will show you how much nobility of heart and grandeur of Character lies hidden beneath the flippant and at times grim exterior of the Man whom you have honoured with your regard.

The writing of the Historie hath caused me much anxiety and deep thought. I desired to present the Truth before you, and not the highly-coloured effusions of a Partisan. I have slurred over nothing, concealed nothing. An you, gracious Mistress, have the patience to read unto the End, I am confident that any Hesitation as to your Future which may still linger in your Heart will vanish with the more intimate Knowledge of the true Facts of the case, as well as of the Man whose faults are of his own Time and of his Entourage, but whose Merits are for the whole World to know and to cherish, for as many Cycles of years as there will be Englishmen to speak the Words of English Poets.

2

Dare I take you back, honoured Mistress, to those humble days, five years ago, when first I entered the Household of your worthy Uncle, Mr. Theophilus Baggs, and of his still more worthy Spouse, Mistress Euphrosine, where for a small—very small—

stipend, and free board and lodging, I copied legal documents, Leases, Wills and Indentures for my Employer?

You, fair Lady, were then the only ray of Sunshine which illumined the darkness of my dreary Life. Yours was a Gaiety which nothing could damp, a Courage and Vitality which not even the nagging disposition of Mistress Euphrosine succeeded in crushing. And when, smarting under her many Chidings, my stomach craving for a small Measure of satisfaction, my Bones aching from the hardness of my bed, I saw your slim Figure flitting, elf-like, from kitchen to living-room, your full young Throat bursting with song like that of a Bird at the first scent of Spring, I would find my lot less hard, the bread less sour, even Mistress Euphrosine's tongue less acrimonious. My poor, atrophied Heart felt the warmth of your Smile.

Then sometimes, when my Work was done and my Employers occupied with their own affairs, You used to allow me to be of service to you, to help you wash the dishes which your dainty Hands should never have been allowed to touch.

Oh! how I writhed when I heard Mistress Euphrosine ordering You about as if You were a kitchen-wench, rather than her husband's Niece, who was honouring his House with your presence! You, so exquisite, so perfect, so cultured, to be the Handmaid of a pair of sour, ill-conditioned Reprobates who were not worthy to tie the lacets of your dainty shoes. With what Joy I performed the menial tasks which never should have been allotted to You, I never until now have dared to tell. I did not think that any Man could find dish-washing and floor-scrubbing quite so enchanting. But then no other Man hath ever to my knowledge performed such tasks under such happy circumstances; with You standing before me, smiling and laughing at my clumsiness, your shapely arms akimbo, your Voice now rippling into Song, now chaffing me with Words full of kindness and good-humour.

I have known many happy Hours since that Day, Mistress, and many Hours full of Sorrow, but none so full of pulsating Life as those which outwardly had seemed so miserable.

And then that wonderful afternoon when Mr. Theophilus Baggs and his Spouse being safely out of the way, we stole out together and spent a few hours at the Play! Do you remember the day on which we ventured on the Escapade? Mr. Baggs and Mistress Euphrosine had gone to Hampton Court: he to see a noble Client and she to accompany him. The day being fine and the Client being a Lady possessed of well-known charms, Mistress Euphrosine would not have trusted her Lord alone in the company of such a forward Minx—at least, those were her Words, which she uttered in my hearing two Days before the memorable Expedition.

Memorable, indeed, it was to me!

Mr. Baggs left a sheaf of Documents for me to copy, which would—he thought—keep me occupied during the whole course of a long Day. You too, fair Mistress, were to be kept busy during the worthy couple's absence, by scrubbing and polishing and sewing—Mistress Euphrosine holding all idleness in abhorrence.

I marvel if you remember it all!

I do, as if it had occurred yesterday! We sat up half the Night previous to our Taskmasters' departure; you polishing and sewing, and I copying away for very life. You remember? Our joint Savings for the past six Months we had counted up together. They amounted to three shillings. One shilling we spent in oil for our lamps, so that we might complete our Tasks during the Night. This left us free for the great and glorious Purpose which we had in our Minds and which we had planned and brooded over for Days and Weeks.

We meant to go to the Play!

It seems strange now, in view of your Renown, fair Mistress, and of mine own intimacy with Mr. Betterton, that You and I had both reached an age of Man and Womanhood without ever having been to the Play. Yet You belonged from childhood to the household of Mistress Euphrosine Baggs, who is own sister to Mr. Betterton. But that worthy Woman abhorred the Stage and all that pertained to it, and she blushed—aye, blushed!—at thought of the marvellous Fame attained by her illustrious Brother.

Do you remember confiding to me, less than a month after I first entered the household of Mr. Baggs, that You were pining to go to the Play? You had seen Mr. Betterton once or twice when he came to visit his Sister—which he did not do very often—but you had never actually been made acquainted with him, nor had you ever seen him act. And You told me how handsome he was, and how distinguished; and your dark Eyes would flash with enthusiasm at thought of the Actor's Art and of the Actor's Power.

I had never seen him at all in those Days, but I loved to hear about him. Strange what a fascination the Stage exercised over so insignificant and so mean a creature as I!

Will you ever forget the dawn of that glorious Day, fair Mistress?

Mr. Baggs and his Spouse went off quite early, to catch the chaise at La Belle Sauvage which would take them to Hampton Court. But however early they went, we thought them mighty slow in making a start. An hundred Recommendations, Orderings, Scoldings, had to be gone through ere the respectable Couple, carrying provisions for the day in a Bandana Handkerchief, finally got on the way.

It was a perfect Morning early in March, with the first scent and feel of Spring in the air. Not a Cloud in the Sky. By Midday our tasks were entirely accomplished and we were free! Free as the Birds in the air, free as two 'prentices out for a holiday! But little did we eat, I remember. We were too excited for hunger; nor had Mistress Euphrosine left much in the larder for us. What did we care? Our Enthusiasm, our Eagerness, were Cook and Scullion for us, that day!

We were going to the Play!

Oh! how we tripped to Cockpit Lane, asking our way from passers-by, for we knew so little of London—fashionable London, that is; the London of Gaiety and Laughter, of careless Thoughts and wayward Moods. Holding hands, we hurried through the Streets. You wore a dark Cape with a Hood to hide your pretty Face and your soft brown Hair, lest some Acquaintance of your Uncle's should chance to see You and betray our guilty secret.

Do you remember how we met Mr. Rhodes, the bookseller, and friend of Mr. Baggs?—he to whom young Mr. Betterton was even then apprenticed. At the corner of Princes Street we came nose to nose with him, and but for great presence of mind on my part when, without an instant's hesitation, I ran straight at him and butted him in the Stomach so that he lost his Balance for the moment and only recovered complete Consciousness after we had disappeared round the corner of the Street, he no doubt would have recognised us and betrayed our naughty Secret.

Oh, what a fright we had! I can see You now, leaning, breathless and panting, against the street corner, your Hand pressed to your Bosom, your Eyes shining like Stars!

As for the rest, it is all confusion in my mind. The Crowd, the Bustle, the Noise, this great Assembly, the like of which I had never seen before. I do not know how we came to our seats. All I know is that we were there, looking down upon the moving throng. I remember that some Worthy of obvious note was sitting next to me, and was perpetually treading upon my toes. But this I did not mind, for he was good enough to point out to me the various Notabilities amongst the Audience or upon the Stage; and I was greatly marvelled and awed by the wonderful familiarity with which he spoke of all these distinguished People.

"There sits General Monk. Brave old George! By gad! 'twere interesting to know what goes on inside that square Head of his! King or Protector, which is it to be? Or Protector and King! George knows; and you mark my words, young Sir, George will be the one to decide. Old Noll is sick; he can't last long. And Master Richard hath not much affection for his Father's Friends—calls them Reprobates and ungodly. Well! can you see George being rebuked by Master Richard for going to the Play?"

And I, not being on such intimate terms with the Lord Protector's Son or with General Monk, could offer no opinion on the subject. And after a while my Neighbour went on glibly:

"Ah! here comes my Lady Viner, flaunting silks and satins. Aye, the fair Alice—his third Wife, mark you!—knows how to spend the money which her Lord hath been at such pains to scrape together. By gad! who'd have thought to see red-haired Polly Ann so soon after the demise of His Grace! See, not an inch of widows' Weeds doth she wear in honour of the old Dotard who did her the infinite favour of dying just in the nick of time...."

And so on, the Man would babble in a continuous stream of talk. You, Mistress, listened to him open-mouthed, your great brown Eyes aglow with curiosity and with excitement. You and I knew but little of those great Folk, and seeing them all around us, prepared for the same enjoyment which we had paid to obtain, made us quite intoxicated with eagerness.

Our Neighbour, who of a truth seemed to know everything, expressed great surprise at the fact that Old Noll—as he so unceremoniously named the Lord Protector—had tolerated the opening of the Cockpit. "But," he added sententiously, "Bill Davenant could wheedle a block of ice out of the devil, if he chose."

4

Of the Play I remember but little. I was in truth much too excited to take it all in. And sitting so near You, Mistress—for the Place was overcrowded—my Knee touching yours, your dear little

6

hand darting out from time to time to grip mine convulsively during the more palpitating moments of the Entertainment, was quite as much as an humble Clerk's brain could hold.

There was a great deal of Music—that I do remember. Also that the entertainment was termed an opera and that the name of the piece was "The Cruelty of the Spaniards in Peru." My omniscient Neighbour told me presently that no doubt the Performance was an artful piece of Flattery on the part of Bill (meaning, I suppose, Sir William Davenant) who, by blackening the Spaniards, made Old Noll's tyranny appear like bountiful Mercies.

But I did not like to hear our Lord Protector spoken of with such levity. Moreover, my Neighbour's incessant Chatter distracted me from the Stage.

What I do remember more vividly than anything else on that memorable Day was your cry of delight when Mr. Betterton appeared upon the Stage. I do not know if you had actually spoken with him before; I certainly had never even seen him. Mr. Betterton was then apprenticed to Mr. Rhodes, the Bookseller, and it was entirely against the Judgment and Wishes of Mistress Euphrosine Baggs, his Sister, that he adopted the Stage as an additional calling. I know that there were many high Words on that subject between Mr. Betterton and Mistress Euphrosine, Mr. Rhodes greatly supporting the young Man in his Desire, he having already formulated schemes of his own for the management of a Theatre, and extolling the virtues of the Actor's Art and the vastly lucrative State thereof.

But Mistress Euphrosine would have none of it. Actors were Rogues and Vagabonds, she said, ungodly Reprobates who were unfit, when dead, to be buried in consecrated ground. She would never consent to seeing a Brother of hers follow so disreputable a Calling. From high words it came to an open Quarrel, and though I had been over a year in the House of Mr. Theophilus Baggs, I had never until this day set eyes on young Mr. Betterton.

He was not taking a very important part in the Opera, but there was no denying the fact that as soon as he appeared upon the Stage his very Presence did throw every other Actor into the shade. The Ladies in the Boxes gave a deep sigh of content, gazing on him with admiring eyes and bestowing loud Applause upon his every Word. And when Mr. Betterton threw out his Arms with a gesture expressive of a noble Passion and spoke the ringing lines: "And tell me then, ye Sons of England..."—his beautiful Voice rising and falling with the perfect cadence of an exquisite Harmony—the uproar of Enthusiasm became wellnigh deafening. The Ladies clapped their Hands and waved their Handkerchiefs, the Gentlemen stamped their feet upon the floor; and some, lifting their Hats, threw them with a flourish upon the Stage, so that anon Mr. Betterton stood with a score or more Hats all round his feet, and was greatly perturbed as to how he should sort them out and restore them to their rightful Owners.

Ah, it was a glorious Day! Nothing could mar the perfection of its Course. No! not even the Rain which presently began to patter over the Spectators, and anon fell in torrents, so that those who were in the Pit had to beat a precipitate retreat, scrambling helter-skelter over the Benches in a wild endeavour to get under cover.

This incident somewhat marred the Harmony of the Ending, because to see Ladies and Gentlemen struggling and scrambling to climb from bench to bench under a Deluge of Rain, was in truth a very droll Spectacle; and the attention of those in the Boxes was divided between the Happenings on the Stage and the antics of the rest of the Audience.

You and I, fair Mistress, up aloft in our humble place, were far better sheltered than the more grand Folk in the Pit. I put your Cloak around your Shoulders to protect You against the Cold, and thus sitting close together, my knee still resting against yours, we watched the Performance until the end.

5

How we went home that afternoon I do not remember. I know that it was raining heavily and that we got very wet. But this caused me no Inconvenience, because it gave me the privilege of placing my Arm round your Shoulders so as to keep your Cloak from falling. Also my Mind was too full of what I had seen to heed the paltry discomfort of a Wetting. My thoughts were of the Play, the Music, the brilliant Assembly; yours, Mistress, were of Mr. Betterton. Of him you prattled all the way home, to the exclusion of every other Topic. And if your enthusiastic Eulogy of that talented Person did at times send a pang of Sorrow through my Heart, You at least were unaware of my Trouble. Not that I took no share in your Enthusiasm. I did it whole-heartedly. Never had I admired a Man before as I did Mr. Betterton on that Day. His Presence was commanding, his Face striking, his Voice at times masterful and full of Power, at others infinitely sweet. My officious and talkative Neighbour, just before the Rain came down and rendered him dumb, had remarked to me with a great air of Knowledge and of Finality: "Mark my word, young Sir, England will hear something presently of Tommy Betterton."

It was not until we reached the corner of Chancery Lane that we were forced to descend to the Realities of Life. We had had a glorious Day, and for many Hours had wholly forgotten the many Annoyances and Discomforts with which our lives were beset. Now we were a little tired and exceedingly wet. Mistress Euphrosine's Scoldings, our oft empty stomachs, hard Beds and cheerless Lives loomed once more largely upon the Horizon of our mental vision.

Our Pace began to slacken; your glib Tongue was stilled. Holding Hands now, we hurried home in silence, our Minds stirred by a still vague Sense of Fear.

Nor was that Fear unjustified, alas! as subsequent Events proved. No sooner had We entered the House than We knew that We were discovered. Mr. Baggs' cloak, hung up in the Hall, revealed the terrifying Fact that he and his indomitable Spouse had unaccountably returned at this hour. No doubt that the Weather was the primary cause of this untoward Event: its immediate result was a Volley of abuse poured upon our Heads by Mistress Euphrosine's eloquent Tongue. We were Reprobates, Spawns and Children of the Devil! We were Liars and Cheats and Thieves! We had deserved God's wrath and eternal punishment! Heavens above! how she did talk! And we, alas! could not escape that vituperative Torrent.

We had fled into the Kitchen as soon as We had realised that we were fairly caught; but Mistress Euphrosine had followed us thither and had closed the door behind her. And now, standing facing Us, her large, gaunt Body barring every egress, she talked and talked until You, fair Mistress, gave way to a passionate Flood of tears.

All our Pleasure, our Joy, had vanished; driven hence by the vixenish Tongue of a soured Harridan. I was beside myself with Rage. But for your restraining influence, I could have struck that shrieking Virago, and for ever after have destroyed what was the very Essence of my Life. For she would have turned me out of Doors then and there, and I should have been driven forth from your Presence, perhaps never to return.

The sight of your Patience and of your Goodness helped to deaden my Wrath. I hung my Head and bit my Tongue lest it should betray me into saying things which I should have regretted to the end of my Days.

And thus that memorable Day came to a close. Somehow, it stands before my mind as would the first legible Page in the Book of my Life. Before it, everything was blurred; but that Page is clear. I can read it now, even after four years. For the first time, destiny had writ on it two Names in bold, indelible Characters—yours, Mistress, and that of Mr. Betterton. Henceforth, not a Day in my Life would pass without one of You looming largely in its Scheme.

Mary Saunderson! Tom Betterton! My very pulses seem to beat to the tune of those two Names! I knew then, by one of those subtle intuitions which no Man has ever succeeded in comprehending, that Heaven itself had intended You for one another. How then could I stand by and see the Wickedness of Man striving to interfere with the decrees of God?

CHAPTER II

THE RIFT WITHIN THE LUTE

1

After that memorable Day, Mistress, we were like naughty Children who were being punished for playing truant out of School. For Weeks and Months our Lives went on with dreary monotony, with never a chance of seeing Something of that outside World of which we had caught a glimpse. You continued to sew and to scrub and to be at the beck and call of a Scold. I went on copying legal Documents till my very Brain appeared atrophied, incapable of a single happy Thought or of a joyous Hope.

Out there in the great World, many things were happening. The Lord Protector died; his Son succeeded. And then England woke to the fact that she had never cared for these Regicides, Republicans and Puritans; that in her Heart she had always loved the martyred King and longed to set his Son once more upon his Throne.

I often thought of my loquacious Neighbour at the Play, with his talk of Old Noll and Master Richard and of George. For George Monk in truth had become the Man of the hour; for he it was who was bringing King Charles back into his Kingdom again.

Two years had gone by since our memorable Day at the Play,

and as that same Neighbour had also foretold, England was hearing a great deal about Tom Betterton. His Name was on every one's lips. Mr. Rhodes, the Bookseller, had obtained a licence from General Monk to get a Company of Actors together, and the palmy Days of the Cockpit had begun. Then it was that some faint Echo of the Life of our great City penetrated as far as the dull Purlieus of Mr. Baggs' Household; then it was that the ring of the Fame of Mr. Betterton even caused Mistress Euphrosine to recall her former arbitrary Judgments.

Every one now was talking of her illustrious Brother. General Monk himself had made a Friend of him, so had Sir John Grenville, who was the King's own Envoy; and those who were in the know prophesied that His Majesty Himself would presently honour the eminent Player with his regard. My Lord Rochester was his intimate Friend; Sir George Etherege was scarce ever seen in public without him. Lord Broghill had vowed that the English Stage was made famous throughout the Continent of Europe by the superlative excellence of Mr. Betterton.

To such Eulogies, coming from the most exalted Personages in the Land, Mistress Euphrosine could not turn an altogether deaf Ear; and being a Woman of character and ambition, she soon realised that her Antagonism to her illustrious Brother not only rendered her ridiculous, but might even prove a bar to Mr. Theophilus Baggs' Advancement.

The first Step towards a Reconciliation was taken when Mr. Baggs and his Spouse went together to the Play to see Mr. Betterton act Solyman in a play called "The Siege of Rhodes." You and I, Mistress, were by great favour allowed to go too, and to take our places in that same Gallery where two Years previously You and I had spent such happy hours. We spoke little to one another, I remember. Our hearts were full of Memories; but I could see your brown Eyes lighten as soon as the eminent Actor walked upon the Stage. The same Glamour which his personality had thrown over You two years ago was still there. Nay! it was enhanced an hundredfold, for to the magnetic presence of the Man was now added the supreme Magic of the Artist. I am too humble a Scrivener, fair Lady, to attempt to describe Mr. Betterton's acting, nor do I think that such Art as his could be adequately discussed. Your enjoyment of it I did fully share. You devoured him with your Eyes while he was on the Stage, and the Charm of his Voice filled the crowded Theatre and silenced every other sound. I knew that the World had ceased to exist for You and that the mysterious and elusive god of Love had hit your Heart with his wayward dart.

I thank God that neither then nor later did any feeling of

Bitterness enter into my Soul. Sad I was, but of a gentle Sadness which made me feel mine own Unworthiness, even whilst I prayed that You might realise your Heart's desire.

Strangely enough, it was at the very moment when I first understood the state of your Feelings that mine eyes, a little dimmed with tears, were arrested by the Sight of a young and beautiful Lady, who sat in one of the Boxes, not very far from our point of vantage. I wondered then what it was about her that thus enchained mine Attention. Of a truth, she was singularly fair, of that dainty and translucent Fairness which I for one have never been able to admire, but which is wont to set Men's pulses beating with an added quickness—at least, so I've heard it said. The Lady had blue Eyes, an exquisitely white Skin, her golden Hair was dressed in the new modish Fashion, with quaint little Ringlets all around her low, square Brow. The face was that of a Child, yet there was something about the firm Chin, something about the Forehead and the set of the Lips which spoke of Character and of Strength not often found in one so young.

Immediately behind her sat a young Cavalier of prepossessing Appearance, who obviously was whispering pleasing Words in the Lady's shell-like ear. I confess that for the moment I longed for the presence of our loquacious Neighbour of two years ago. He, without doubt, would have known who the noble young Lady was and who was her attentive Cavalier. Soon, however, the progress of the Play once more riveted mine Attention upon the Stage, and I forgot all about the beautiful Lady until it was time to go. Then I sought her with mine Eyes; but she had already gone. And I, whilst privileged to arrange your Cloak around your shoulders, realised how much more attractive brown Hair was than fair, and how brilliant could be the sparkle of dark Eyes as against the more languorous expression of those that are blue.

2

I was not present at the time that You, Mistress, first made the acquaintance of Mr. Betterton. He came to the House originally for the sole purpose of consulting with his Brother-in-law on a point of Law, he having an idea of joining Sir William Davenant in the Management of the new Theatre which that Gentleman was about to open in Lincoln's Inn Fields.

The season in London promised to be very brilliant. His

12

Majesty the King was coming into his own once more. Within a Month or two at the latest, he would land at Dover, and as even through his misfortunes and exile he had always been a great Patron of the Arts of Drama and Literature, there was no doubt that he would give his gracious Patronage to such enterprises as Sir William Davenant and Mr. Killigrew, not to mention others, had already in view.

No doubt that Sir William Davenant felt that no Company of Actors could be really complete without the leadership of Mr. Betterton; and we all knew that both he and Mr. Killigrew were literally fighting one another to obtain the great Actor's services.

In the end, of course, it was Sir William who won, and thus Mr. Betterton came to visit Mr. Theophilus Baggs to arrange for an Indenture whereby he was to have a Share of the Profits derived from the Performances at the new Theatre in Lincoln's Inn Fields.

You, Mistress, will remember that Day even better than I do, for to me it only marked one more Stage on the dreary road of my uneventful Life, whilst for You it meant the first Pearl in that jewelled Crown of Happiness which Destiny hath fashioned for You. Mr. Baggs had sent me on that day to Richmond, to see a Client of his there. Whether he did this purposely, at the instance of Mistress Euphrosine, in order to get me out of the way, I know not. In her Estimation I was supposed to have leanings for the Actor's profession in those days—surely a foolish Supposition, seeing how unprepossessing was my Appearance and how mediocre my Intellect.

Without doubt, however, could she have read the Secrets of your Soul, dear Mistress, she would have sent You on an errand too, to a remote corner of England, or had locked You up in your Room, ere you came face to face with the great Man whose Personality and Visage were already deeply graven upon your Heart.

But her futile, unamiable Mind was even then torn between the desire to make a brave show of Prosperity before her illustrious Brother and to welcome him as the Friend and Companion of great Gentlemen, and the old puritanical Spirit within her which still looked upon Actors as Rogues and Vagabonds, Men upon whom God would shower some very special, altogether terrible Curses because of their loose and immoral Lives.

Thus Mistress Euphrosine's treatment of the distinguished Actor was ever contradictory. She did her best to make him feel that she despised him for his Calling, yet nevertheless she fawned upon him because of his connection with the Aristocracy. Even subsequently, when Mr. Betterton enjoyed not only the Patronage but the actual Friendship of His Majesty the King, Mistress

13

Euphrosine's attitude towards him was always one of pious scorn. He might be enjoying the protection of an earthly King, but what was that in comparison with his Sister's intimacy with God? He might consort with Dukes, but she would anon make one in a company of Angels, amongst whom such Reprobates as Actors would never find a place.

That, I think, was her chief Attitude of Mind, one that caused me much Indignation at the time; for I felt that I could have knelt down and worshipped the heaven-born Genius who was delighting the whole Kingdom with his Art. But Mr. Betterton, with his habitual kindliness and good humour, paid no heed to Mistress Euphrosine's sour Disposition towards him, and when she tried to wither him with lofty Speeches, he would quickly make her ridiculous with witty Repartee.

He came more and more frequently to the House, and mine Eyes being unusually sharp in such matters, I soon saw that You had wholly won his regard. Those then became happy times. Happy ones for You, Mistress, whose Love for a great and good Man was finding full Reciprocity. Happy ones for him, who in You had found not only a loving Heart, but rare understanding, and that great Talent which he then and there set himself to develop. They were happy times also for me, the poor, obscure Scrivener with the starved Heart and the dreary Life, who now was allowed to warm his Soul in the Sunshine of your joint Happiness.

It was not long before Mr. Betterton noticed the profound Admiration which I had for him, not long before he admitted me to his Friendship and Intimacy. I say it with utmost pride, that I was the first one with whom he discussed the question of your Career and to whom he confided the fact that You had a conspicuous talent for the Stage, and that he intended to teach and to train You until You could appear with him on the Boards. You may imagine how this Idea staggered me at first—aye! and horrified me a little. I suppose that something of the old puritanical middle-class Prejudice had eaten so deeply into my Soul that I could not be reconciled to the idea of seeing any Woman—least of all you, Mistress—acting a part upon the Stage. Hitherto, young Mr. Kynaston and other boy-actors had represented with perfect grace and charm all the parts which have been written for Women; and I could not picture to myself any respectable Female allowing herself to be kissed or embraced in full view of a large Audience, or speaking some of those Lines which our great Dramatists have thought proper to write.

But Mr. Betterton's Influence and his unanswerable Arguments soon got the better of those old-fashioned Ideas, and anon I found myself looking eagerly forward to the happy time when You would be freed from the trammels of Mistress Euphrosine's Tyranny and, as the Wife and Helpmate of the greatest Actor of our times, take your place beside him among the Immortals.

3

It was not until the spring of the following Year that I first noticed the cloud which was gathering over your happiness. Never shall I forget the day when first I saw Tears in your Eyes.

You had finally decided by then to adopt the Stage as your Profession, and at the instance of Mr. Betterton, Sir William Davenant had promised You a small part in the new Play, wherewith he was about to open his new Theatre in Lincoln's Inn Fields. The piece chosen was called "Othello," written by one William Shakespeare, and Sir William had finally decided that the parts written in this Play by the Author for Women should be enacted by Women; an arrangement which was even then being worked quite successfully by Mr. Killigrew at his Theatre in Clare Market.

I knew that a brilliant Future lay before You; but Mistress Euphrosine, who had constituted herself your Guardian and Mentor, tried in vain to turn You from your Career. The day when You made your Decision was yet another of those momentous ones which will never fade from my Memory. You had hitherto been clever enough to evade Mistress Euphrosine's Vigilance whilst you studied the Art of speaking and acting under the guidance of Mr. Betterton. She thought that his frequent Visits to the House were due to his Regard for her, whereas he came only to see You and to be of service to You in the pursuit of your Studies.

But the time came when You had to avow openly what were your Intentions with regard to the Future. Sir William Davenant's Theatre in Lincoln's Inn Fields was to be opened in June, and You, Mistress, were, together with his principal Actresses, to be boarded after that by him at his own House, in accordance with one of the Provisions of the Agreement. The Question arose as to where You should lodge, your poor Mother having no home to offer You. Mistress Euphrosine made a great Show of her Abhorrence of the Stage and all the Immorality which such a Career implied. My cheeks blush with shame even now at the recollection of the abominable language which she used when first You told her what You meant to do, and my Heart is still filled with admiration at your Patience and Forbearance with her under such trying circumstances.

Fortunately for us all, Mr. Betterton arrived in the midst of all this wrangle. He soon succeeded in silencing Mistress Euphrosine's exacerbating tongue, and this not so much by the magic of his Persuasion as by the aid of the golden Key which is known to open every door—even that which leads to a scolding Harridan's heart. Mr. Betterton offered his Sister a substantial Sum of Money if she in return would undertake to give You a comfortable lodging until such time as he himself would claim You as his Wife. He stipulated that You should be made comfortable and that no kind of menial work should ever be put upon You.

"Mistress Saunderson," he said impressively, "must be left absolutely free to pursue her Art, unhampered by any other consideration."

Even so, Mistress Euphrosine could not restrain her malicious tongue, and the whole equitable arrangement might even then have fallen through but for your gentleness and quiet determination. Finally, Mistress Euphrosine gave in. She accepted the liberal terms which her illustrious Brother was offering her for your Maintenance, but she reserved unto herself the right of terminating the Arrangement at her will and pleasure. Obviously, she meant to be as disagreeable as she chose; but You had to have a respectable roof over your head until such time as You found a Haven under the ægis of your future Husband's Name.

After that, it seemed as if no cloud could ever come to obscure the Heavens of your happiness. Nevertheless, it was very soon after that Episode that I chanced upon You one evening, sitting in the parlour with the Book of a Play before You, yet apparently not intent upon reading. When I spoke your name You started as if out of a Dream and quickly You put your handkerchief up to your eyes.

I made no remark then; it would have been insolence on my part to intrude upon your private Affairs. But I felt like some faithful cur on the watch.

For awhile dust was thrown in my eyes from the fact that Mr. Betterton announced to us his projected trip abroad, at the instance of Sir William Davenant, who desired him to study the Scenery and Decorations which it seems were noted Adjuncts to the Stage over in Paris. If Mr. Betterton approved of what he saw there, he was to bring back with him a scheme for such Scenery to be introduced at the new Theatre in Lincoln's Inn Fields, which would be a great triumph over Mr. Killigrew's Management, where no such innovations had ever been thought of.

Naturally, Mr. Betterton, being a Man and an Artist, was eager and excited over this journey, which showed what great confidence Sir William Davenant reposed in his Judgment. This, methought, accounted for the fact that You, Mistress, seemed so much more dejected at the prospect of his Absence than he was. I also was satisfied that this Absence accounted for your tears.

Fool that I was! I should have guessed!

Mr. Betterton was absent two months, during which time I oft chanced upon You, dear Mistress, with a book lying unheeded on your lap and your dark eyes glistening with unnatural brilliancy. But I still believed that it was only Mr. Betterton's Absence that caused this sadness which had of late fallen over your Spirits. I know that he did not write often, and I saw—oh! quite involuntarily—that when his Letters came they were unaccountably short.

Then, one day—it was in May—seeing You more than usually depressed, I suggested that as the weather was so fine we should repair to the Theatre in Clare Market, and there see Mr. Killigrew's company enact "The Beggar's Bush," a play in which Major Mohun was acting the part of Bellamente with considerable success.

Had I but known what we were destined to see in that Theatre, I swear to God that I would sooner have hacked off my right leg than to have taken You thither. Yet We both started on our way, oblivious of what lay before Us. Time had long since gone by when such expeditions had to be done in secret. You, Mistress, were independent of Mistress Euphrosine's threats and tantrums, and I had come to realise that my Employer could nowhere else in the whole City find a Clerk who would do so much for such very scanty pay, and that he would never dismiss me, for fear that he would never again meet with such a willing Drudge.

So, the day being one on which Mr. Baggs and Mistress Euphrosine were absenting themselves from home, I persuaded You easily enough to come with me to the Play.

Your spirits had risen of late because you were expecting Mr. Betterton's home-coming. In fact, You had received authentic news that he would probably be back in England within the week.

4

At once, when I took my seat in the Gallery beside you, I noticed the beautiful fair Lady in the Box, whom I had not seen since that marvellous day a year ago, when you and I sat together at the Play. She was more radiantly beautiful than ever before.

Discreet enquiries from my Neighbour elicited the information that she was the Lady Barbara Wychwoode, daughter of the Marquis of Sidbury, and the acknowledged Belle among the Debutantes of the season. I understood that nothing had been seen of the Lady for the past year or more, owing to the grave and lingering illness of her Mother, during the whole course of which the young Girl had given up her entire life to the tending of the Invalid.

Now that his Lordship was a Widower, he had insisted on bringing his Daughter to London so that she might be brought to the notice of His Majesty and take her place at Court and in Society, as it beseemed her rank. That place the Lady Barbara conquered quickly enough, by her Beauty, her Charm and her Wit, so much so that I was told that all the young Gallants in the City were more or less over head and ears in love with her, but that her affections had remained steadfastly true to the friend and companion of her girlhood, the young Earl of Stour who, in his turn had never swerved in his Allegiance and had patiently waited for the day when her duty to her Mother would cease and her love for him be allowed to have full sway.

All this, of course, sounded very pretty and very romantic; and you, Mistress, gave ungrudging admiration to the beautiful girl who was the cynosure of all eyes. She sat in the Box, in the company of an elderly and distinguished Gentleman, who was obviously her Father, and of another Man, who appeared to be a year or two older than herself and whose likeness of features to her own proclaimed him to be her Brother. At the rear of the box a number of brilliant Cavaliers had congregated, who had obviously come in order to pay court to this acknowledged Queen of Beauty. Foremost among these we noticed a tall, handsome young Man whose noble features looked to me to suggest a somewhat weak yet obstinate disposition. He was undeniably handsome: the huge, fair periwig which he wore lent a certain manly dignity to his countenance. We quickly came to the conclusion that this must be the Earl of Stour, for it was obvious that the Lady Barbara reserved her most welcoming smile and her kindliest glances for him.

18

The company in the Box kept us vastly amused for a time, in the intervals of watching the Actors on the Stage; and I remember that during the second Act the dialogue in the Play being somewhat dull, both You and I fell to watching the Lady Barbara and her throng of Admirers. Suddenly we noticed that all these Gentlemen gave way as if to a New-comer who had just entered at the rear of the Box and was apparently desirous of coming forward in order to pay his respects. At first we could not see who the New-comer was, nor did we greatly care. The next moment, however, he was behind the Lady Barbara's chair. Anon he stooped forward in order to whisper something in her ear.

And I saw who it was.

It was Mr. Betterton.

For the moment, I remember that I felt as if I were paralysed; either that or crazed. I could not trust mine eyes.

Then I turned my head and looked at You.

You too had seen and recognised. For the moment You did not move, but sat rigid and silent. Your face had become a shade or two paler and there was a scarce perceptible tremor of your lips.

But that was all. I alone knew that You had just received a stab in your loving and trusting Heart, that something had occurred which would for ever mar the perfect trustfulness of your early love ... something which you would never forget.

5

You sat out the rest of the Play, dear Mistress, outwardly quite serene. Never, I think, has my admiration for your Character and for your Worth been more profound. I believe that I suffered almost as much as You. I suffered because many things were made clear to me then that I had ignored before. Your tears, your many Silences, that look of trustful happiness now gone from your eyes. I understood that the Incident was only the confirmation of what you had suspected long since.

But you would not let any one see your heart. No! not even me, your devoted Bondsman, who would gladly die to save You from pain. Yet I could not bring my heart to condemn Mr. Betterton utterly. I did not believe even then that he had been unfaithful—led away no doubt by the glamour of the society Beauty, by the talk and the swagger of all the idle Gentlemen about town—but not unfaithful. His was not a Nature to love more than the once, and he loved You, Mistress—loved You from the moment that he set eyes on You, from the moment that he knew your Worth. His fancy had perhaps been captured by the beautiful Lady Barbara, his Heart wherein your image was eternally enshrined, had been momentarily bewitched by her wiles; but he was not responsible for these Actions—that I could have sworn even then.

Mr. Betterton is above all an Artist, and in my humble judgment Artists are not to be measured by ordinary standards. Their mind is more fanciful, their fancy more roving; they are the Butterflies of this World, gay to look at and light on the wing.

You never told me, Mistress, what course You adopted after that eventful afternoon; nor would I have ventured to pry into your secrets. That You and Mr. Betterton talked the whole matter over, I make no doubt. I could even tell You, methinks, on which day the heart to heart talk between You took place. That there were no Recriminations on your part I dare aver; also that Mr. Betterton received his final dismissal on that day with a greater respect than ever for You in his Heart, and with deep sorrow weighing upon his Soul.

After that, his visits to the house became more and more infrequent; and at first You would contrive to be absent when he came. But, as I have always maintained, his love for You still filled his innermost Being, even though the Lady Barbara ruled over his fancy for the time. He longed for your Presence and for your Friendship, even though at that time he believed that You had totally erased his image from your Heart.

And so, when he came, and I had perforce to tell him that You were absent, he would linger on in the hope that You would return, and he would go away with a bitter sigh of regret whenever he had failed to catch a glimpse of You.

You never told me in so many Words that you had definitely broken off your Engagement to Mr. Betterton, nor do I believe that such was your intention even then. Mistress Euphrosine certainly never realised that You were smarting under so terrible a blow, and she still spoke glibly of your forthcoming marriage.

It was indeed fortunate for You, fortunate for us all, that both she and Mr. Baggs were too self-absorbed—he in his Business and she in her Piety—and too selfish, to be aware of what went on around them. Their self-absorption left You free to indulge in the luxury of suffering in silence; and I was made almost happy at times by an occasional surreptitious pressure of your Hand, a glance from your Eyes, telling me that my Understanding and Sympathy were not wholly unwelcome.

CHAPTER III

A CRIMINAL FOLLY

1

In June, you made your debut upon the stage, dear Mistress. Though You only played a small Part, your Grace and Charm soon won universal approval. I have so often told You of my feelings, my hopes, my tremors and my joy on the occasion when first I saw You upon the boards, that I will not weary You with the re-telling of them once again. Securely hidden behind a pillar, I only lived through the super-acuteness of my Senses, which drank in your Presence from the moment when You stepped out from behind the Curtain and revealed your gracious personality to an admiring Audience.

As long as I live, every word which You spoke on that day will continue to ring in mine ear, and ere mine eyes close for ever in their last long Sleep, I shall see your exquisite Image floating dreamlike before their gaze.

2

From that day onward, I saw you more seldom than I had been wont to do before. Your Success at the new Theatre had been so pronounced that Sir William Davenant soon entrusted You with more important parts. Thus your time was greatly taken up both with Performances and with Rehearsals and with the choosing and trying on of dresses. Of necessity, your work threw you often in the company of Mr. Betterton, he being the leading Actor in Sir William's Company, and the most popular as he was the most eminent of His Majesty's Well-Beloved Servants. In fact, his Fame at this time was reaching its Apogee. He was reckoned one of the Intimates of His Majesty himself; Gentlemen and Noblemen sought his company; great Ladies were zealous to win his favours.

Needless to say that concurrently with his rise to pre-eminence, an army of Enemies sprung up around him. Hungry curs will ever bay at the moon. Set a cat upon a high post and in a

21

moment others will congregate down below and spit and yowl at their more fortunate kind. Scandal and spite, which had never been so rife as in these days, fastened themselves like evil tentacles on Mr. Betterton's fair Name.

He was too proud to combat these, and You too proud to lend an ear to them. You met him now upon an easy footing of Friendship, of gentle gratitude as of a successful Pupil towards a kindly Teacher. To any one who did not know You as I do, You must at that time have seemed completely happy. You were independent now, earning a good salary, paying Mistress Euphrosine liberally for the lodgings which she placed at your disposal; free to come and go as You pleased, to receive the visits of Gentlemen who were desirous of paying their respects to You. You were, in fact, Mistress Saunderson, the well-known Actress, who was busy climbing—and swiftly, too—the Ladder of Fame.

Of your proposed Marriage with Mr. Betterton there was of course no longer any talk. For some reason best known to herself, and which I myself never tried to fathom, even Mistress Euphrosine had ceased to speak of it.

Did she, within the depths of her ambitious and avaricious Heart, harbour the belief that her Brother would one day wed one of those great Ladies, who were wont to hang entranced upon his lips, when he spoke the immortal words of the late Mr. William Shakespeare or of Mr. John Dryden? I know not; nor what benefit she would have derived from it if such an unlikely Event had indeed taken place.

Towards me, she was still frigidly contemptuous. But as to that, I did not care. I was determined to endure her worst gibes for the sake of dwelling under the same roof which still had the privilege of sheltering You.

3

It was one day early in September—just something over a year ago, in fact—that my Lord Stour called at the house of Mr. Theophilus Baggs. I knew him at once for the Cavalier who was ever in attendance upon the Lady Barbara Wychwoode and whom rumour had assigned to her as her future Husband.

Frankly, I had never liked him from the first. I thought him overbearing and arrogant. His manner towards those who were inferior to him in station was always one of contempt. And I often wondered how Mr. Theophilus Baggs, who was an Attorney of some standing in the City of London, could endure the cool insolence wherewith young Gentlemen like my Lord Stour and others were wont to treat him. Not only that, but he seemed to derive a sort of gratification from it, and was wont to repeat—I was almost going to say that he would boast of—these acts of overbearance to which he was so often subjected.

"Another of the stiff-necked sort," he would say after he had bowed one of these fine Gentlemen obsequiously out of his office. "An honest, God-fearing Man is as dirt beneath the feet of these Gallants."

My Lord Stour, of a truth, was no exception to the rule. I have since been assured that he was quite kindly and gracious in himself, and that his faults were those of the Milieu in which he had been brought up, rather than of himself.

Of course, You, dear Mistress, were out of the house during the whole of that never-to-be-forgotten day of which I am about to speak, and therefore knew nothing of the terrible Event which then occurred and which, in my humble judgment, completely revolutionized Mr. Betterton's character for the time being. But Fate had decreed that I should see it all. Every moment of that awful afternoon is indelibly graven upon my Memory. I had, however, neither the Chance nor the Opportunity to speak to You of it all. At first I did not think that it would be expedient. The humiliation which Mr. Betterton was made to endure on that day was such that I could not bear to speak of it, least of all to You, who still held him in such high esteem. And later on, I still thought it best to be silent. Mr. Betterton and You seemed to have drifted apart so completely, that I did not feel that it would do any good to rake up old hurts, and to submit them to the cruel light of day.

But now everything is changed. The Lady Barbara's influence over Mr. Betterton has gone, never to return; whilst his Heart once more yearns for the only true Love which has ever gladdened it.

4

My Lord Stour came to call upon Mr. Theophilus Baggs at three o'clock of the afternoon. Kathleen, the maid of all work, opened the door to him, and Mistress Euphrosine received him in the Parlour, where I was also sitting at my desk, engaged in copying out a lengthy Indenture.

"Master Baggs awaits me, I think," my Lord said as he entered the room.

Mistress Euphrosine made a deep curtsey, for she was ever fond of the Aristocracy.

"Will you deign to enter, my Lord?" she said. "My husband will wait upon your pleasure."

"Tell him to be quick, then," said my Lord; "for I have not a great deal of time to spare."

He seated himself beside the table and drew off his gloves. He had taken absolutely no notice of my respectful salutation.

Mistress Euphrosine sailed out of the room and a moment or two later Mr. Baggs came in, carrying a sheaf of papers and looking very fussy and obsequious.

My Lord did not rise to greet him, only turned his head in his direction and said curtly:

"You are Mr. Theophilus Baggs, Attorney-at-law?"

"At your Lordship's service," replied my employer.

"Brother-in-law of Tom Betterton, the Actor, so I am told," my Lord went on with quiet condescension.

This innocent remark, however, appeared to upset Mr. Baggs. He stammered and grew as red as a turkey-cock, not realizing that his connection with the great Actor was truly an honour upon his Name. He hemmed and hawed and looked unutterably foolish, as he mumbled confusedly:

"Er ... that is ... only occasionally, my Lord ... very occasionally, I may say ... that is ... I..."

"Pray calm yourself," broke in my Lord haughtily. "I admire the fellow's acting ... the Man himself does not exist for me."

"You are most gracious, my Lord," murmured Mr. Baggs promptly, whilst I could have struck him for his obsequiousness and his Lordship for his arrogance.

It seems that the matter which had brought Lord Stour to Mr. Baggs' office was one of monies connected with the winding-up of the affairs of the late Earl, uncle of the present Peer. I was busy with my work during the time that these affairs were being discussed and did not pay much heed to the conversation. Only two fragments thereof struck mine ear. I remember, chiefly because they were so characteristic of the two men—the Aristocrat and the Plebeian—and of the times in which we live.

At one time Mr. Baggs ventured to enquire after the health of the Honourable Mrs. Stourcliffe, his Lordship's mother; and you should have heard the tone of frigid pride wherewith my Lord seemed to repel any such presumptuous enquiries.

The other fragment which I overheard was towards the end of

the interview, when Mr. Theophilus Baggs, having counted over the Money before his Lordship, placed a Paper before him and bade me bring him a pen.

"What's this?" queried my Lord, astonished.

"Oh!" Mr. Baggs stammered, with his habitual humility of demeanour, "a mere formality, my Lord ... er ... h'm ... only a ... er ... receipt."

"A receipt?" my Lord asked, with an elevation of his aristocratic brows. "What for?"

"Er ... er..." Mr. Baggs stammered. "For the monies, my Lord. That is ... er ... if you will deign to count it over yourself ... and see that it is correct."

At this, my Lord rose from his seat, waved me aside, took and pocketed the money. Then he said coolly to Mr. Baggs:

"No, Sir; I do not care to count. My Uncle knew You to be honest, or he would not have placed his affairs in your hands. That is sufficient for me. I, on the other hand, have received the money.... That is sufficient for You."

"But——!" ejaculated Mr. Baggs, driven out of his timidity by such summary procedure.

"Egad, Sir!" broke in my Lord, more haughtily than before. "Are you perchance supposing that I might claim money which I have already had?"

"No ... no!" protested Mr. Baggs hastily. "I assure you, my Lord ... er ... that it is ... h'm ... a mere formality ... and..."

"My word," retorted my Lord coolly, "is sufficient formality."

Whereupon he turned to the door, taking no more notice of me than if I were the doormat. He nodded to Mr. Baggs, who was of a truth too deeply shaken to speak, and with a curt "I wish you good-day, Mr. Notary!" strode out of the room.

I doubt not, Mistress, that You and many others of gentle Manners if not of gentle Birth, would think that in recounting this brief interview between my employer and the young Earl of Stour, I have been guilty of exaggeration in depicting my Lord's arrogance. Yet, on my word, it all occurred just as I have told it. No doubt that Mr. Baggs' obsequiousness must have been irritating, and that it literally called forth the haughty Retort which otherwise might have remained unspoken. I myself, humble and insignificant as I am, have oft felt an almost uncontrollable impulse to kick my worthy Employer into some measure of manliness.

For let me assure You that, though subsequently I became more closely acquainted with my Lord Stour, I never heard him use such haughty language to any of his Dependents, nor do I think that so gentle a Lady as Lady Barbara Wychwoode would have bestowed her fondness and regard upon him had his Nature been as supercilious and as insolent as his Words.

5

That afternoon was indeed destined to be fuller of events than I ever could have anticipated. No sooner had I closed the door upon my Lord Stour, when I heard footsteps ascending the stairs, and then my Lord's voice raised once more, this time with a tone of pleasure mingled with astonishment.

"Wychwoode, by gad!" he exclaimed. "And what in Heaven's name have you come to do in the old fox's lair?"

I did not hear the immediate reply. More fussy than ever, Mr. Baggs had aleady signed to me to reopen the door.

"Lord Douglas Wychwoode," he murmured hurriedly in my ear. "One of the younger sons of the Marquis of Sidbury. I am indeed fortunate to-day. The scions of our great Nobility do seek my help and counsel..." and more such senseless words did he utter, whilst the two young Gentlemen paused for a moment upon the landing, talking with one another.

"I thought you still in France," Lord Douglas said to his friend. "What hath brought you home so unexpectedly?"

"I only arrived this morning," the other replied; "and hoped to present my respects this evening, if your Father and the Lady Barbara will receive me."

"Indeed, they'll be delighted. Cela va sans dire, my friend. My sister has been rather pensive of late. Your prolonged absence may have had something to do with her mood."

"May you speak the truth there!" my Lord Stour remarked with a sigh.

"But now you have not told me," rejoined Lord Douglas, as he and his friend finally went into the room and curtly acknowledged Mr. Baggs' reiterated salutations, "what hath brought you to the house of this bobbing old Thief yonder."

"Private business," replied Lord Stour. "And you?"

"The affairs of England," said the other, and tossed his head proudly like some young Lion scenting battle.

Before his friend could utter another remark, Lord Douglas strode rapidly across the room, took some papers out of the inner pocket of his coat, and called to Mr. Baggs to come up closer to him.

"I want," he said in a quick and peremptory whisper, "a dozen copies of this Deed done at once and by a sure hand. Can you do it?"

"Yes, I think so," replied Mr. Baggs. "May I see what the paper is?"

I was watching the pair of them; so was my Lord Stour. On his face there came a sudden frown as of disapproval and anxiety.

"Wychwoode——!" he began.

But the other did not heed him. His eyes—which were so like those of his Sister—were fixed with an eager, questioning gaze upon my Employer. The latter's face was absolutely expressionless and inscrutable whilst he scanned the paper which Lord Douglas, after a scarce perceptible moment of hesitation, had handed to him for perusal.

"Yes," he said quietly, when he had finished reading. "It can be done."

"At once?" asked Lord Douglas.

"At once. Yes, my Lord."

"By a sure hand?"

"Discretion, my Lord," replied Mr. Baggs, with the first show of dignity I have ever seen him display, "is a virtue in my profession, the failing in which would be a lasting disgrace."

"I rely even more upon your convictions, Mr. Baggs," Lord Douglas rejoined earnestly, "than upon your virtues."

"You and your friends, my Lord, have deigned to talk those matters over with me many a time before. You and they know that You can count on me."

Mr. Baggs spoke with more Quietude and Simplicity than was his wont when dealing with some of these noble Lords. You may be sure, dear Mistress, that I was vastly astonished at what I heard, still more at what I guessed. That Mr. Baggs and his Spouse belonged to the old Puritan Party which had deplored the Restoration of the Kingship, I knew well enough. I knew that both he and Mistress Euphresine looked with feelings akin to horror upon a system of Government which had for its supreme head a King, more than half addicted to Popery and wholly to fast living, with women, gambling and drinking all the day. But what I had never even remotely guessed until now was that he had already lent a helping hand to those numerous Organisations, which had for their object the overthrow of the present loose form of Government, if not that of the Monarchy itself.

I did not know, in fact, that beneath a weak and obsequious exterior, my Employer hid the stuff of which dangerous Conspirators are often made.

For the nonce, however, I imagine that he contented himself

27

with writing out Deeds and Proclamations for the more important Malcontents, of whom apparently my Lord Douglas Wychwoode was one. He had never taken me into his confidence, even though he must have known that he could always rely upon my Discretion. What caused him to trust me now more than he had done before, I do not know. Perhaps he had come to a final decision to throw in his lot with the ultra-Protestant party, who viewed with such marked disfavour the projects of the King's marriage with the Popish Princess of Portugal. Certain it is that he came to me without any hesitation with the Papers which Lord Douglas had just entrusted to him, and that he at once ordered me to make the twelve copies which his Lordship desired.

I retired within the window-recess which You know so well, and wherein I am wont to sit at my copying work. Mr. Baggs then set me to my task, after which he drew the screen across the recess, so that I remained hidden from the view of those who were still in the room. I set to with a Will, for my task was a heavy one. Twelve copies of a Manifesto, which in itself covered two long pages.

A Manifesto, in truth!

I could scarce believe mine eyes as I read the whole rambling, foolish, hot-headed Rigmarole. Did I not have the Paper actually in my hand, had I not seen Lord Douglas Wychwoode handing it himself over to Mr. Baggs, I could not have believed that any Men in their sober senses could have lent a hand to such criminal Folly.

Folly it was; and criminal to boot!

The whole matter is past History now, and there can be no harm in my relating it when so much of it hath long ago been made public.

That Manifesto was nothing more or less than an Appeal to certain Sympathizers to join in one of the maddest enterprises any man could conceive. It seems that my Lady Castlemaine's house was to be kept watched by Parties of these same Conspirators, until one night when the King paid her one of his customary evening Visits. Then the signal was to be given, the House surrounded, my Lady Castlemaine kidnapped, His Majesty seized and forced to abdicate in favour of the young Duke of Monmouth, who would then be proclaimed King of England, with the Prince of Orange as Regent.

Now, have you ever heard of anything more mad? I assure You that I was literally staggered, and as my Pen went wearily scratching over the Paper I felt as if I were in a dream, seeing before me visions of what the end of such a foolish Scheme would be: the Hangman busy, the Prisons filled, sorrow and desolation in many homes that had hoped to find peace at last after the turmoil of the past twenty years. For the appeals were directed to well accredited people outside London, some of whom were connected with the best known Families in the Country. I must, of course, refrain from mentioning names that have been allowed to fall into oblivion in connection with the affair; but You, dear Mistress, would indeed be astonished if You heard them now.

And what caused me so much worry, whilst I wrote on till my hand felt cramped and stiff, was mine own Helplessness in the matter. What could I do, short of betraying the trust which was reposed in me?—and this, of course, was unthinkable.

I wrote on, feeling ever more dazed and dumb. From the other side of the screen the Voices of the two young Gentlemen came at times to mine ear with unusual clearness, at others only like an intermittent hum. Mr. Baggs had apparently left the room, and the others had no doubt become wholly oblivious of my Presence. Lord Douglas Wychwoode had told his Friend something of his madcap Schemes; his voice sounded both eager and enthusiastic. But my Lord Stour demurred.

"I am a Soldier," he said at one time; "not a Politician."

"That's just it!" the other argued with earnestness. "It is Men like you that we want. We must crush that spendthrift Wanton who holds the King in her thrall, and we must force a dishonoured Monarch to give up the Crown of England to one who is worthier to wear it, since he himself, even in these few brief months, has already covered it with infamy."

"You have set yourself a difficult task, my friend," my Lord Stour urged more soberly; "and a dangerous one, too."

"Only difficult and dangerous," retorted Lord Douglas, "whilst such Men as you still hold aloof."

"I tell you, I am no Politician," his Friend rejoined somewhat impatiently.

"But You are a Man, and not a senseless profligate—an earnest Protestant, who must loathe that cobweb of Popery which overlies the King's every Action, and blurs his vision of duty and of dignity."

"Yes—but——"

Then it was that Lord Douglas, with great patience and earnestness, gave to his Friend a detailed account of his criminal Scheme—for criminal it was, however much it might be disguised under the cloak of patriotism and religious fervour. How Lord Stour received the communication, I could not say. I had ceased to listen and was concentrating my mind on my uncongenial task. Moreover, I fancy that Lord Stour did not say much. He must have disapproved of it, as any right-minded Man would, and no doubt tried his best to bring Lord Douglas to a more rational state of mind. But this is mere conjecture on my part, and, of course, I could not see his face, which would have been a clear index to his thoughts. At one time I heard him exclaim indignantly:

"But surely You will not entrust the distribution of those Manifestos, which may cost you your head, to that obsequious and mealy-mouthed notary?"

Mr. Baggs should have heard the contempt wherewith my Lord uttered those words! It would have taught him how little regard his servile ways had won for him, and how much more thoroughly would he have been respected had he adopted a more manly bearing towards his Clients, however highly these may have been placed.

After this, Lord Douglas Wychwoode became even more persuasive and eager. Perhaps he had noted the first signs of yielding in the Attitude of his Friend.

"No, no!" he said. "And that is our serious trouble. I and those who are at one with me feel that we are surrounded with spies. We do want a sure Hand—a Hand that will not err and that we can trust—to distribute the Manifestos, and, if possible, to bring us back decisive Answers. Some of the Men with whom we wish to communicate live at some considerable distance from town. We only wish to approach influential people; but some of these seldom come to London; in fact, with the exception of the Members of a venal Government and of a few effete Peers as profligate as the King himself, but few Men, worthy of the name, do elect to live in this degenerate City."

His talk was somewhat rambling; perhaps I did not catch all that he said. After awhile Lord Stour remarked casually:

"And so You thought of me as your possible Emissary?"

"Was I wrong?" retorted Lord Douglas hotly.

"Nay, my friend," rejoined the other coldly. "I am honoured by this trust which You would place in me; but——"

"But You refuse?" broke in Lord Douglas with bitter reproach.

I imagine that my Lord Stour's reply must have been an unsatisfactory one to his Friend, for the latter uttered an exclamation of supreme impatience. I heard but little more of their conversation just then, for the noise in the Street below, which had been attracting my Attention on and off for some time, now grew in intensity, and, curious to know what it portended, I rose from my chair and leaned out of the window to see what was happening.

From the window, as You know, one gets a view of the corner of our Street as it debouches into Fleet Street by the Spread Eagle tavern, and even the restricted View which I thus had showed me at once that some kind of rioting was going on. Not rioting of an ordinary kind, for of a truth we who live in the heart of the City of

London are used to its many cries; to the "Make way there!" of the Sedan Chairman and the "Make room there!" of the Drivers of wheel-barrows, all mingling with the "Stand up there, you blind dog!" bawled by every Carman as he tries to squeeze his way through the throngs in the streets.

No! this time it seemed more than that, and I, who had seen the crowds which filled the Streets of London from end to end on the occasion of the death of the Lord Protector, and had seen the merry-makers who had made those same streets impassable when King Charles entered London a little more than a year ago, I soon realized that the Crowd which I saw flocking both up and down Fleet Street was in an ugly mood.

At first I thought that some of those abominable vagabonds from Whitefriars—those whom we call the Alsatians, and who are in perpetual conflict with the law—had come out in a body from their sink of iniquity close by and had started one of their periodical combats with the Sheriffs' Officers; but soon I recognized some faces familiar to me among the crowd as they ran past the corner— Men, Women and Boys who, though of a rough and turbulent Character, could in no way be confounded with the law-breaking Alsatians.

There was, for instance, the Tinker, whom I knew well by sight. He was running along, knocking his skillets and frying-pans against one another as he passed, shouting lustily the while. Then there was a sooty chimney-sweep, whom I knew to be an honest Man, and the broom Men with their Boys, and many law-abiding Pedestrians who, fearful of the crowd, were walking in the traffic way, meekly giving the wall to the more roisterous throng. They all seemed to be a part of that same Crowd which was scampering and hurrying up and down Fleet Street, shouting and causing a disturbance such as I do not remember ever having seen before.

I should have liked to have gazed out of the Window until I had ascertained positively what the noise was about; but I remembered that my task was only half-accomplished and that I had at the least another half-dozen Manifestos to write out. I was on the point of sitting down once more to my Work when I heard Lord Douglas Wychwoode's voice quite close to the screen, saying anxiously, as if in answer to some remark made by his friend:

"I trust not. My Sister is out in her chair somewhere in this neighbourhood, and only with her two Bearers."

Apparently the two Gentlemen's attention had also been arrested by the tumult. The next moment Mr. Theophilus Baggs came in, and immediately they both plied him simultaneously with questions. "What were those strange cries in the street? Was there

31

likely to be a riot? What was the cause of the tumult?" All of which Mr. Baggs felt himself unable to answer. In the end, he said that he would walk down to the corner of the Street and ascertain what was happening.

Ensconced within the window recess and hidden from view by the screen, I soon gave up all attempt at continuing my work. Somehow, the two Gentlemen's anxiety about the Lady Barbara had communicated itself to me. But my thoughts, of course, were of You. Fortunately for my peace of mind, I knew that You were safe; at some distance, in fact, from the scene of the present tumult. Nevertheless, I had already made up my mind that if the rioting spread to the neighbouring streets, I would slip out presently and go as far as Dorset Gardens, where you were busy at rehearsal, and there wait for you until you came out of the Theatre, when, if you were unattended, I could escort you home.

I could not myself have explained why the Noise outside and the obvious rough temper of the People should have agitated me as they undoubtedly did.

Anon, Mr. Baggs returned with a veritable sackful of news.

"There is a great tumult all down the neighbourhood," said he, "because Lady Castlemaine is even now at the India House drinking tea, and a lot of rowdy folk have made up their minds to give her a rough welcome when she comes out. She is not popular just now, my Lady Castlemaine," Mr. Baggs continued complacently, as he gave a look of understanding to Lord Douglas Wychwoode, "And I fancy that she will experience an unpleasant quarter of an hour presently."

"But, surely," protested my Lord Stour, "a whole mob will not be allowed to attack a defenceless woman, however unpopular she may be!"

"Oh, as to that," rejoined Mr. Baggs with an indifferent shrug of the shoulders, "a London mob is not like to be squeamish when its temper is aroused; and just now, when work is scarce and food very dear, the sight of her Ladyship's gorgeous liveries are apt to exasperate those who have an empty stomach."

"But what will they do to her?" urged my Lord, whose manly feelings were evidently outraged at the prospect of seeing any Woman a prey to an angry rabble.

"That I cannot tell you, my Lord," replied Mr. Baggs. "The crowd hath several ways of showing its displeasure. You know, when a Frenchman or some other Foreigner shows his face in the Streets of London, how soon he becomes the butt of passing missiles. The sweep will leave a sooty imprint upon his coat; a baker's basket will cover him with dust; at every hackney-coach

32

stand, some facetious coachman will puff the froth of his beer into his face. Well! you may draw your own conclusions, my Lord, as to what will happen anon, when my Lady Castlemaine hath finished drinking her dish of tea!"

"But surely no one would treat a Lady so?" once more ejaculated my Lord Stour hotly.

"Perhaps not," retorted Mr. Baggs drily. "But then you, see, my Lord, Lady Castlemaine is ... Well; she is Lady Castlemaine ... and at the corner of our street just now I heard murmurs of the Pillory or even worse for her——"

"But this is monstrous—infamous——!"

"And will be well deserved," here broke in Lord Douglas decisively. "Fie on You, Friend, to worry over that baggage, whilst we are still in doubt if my Sister be safe."

"Yes!" murmured Lord Stour, with a sudden note of deep solicitude in his voice. "My God! I was forgetting!"

He ran to the window—the one next to the recess where I still remained ensconced—threw open the casement and gazed out even more anxiously than I had been doing all along. Mr. Baggs in the meanwhile endeavoured to reassure Lord Douglas.

"If," he said, "her Ladyship knows that your Lordship hath come here to visit me, she may seek shelter under my humble roof."

"God grant that she may!" rejoined the young Man fervently.

We all were on tenterhooks, I as much as the others; and we all gazed out agitatedly in the direction of Fleet Street. Then, all at once, my Lord Stour gave a cry of relief.

"There's the chaise!" he exclaimed. "It has just turned the corner of this street.... No! not that way, Douglas ... on your right.... That is Lady Barbara's chaise, is it not?"

"Yes, it is!" ejaculated the other. "Thank Heaven, her man Pyncheon has had the good sense to bring her here. Quick, Mr. Notary!" he added. "The door!"

The next moment a Sedan chair borne by two men in handsome liveries of blue and silver came to a halt just below. Already Mr. Baggs had hurried down the stairs. He would, I know, yield to no one in the privilege of being the first to make the Lady Barbara welcome in his House. The Excitement and Anxiety were momentarily over, and I could view quite composedly from above the beautiful Lady Barbara as she stepped out of her Chair, a little flurried obviously, for she clasped and unclasped her cloak with a nervy, trembling hand.

A second or two later, I heard her high-heeled shoes pattering up the stairs, whilst her Men with the Chair sought refuge in a quiet tavern higher up in Chancery Lane.

33

CHAPTER IV

MORE THAN A PASSING FANCY

1

I would that You, fair Mistress, had seen the Lady Barbara Wychwoode as I beheld her on that never-to-be-forgotten afternoon, her Cheeks of a delicate pallor, her golden Hair slightly disarranged, her Lips trembling with excitement. You, who are so inexpressibly beautiful, would have been generous enough to give ungrudging Admiration to what was so passing fair.

She was panting a little, for obviously she had been scared, and clung to her Brother as if for protection. But I noticed that directly she entered the room her Eyes encountered those of my Lord Stour, and that at sight of him a happy smile at once overspread and illumined her Face.

"I am so thankful, Douglas, dear," she said, "that Pyncheon happened to know you were here. He also knew the way to Mr. Baggs' house, and as soon as he realized that the crowd in Fleet Street was no ordinary one, he literally took to his heels and brought me along here in amazingly quick time. But, oh!" she added lightly, "I can tell You that I was scared. My heart went thumping and I have not yet recovered my breath."

Her cheeks now had become suffused with a blush and her blue eyes sparkled, more with excitement than fear, I imagined. Certain it is that her Beauty was enhanced thereby. But Lord Douglas, with a Brother's privilege, shrugged his shoulders and said with a show of banter:

"Methinks, Babs, dear, that your heart hath chiefly gone a-thumping because you are surprised at finding Stour here."

She gave a gay little laugh—the laugh of one who is sure of Love and of Happiness; the same laugh, dear Mistress, for which I have hearkened of late in vain from You.

"I only arrived in London this morning," my Lord Stour explained.

"And hastened to pay your respects to the law rather than to me," Lady Barbara taunted him lightly.

"I would not have ventured to present myself at this hour," he rejoined. "And, apparently, would have found the Lady Barbara from home."

"So a beneficent Fairy whispered to You to go and see Mr. Notary, and thus arranged everything for the best."

"The beneficent Fairy had her work cut out, then," Lord Douglas remarked, somewhat impatiently, I thought.

"How do you mean?" she retorted.

"Why," said he, "in order to secure this tryst, the beneficient Fairy had first to bring me hither as well as Stour, and Lady Castlemaine to the India House. Then she had to inflame the temper of a whole Crowd of Roisterers sufficiently to cause the worthy Pyncheon to take to his heels, with you in the chair. In fact, the good Fairy must have been to endless trouble to arrange this meeting 'twixt Lady Barbara and her Lover, when but a few hours later that same meeting would have come about quite naturally."

"Nay, then!" she riposted with perfect good humour, "let us call it a happy Coincidence, and say no more about it."

Even then her Brother uttered an angry exclamation. He appeared irritated by the placidity and good humour of the others. His nerves were evidently on edge, and while my Lord Stour, with the egoism peculiar to Lovers, became absorbed in whispering sweet nothings in Lady Barbara's ears, Lord Douglas took to pacing up and down the Room like some impatient Animal.

I watched the three of them with ever-growing interest. Being very sensitive to outward influences, I was suddenly obsessed with the feeling that through some means or other these three Persons, so far above me in station, would somehow become intermixed with my Life, and that it had suddenly become my Duty to watch them and to listen to what they were saying.

I had no desire to pry upon them, of course; so I pray You do not misunderstand nor condemn me for thus remaining hidden behind the screen and for not betraying my Presence to them all. Certainly my Lord Stour and Lord Douglas Wychwoode had known at one time that I was in the Room. They had seen me installed in the window-recess, with the treasonable Manifestos which I had been set to copy. But since then the two Gentlemen had obviously become wholly oblivious of my Presence, and the Lady Barbara did not of course even know of my Existence, whilst I did not feel disposed to reveal myself to any of them just yet.

2

Lord Douglas, thereafter, was for braving the Rioters and for returning home. But Lady Barbara and Lord Stour, feeling happy in one another's Company, were quite content to bide for a time under Mr. Baggs' sheltering roof.

"You must have patience, Douglas," she said to her Brother. "I assure you that the Streets are not safe. Some rowdy Folk have set themselves to attacking every chair they see and tearing the gold and silver lace from the Chairmen's liveries. Even the side-streets are thronged. Pyncheon will tell you of the difficulty he had in bringing me here."

"But we cannot wait until night!" Lord Douglas urged impatiently.

"No!" said she. "Only an hour or two. As soon as the people have seen Lady Castlemaine and have vented their wrath on her, they will begin to disperse, chiefly into the neighbouring Taverns, and then we can slip quietly away."

"Or else," broke in Lord Stour hotly, "surely the watchmen will come anon and disperse that rabble ere it vents its spite upon a defenceless Woman!"

"A defenceless Woman, you call her, my Lord?" Lady Barbara retorted reproachfully. "She is the most dangerous Enemy England hath at this moment!"

"You are severe, Lady Barbara——"

"Severe!" she exclaimed, with a vehement tone of resentment. "Ah! you have been absent, my Lord. You do not know—You do not understand! Over abroad You did not realise the Misery, the Famine, that is stalking our land. Money that should be spent on reclaiming our Industries, which have suffered through twenty years of civil strife, or in helping the poor to tide over these years of lean Harvests, is being lavished by an irresponsible Monarch upon a greedy Wanton, who——"

"Barbara!"

She paused, recalled to herself by the stern voice of her Brother. She had allowed her Indignation to master her maidenly reserve. Her cheeks were aflame now, her lips quivering with Passion. Of a truth, she was a Woman to be admired, for, unlike most of her sex, she had profound feelings of Patriotism and of Charity; she had valour, enthusiasm, temperament, and was not ashamed to speak what was in her mind. I watched my Lord Stour while she spoke, and saw how deeply he worshipped her. Now she encountered his Gaze, and heavy tears came into her Eyes.

"Ah, my Lord," she said gently, "you will see sadder sights in the Streets of London to-day than ever you did in the Wars after the fiercest Battles."

"'Tis no use appealing to him, Babs," Lord Douglas interposed with obvious exacerbation. "A moment ago I told him of our Plans. I begged him to lend us his sword and his hand to strike a blow at the Profligacy and Wantonness which is sending England to perdition worse than ever before——"

Lady Barbara turned great, reproachful eyes on my Lord.

"And you refused?" she whispered.

My Lord looked confused. All at once, I knew that he was already wavering. A weak Man, perhaps; he was deeply, desperately enamoured. I gathered that he had not seen the Lady Barbara for some months. No doubt his Soul hungered for her Smiles. He was the sort of Man, methinks, who would barter everything—even Honour—for the Woman he loved. And I do not think that he cared for much beyond that. His Father, an you remember, fought on the Parliament side. I do not say that he was one of the Regicides, but he did not raise a finger to help or to serve his King. And he had been a rigid Protestant. All the Stourcliffes of Stour were that; and the present Earl's allegiance to King Charles could only have been very perfunctory. Besides which, this is the age of Conspiracies and of political Factions. I doubt not but it will be another twenty years before the Country is really satisfied with its form of Government. I myself—though God knows I am but a humble Clerk—could wish that this Popish marriage for the King had not been decided on. We do not want religious factions warring with one another again.

But all this is beside the mark, nor would I dwell on it save for my desire to be, above all, just to these three People who were destined to do the Man I love best in the world an irreparable injury.

As I said before, I could see that my Lord Stour was hesitating. Now Lady Barbara invited him to sit beside her upon the Sofa, and she began talking to him quietly and earnestly, Lord Douglas only putting in a word or so now and again. What they said hath little to do with the portent of my Narrative, nor will I plague You with the telling of it. Those people are nothing to You; they have nothing to do with humble Plebeians like ourselves; they are a class apart, and we should never mix ourselves up with them or their affairs, as Mr. Betterton hath since learned to his hurt.

While they were talking together, the three of them, I tried once more to concentrate my mind upon my work, and finished off another two or three copies of the treasonable Manifesto.

All this while, you must remember that the noise and rowdiness in the streets had in no way diminished. Rather had it grown in intensity. The people whom I watched from time to time and saw darting down Chancery Lane or across the corner of Fleet Street, looked more excited, more bent on mischief, than before. I had seen a few stones flying about, and once or twice heard the ominous crash of broken glass.

Then suddenly there came an immense Cry, which was not unlike the snarling of hundreds of angry Beasts. I knew what that meant. My Lady Castlemaine was either on the point of quitting the India House or had been otherwise spied by the Populace. I could no longer restrain my Curiosity. Once more I cast my papers aside and leaned out of the window. The shouting and booing had become more and more ominous. Apparently, too, a company of the City Watchmen had arrived. They were trying to force through the throng, and their calls of "Make way there!" sounded more and more peremptory. But what was a handful of Watchmen beside an excited crowd of Rioters determined to wreak their temper upon an unpopular bit of baggage? I doubt not but that His Majesty's Body-guard could alone restore order now and compass the safety of the Lady.

As I leaned out of the Window I could see stones and miscellaneous missiles flying in every direction; and then suddenly I had a clear vision of a gorgeous Sedan Chair escorted by a dozen or more City Watchmen, who were trying to forge a way for it through the Crowd. They were trying to reach the corner of our Street, hoping no doubt to turn up this way and thus effect an escape by way of the Lower Lincoln's Inn Fields and Drury Lane, while the Crowd would of necessity be kept back through the narrowness of the Streets and the intricacies of the Alleys.

The whole point now was whether the Chairmen could reach our corner before the Roisterers had succeeded in beating back the Watchmen, when of course they meant to tear Lady Castlemaine out of her chair. Poor, wretched Woman! She must have been terribly frightened. I know that I myself felt woefully agitated. Leaning out toward the street, I could see Lady Barbara's pretty head at the next window and my Lord Stour and Lord Douglas close beside her. They too had forgotten all about their talk and their plans and Conspiracies, and were gazing out on the exciting Spectacle with mixed feelings, I make no doubt. As for me, I feel quite sure that but for my sense of utter helplessness, I should have rushed out even then and tried to lend a hand in helping an unfortunate Woman out of so terrible a Predicament, and I marvelled how deep must have been the hatred for her, felt by Gentlemen like my Lord Stour and Lord Douglas Wychwoode, that their Sense of Chivalry forsook them so completely at this Hour, that neither of them attempted to run to her aid or even suggested that she should find shelter in this House.

As for Mr. Baggs, he was not merely idly curious; he was delighted at the idea that my Lady Castlemaine should be maltreated by the mob; whilst Mistress Euphrosine's one idea was the hope that if the Rioters meant to murder the Baggage, they would not do so outside this door. She and Mr. Baggs had come running into the Parlour the moment the rioting reached its height, and of a truth, dear Mistress, you would have been amused to see us all at the three front windows of the house—three groups watching the distant and wildly exciting happenings in Fleet Street. There was I at one window; Mr. and Mrs. Baggs at the other; Lady Barbara and the two Gallants at the third. And the ejaculations which came from one set of Watchers or the other would fill several pages of my narrative.

Mistress Euphrosine was in abject fear. "Oh! I hope," cried she now and again, "that they won't come this way. There'll be murder upon our doorstep!"

My Lord Stour had just one revulsion of feeling in favour of the unfortunate Castlemaine. "Come, Douglas!" he called at one time. "Let's to her aid. Remember she is a Woman, after all!"

But Lady Barbara placed a restraining hand upon his arm, and Lord Douglas said with a rough laugh: "I would not lift a finger to defend her. Let the Devil befriend her, an he list."

And all the while the mob hissed and hooted, and stones flew like hail all around the Chaise.

"Oh! they'll murder her! They'll murder her!" called Mistress Euphrosine piously.

"And save honest men a vast deal of trouble thereby," Mr. Baggs concluded sententiously.

The Watchmen were now forging ahead. With their sticks and staves they fought their way through bravely, heading the chair towards our street. But even so, methought that they stood but little Chance of saving my Lady Castlemaine in the end. The Crowd had guessed their purpose already, and were quite ready to give Chase.

The Chairmen with their heavy burden could be no match against them in a Race, and the final capture of the unfortunate Woman was only now a question of time.

Then suddenly I gave a gasp. Of a truth I could scarce believe in what I saw. Let me try and put the picture clearly before you, dear Mistress; for in truth You would have loved to see it as I did then. About half a dozen Watchmen had by great exertion succeeded in turning the corner of our Street. They were heading towards us with only a comparatively small knot of roisterers to contend against, and the panting, struggling Chairmen with the Sedan Chair were immediately behind them.

As far as I could see, the Crowd had not expected this Manoeuvre, and the sudden turning off of their prey at right angles disconcerted the foremost among them, for the space of a second or two. This gave the Chairmen a brief start up the street. But the very next moment the Crowd realized the situation, and with a wild war-cry, turned to give Chase, when a Man suddenly stepped out from nowhere in particular that I could see, unless it was from the Spread Eagle tavern, and stood at the bottom of the street between two posts, all alone, facing the mob.

His Appearance, I imagine, had been so unexpected as well as so sudden, that the young Roisterers in the front of the Crowd paused—like a Crowd always will when something totally unexpected doth occur. The Man, of course, had his back towards us, but I had recognized him, nor was I surprised that his Appearance did have the effect of checking for an instant that spirit of Mischief which was animating the throng. Lady Barbara and the young Gentlemen at the other window were even more astonished than I at this wholly unforeseen occurrence. They could not understand the sudden checking of the Rioters and the comparative silence which fell upon the forefront of their ranks.

"What does it all mean?" my Lord Stour exclaimed.

"A Man between the chair and its pursuers," Lord Douglas said in amazement.

"Who is it?" queried Lady Barbara.

"Not a Gentleman," rejoined Lord Douglas; "for he would not thus stop to parley with so foul a mob. Meseems I know the figure," he added, and leaned still further out of the window, the better to take in the whole of the amazing scene. "Yes—by gad! ... It is..."

Here Mistress Euphrosine's cry of horror broke in upon us all.

"Alas!" she ejaculated piously. "'Tis that reprobate Brother of mine!"

"So it is!" added Mr. Baggs drily. "'Tis meet he should raise his voice in defence of that baggage."

40

"But, who is it?" insisted my Lord Stour impatiently.

"Why, Betterton the Actor," replied Lord Douglas with a laugh. "Do you not know him?"

"Only from seeing him on the stage," said the other. Then he added: "An Actor confronting a mob! By gad! the fellow hath pluck!"

"He knows," protested Mr. Baggs acidly, "that the mob will not hurt him. He hath so oft made them laugh that they look upon him as one of themselves."

"Listen!" said Lady Barbara. "You can hear him speak quite plainly."

Whereupon they all became silent.

All this, of course, had occurred in far less time than it takes to describe. Not more than a few seconds had gone by since first I saw Mr. Betterton step out from Nowhere in particular into the Street. But his Interposition had given my Lady Castlemaine's Chairmen and also the Watchmen, who were guarding her, a distinct advance. They were making the most of the respite by hurrying up our street as fast as they were able, even while the Crowd—that portion of it that stood nearest to Mr. Betterton and could hear his Voice—broke into a loud laugh at some Sally of his which had apparently caught their Fancy.

From the distance the cry was raised: "To the pillory, the Castlemaine!"

It was at this point that my Lady Barbara bade every one to listen, so that we all could hear Mr. Betterton's rich and powerful Voice quite plainly.

"Come, come, Friends!" he was saying; "the Lady will get there without your help some day, I'll warrant. Aye! and further too, an the Devil gives her her due! Now, now," he continued, when cries and murmurs, boos and hisses, strove to interrupt him. "You are not going to hiss a hard-working Actor off the Stage like this. Do, in the name of Sport, which every sound-minded Englishman loves, after all, await a fitter opportunity for molesting a defenceless Woman. What say You to adjourning to the Spread Eagle tavern, where mine Host hath just opened a new cask of the most delicious beer You have ever tasted? There's a large room at the back of the bar—You know it. Well! every one who goes there now—and there's room for three or four hundred of You—can drink a pint of that beer at my expense. What say You, Friends? Is it not better than to give chase to a pack of Watchmen and a pair of liveried Chairmen who are already as scared as rabbits? See! they are fast disappearing up the street. Come! who will take a pint of beer at the invitation of Tom Betterton? You know him! Is he not a jolly, good fellow?..."

Of course, he did not deliver this speech uninterruptedly. It was only snatches of it that came to our ear. But we Listeners soon caught the drift of it, and watched its reception by the Crowd. Well! the Fire-eaters gradually cooled down. The prospect of the ale at the Spread Eagle caused many a smack of the lips, which in its turn smothered the cries of Rage and Vituperation. Anon, One could perceive one forearm after another drawn with anticipatory Pleasure across lips that had ceased to boo.

Just then, too, Heaven interposed in a conciliatory spirit in the form of a few drops of heavy Rain, presaging a Storm. The next moment the stampede in the direction of the Spread Eagle tavern had begun, whilst my Lady Castlemaine's Chairmen trudged unmolested past our door.

My Lord Stour gave a loud laugh.

"'Twas well thought on," he exclaimed. "The Mountebank hath found a way to stop the Rabble's howls, whilst my Lady Baggage finds safety in flight."

But Lady Barbara added thoughtfully: "Methinks 'twas plucky to try and defend a Woman single-handed."

4

I watched the turbulent throng, filing now in orderly procession through the hospitably open doors of the Spread Eagle tavern. Mr. Betterton remained for awhile standing at the door, marshalling the more obstreperous of his invited Guests and parleying with Mr. Barraclough, the Host of the Spread Eagle—no doubt making arrangements for the quenching of three or four hundred thirsts at his expense. Then he suddenly turned on his heel and came up the Street. Lord Douglas gave one of his rough, grating laughs, and said:

"So now I see that, like a wise man, Mr. Betterton mistrusts his Popularity and proposes to seek refuge from his ebullient Friends."

"I believe," said Mistress Euphrosine to her Lord in an awed whisper; "I believe that Thomas is coming here."

Which possibility greatly disconcerted Mr. Baggs. He became quite agitated, and exclaimed fussily:

"I'll not have him here ... I'll not ... Not while her Ladyship is here ... I'll not allow it!"

"And pray why not, Mr. Notary?" Lady Barbara put in

haughtily. "Mr. Betterton sups twice a week with His Majesty. Surely then you may invite him without shame under your roof!"

"And I've never seen the great Actor close to," remarked Lord Stour lightly. "I've oft marvelled what he was like in private life."

"Oh!" said Lord Douglas, with a distinct note of acerbity in his voice, "he is just like any other Fellow of his degree. These Mountebanks have of late thought themselves Somebodies, just because 'tis the fashion for Gentlemen to write plays and to go to the Theatre. My Lord Rochester, Sir George Etherege and the others have so spoilt them by going about constantly with them, that the Fellows scarce know their place now. This man Betterton is the worst of the lot. He makes love to the Ladies of the Court, forgets that he is naught but a Rogue and a Vagabond and not worthy to be seen in the company of Gentlemen. Oh! I've oft had an itching to lay a stick across the shoulders of some of these louts!"

I would that I could convey to you, dear Mistress, the tone of Spite wherewith Lord Douglas spoke at this moment, or the look of Contempt which for the moment quite disfigured his good-looking Face. That he had been made aware at some time of Mr. Betterton's admiration for Lady Barbara became at once apparent to me, also that he looked upon that admiration as a Presumption and an Insult.

I was confirmed in this Supposition by the look which he gave then and there to his Sister, a look which caused her to blush to the very roots of her hair. I fancy, too, that he also whispered something on that Subject to my Lord Stour, for a dark frown of Anger suddenly appeared upon the latter's Face and he muttered an angry and rough Ejaculation.

As for me, I am an humble Clerk, a peaceful Citizen and a practising Christian; but just at that moment I felt that I hated Lord Douglas Wychwoode and his Friend with a bitter and undying hatred.

5

Meseemed as if the air within the room had become surcharged with a subtle and heady fluid akin to an Intoxicant, so many Passions were even then warring in the innermost hearts of us all. There was Hatred and Spite, and Fervour and Love. We were all of us alive at that moment, if You know what I mean. We were

Individuals who felt and thought individually and strongly; not just the mere sheeplike Creatures swayed hither and thither by the Modes and Exigencies of the hour. And I can assure you that even then, when we heard Mr. Betterton's quick step ascending the stairs, we all held our breath and watched the door as if something Supernatural was about to be revealed to us.

The next moment that door was thrown open and Mr. Betterton appeared upon the threshold.

Ah! if only You had seen him then, Mistress, your heart would have rejoiced, just as mine did, at the sight. Personally, I could never tell You if Mr. Betterton is tall or short, handsome or ill-favoured; all that I know is that when he is in a room you cannot look at any one else; he seems to dwarf every other Man by the Picturesqueness of his Personality.

And now—oh! You should have seen him as he stood there, framed in the doorway, the grey afternoon light of this dull September day falling full upon his Face, with those glittering Eyes of his and the kindly, firm Mouth, round which there slowly began to spread a gently mocking Smile. He was richly dressed, as was his wont, with priceless lace frills at throat and wrists, and his huge Periwig set off to perfection the nobility of his brow.

With one swift gaze round the room, he had taken in the full Situation. You know yourself, dear Mistress, what marvellous Powers of Intuition he has. His glance swept over Lady Barbara's exquisite comeliness, her somewhat flurried mien and wide, inquisitive eyes; over Lord Douglas, sullen and contemptuous; my Lord Stour, wrathful and suspicious; Mistress Euphrosine and Mr. Baggs, servile and tremulous. I doubt not that his keen Eyes had also spied me watching his every Movement from behind the screen.

The mocking Smile broadened upon his Face. With one shapely leg extended forward, his right arm holding his hat, his arm executing a superb flourish, he swept to the assembled Company an elaborate Bow.

"My Lords, your servant," he said. Then bowed more gravely to Lady Barbara and added, with a tone of subtle and flattering deference: "I am, as always, your Ladyship's most humble and most devoted Slave."

Whereupon her Ladyship swept him one of those graceful Curtsies which I understand have become the Mode in fashionable Society of late. But the young Gentlemen seemed to have lost count of their Manners. They were either too wrathful or too much taken aback to speak. Mistress Euphrosine, with her nose in the air, was preparing to sail majestically out of the room.

Mr. Betterton then stepped in. He threw down his hat and playfully made pretence to intercept Mistress Euphrosine.

"Sister, I do entreat You," he said with mock concern, "do not carry your well-shaped nose so high. The scent of Heaven will not reach your nostrils, try how you may.... 'Tis more likely that you will smell the brimstone which clings to my perruque."

And before Mistress Euphrosine had time to think of a retort, he had turned to her Ladyship with that gentle air of deference which became him so well.

"How comes it," he asked, "that I have the privilege of meeting your Ladyship here?"

"A mere accident, Sir," my Lord Stour interposed, somewhat high-handedly I thought. "Her Ladyship, fearing to be molested by the Crowd, came to meet Lord Douglas here."

"I understand," murmured Mr. Betterton. And I who knew him so well, realized that just for the moment he understood nothing save that he was in the presence of this exquisitely beautiful Woman who had enchained his Fancy. He stood like one transfixed, his eyes fastened almost in wonderment upon the graceful Apparition before him. I should not be exaggerating, fair Mistress, if I said that he seemed literally to be drinking in every line of her dainty Figure; the straight, white throat, the damask cheek and soft, fair hair, slightly disarranged. He had of a truth lost consciousness of his surroundings, and this to such an extent that it apparently set my Lord Stour's nerves on edge; for anon he said with evident Irritation and a total Disregard both of polite Usage and of Truth, since of course he knew quite well to whom he was speaking:

"I did not catch your name, Sir; though you seem acquainted with her Ladyship."

He had to repeat the Query twice, and with haughty impatience, before Mr. Betterton descended from the Clouds in order to reply.

"My name is Betterton, Sir," he said, no less curtly than my lord.

"Betterton? Ah, yes!" his Lordship went on, with what I thought was studied Insolence, seeing that he was addressing one of the most famous Men in England. "I have heard the Name before ... but where, I cannot remember.... Let me see, you are...?"

"An Actor, Sir," Mr. Betterton gave haughty answer. "Therefore an Artist, even though an humble one; but still a World contained in one Man."

Then his manner changed, the stiffness and pride went out of it and he added in his more habitual mode of good-natured banter, whilst pointing in the direction of Mistress Euphrosine:

"That, however, is not, I imagine, the opinion which my worthy Sister—a pious Lady, Sir—hath of my talents. She only concedes me a Soul when she gloats over the idea that it shall be damned."

"You are insolent!" quoth Mistress Euphrosine, as she stalked majestically to the door. "And I'll not stay longer to hear you blaspheme."

Even so, her Brother's lightly mocking ripple of Laughter pursued her along the course of her dignified exit through the door.

"Nay, dear Sister," he said. "Why not stay and tell these noble Gentlemen your doubts as to which half of me in the hereafter will be stoking the Fires of Hell and which half be wriggling in the Flames?" Then he added, turning gaily once more to the Visitors as Mistress Euphrosine finally departed and banged the door to behind her: "Mistress Baggs, Sir, is much troubled that she cannot quite make up her mind how much of me is Devil and how much a lost Soul."

"Of a surety, Sir," retorted Lord Douglas, with the same tone of malicious Spite wherewith he had originally spoken of Mr. Betterton, "every Gentleman is bound to share your worthy Sister's doubts on that point ... and as to whether your right Hand or your sharp Tongue will fizzle first down below."

There was a moment's silence in the room—oh! the mere fraction of a second—whilst I, who knew every line of Mr. Betterton's face, saw the quick flash of Anger which darted from his eyes at the insolent speech. Lady Barbara too had made an instinctive movement, whether towards him in protection or towards her Brother in reproach, I could not say. Certain it is that that Movement chased away in one instant Mr. Betterton's flaming wrath. He shrugged his shoulders and retorted with quiet Mockery:

"Your Lordship, I feel sure, will be able to have those doubts set at rest presently. I understand that vast intelligence will be granted to Gentlemen down there."

At once my Lord's hand went to his sword.

"Insolent!—" he muttered; and my Lord Stour immediately stepped to his Friend's side.

Like the Fleet Street crowd awhile ago, these two Gentlemen meant mischief. For some reason which was not far to seek, they were on the verge of a Quarrel with Mr. Betterton—nay! I believe that they meant to provoke him into one. In wordy Warfare, however, they did not stand much chance against the great Actor's caustic Wit, and no doubt their sense of Impotence made them all the more wrathful and quarrelsome.

Mr. Baggs, of course, servile and obsequious as was his wont, was ready enough to interpose. A Quarrel inside his house, between valued Clients and his detested Brother-in-law, was not at all to his liking.

"My Lords ..." he mumbled half-incoherently, "I implore you ... do not heed him ... he..."

His futile attempts at Conciliation tickled Mr. Betterton's sense of humour. The last vestige of his Anger vanished in a mocking Smile.

"Nay, good Master Theophilus," he said coolly, "prithee do not interfere between me and the Wrath of these two Gentlemen. Attend to thine own Affairs ... and to thine own Conspiracies," he added—spoke suddenly under Mr. Baggs' very nose, so that the latter gave a jump and involuntarily gasped:

"Conspiracies? ... What—what the devil do you mean, Sir, by Conspiracies?"

"Oh, nothing—nothing—my good Friend," replied Mr. Betterton lightly. "But when I see two hot-headed young Cavaliers in close conversation with a seedy Lawyer, I know that somewhere in the pocket of one of them there is a bit of Handwriting that may send the lot of them to the Tower first and to—well!—to Heaven afterwards."

My Heart was in my Mouth all the time that he spoke. Of course he could not know how near the Truth he was, and I firmly believe that his banter was a mere Arrow shot into the air; but even so it grazed these noble Lords' equanimity. Lord Douglas had become very pale, and my Lord Stour looked troubled, or was it my fancy? But I am sure that her Ladyship's blue eyes rested on Mr. Betterton with a curious searching gaze. She too wondered how much Knowledge of the Truth lay behind his easy Sarcasm.

Then Lord Douglas broke into a laugh.

"There, for once, Sir Actor," he said lightly, "your perspicacity is at fault. My Lord the Earl of Stour and I came to consult your Brother-in-law on a matter of business."

"And," exclaimed Mr. Betterton with mock concern, "I am detaining you with my foolish talk. I pray you, Gentlemen, take no further heed of me. Time treads hard on your aristocratic Heels, whilst it is the Slave of a poor, shiftless Actor like myself."

"Yes, yes," once more interposed the mealy-mouthed Mr. Baggs. "I pray you, my Lords—your Ladyship—to come to my inner office——"

There was a general movement amongst the Company, during which I distinctly heard Lord Douglas Wychwoode whisper to my Lord Stour:

"Can you wonder that I always long to lay a stick across that

47

Man's shoulders? His every word sounds like insolence ... And he has dared to make love to Barbara...."

Her Ladyship, however, seemed loth to linger. The hour, of a truth, was getting late.

"Father will be anxious," she said. "I have stayed out over long."

"Are the streets safe, I wonder?" my Lord Stour remarked.

"Perfectly," broke in Mr. Betterton. "And if her Ladyship will allow me, I will conduct her to her Chair."

Again my Lord Stour flashed out angrily, and once more the brooding Quarrel threatened to burst the bounds of conventional Intercourse. This time the Lady Barbara herself interposed.

"I pray you, my good Lord," she said, "do not interfere. Mr. Betterton and I are old Friends. By your leave, he shall conduct me to my chair. Do we not owe it to him," she added gaily, "that the streets are quiet enough to enable us all to get home in peace?"

Then she turned to Mr. Betterton and said gently:

"If You would be so kind, Sir—my men are close by—I should be grateful if You will tell them to bring my chair along."

She held out her hand to him and he bowed low and kissed the tips of her fingers. Then he went.

6

Lord Douglas' spiteful glance followed the distinguished Actor's retreating figure until the door had closed upon him. Then he said drily:

"Perhaps you are right, Babs. He may as well fetch your chair. It is raining hard and one Lacquey is as good as another."

He turned to Mr. Baggs, who, standing first on one leg then on the other, presented a truly pitiable spectacle of Servility and Unmanliness. I think he had just come to realize that I had been in the room behind the screen all this while, and that my Presence would be unwelcome to their Lordships if they knew that I had overheard all their Conversation. Certain it is that I saw him give a quick glance in my direction, and then he became even more fussy and snivelling than before.

"In my inner Office," he murmured. "I pray you to honour me, my Lords.... A glass of wine, perhaps ... until the copies are finished. I should be so proud ... and ... and ... we should be quite undisturbed ... whereas here ... I only regret..."

I despised him for all that grovelling, and so did the Gentlemen, I make no doubt. Nevertheless, they were ready to follow him.

"We must wait somewhere," Lord Douglas said curtly. "And I should be glad of a glass of wine."

Lady Barbara was standing in the window-recess, waiting for her chair. She insisted on my Lord Stour going with her Brother into the inner room. Undoubtedly, she did not wish either of them to meet Mr. Betterton again.

"I promise you," she said with quiet Determination, "that I'll not stop to speak with him. I'll watch through the window until my Men bring the chair; then I will go down at once."

"But——" protested his Lordship.

"I entreat you to go, my Lord," she reiterated tartly. "And you too, Douglas. My temper is on edge, and if I am not left to myself for a few moments I shall have an attack of Nerves."

She certainly spoke with unwonted Sharpness. Thus commanded, it would have been churlish to disobey. The young Gentlemen, after a second or two longer of Hesitation, finally followed Mr. Baggs out of the room.

Now, I could not see the Lady Barbara, for she was ensconced in a window-recess, just as I was; but I heard her give a loud Sigh of Impatience. There was no doubt that her Nerves had been jarred. Small wonder, seeing all that she had gone through—the noise and rioting in the streets, her Terror and her Flight; her unexpected meeting with her Lover; then the advent of Mr. Betterton and that brooding Quarrel between him and the two Gentlemen, which threatened to break through at any moment.

The next minute I saw her Ladyship's chair brought to a halt down below, and she crossed the Line of my Vision between the window and the sofa, where she had left her cloak. She picked it up and was about to wrap it round her shoulders, when the door was flung open and Mr. Betterton came in. He gave a quick glance round the room and saw that the Lady Barbara was alone—or so he thought, for, of course, he did not see me. He carefully closed the door behind him and came quickly forward, ostensibly to help her Ladyship on with her cloak.

"It is kind of you, Sir, thus to wait on me," she said coldly. "May I claim your Arm to conduct me to my chair?"

She was standing close in front of him just then, with her back to him and her hands raised up to her shoulders in order to receive her cloak, which he had somewhat roughly snatched out of her grasp.

"My Arm?" he riposted, with a vibrating note of passion in his

49

mellow voice. "My Life, myself, are all at your Ladyship's service. But will not you wait one little moment and say one kind word to the poor Actor whose Art is the delight of Kings, and whose Person is the butt of every Coxcomb who calls himself a Gentleman?"

He flung the cloak upon a chair and tried to take her hand, which, however, she quickly withdrew, and then turned, not unkindly, to face him.

"My Brother is hasty, Sir," she said more gently. "He has many prejudices which, no doubt, time and experience of life will mend. As for me," she added lightly, "I am quite ready to extend the hand of Friendship, not only to the Artist but to the Man."

She held out her hand to him. Then, as he did not take it, but stood there looking at her with that hungry, passionate look which revealed the depth of his Admiration for her, she continued with a bantering tone of reproach:

"You will not take my hand, Sir?"

"No," he replied curtly.

"But I am offering You my Friendship," she went on, with a quick, nervy little laugh; for she was Woman enough, believe me, to understand his look.

"Friendship between Man and Woman is impossible," he said in a strange, hoarse voice, which I scarce recognized as his.

"What do you mean?" she retorted, with a sudden stiffening of her Figure and a haughty Glance which he, of a truth, should have known boded no good for his suit.

"I mean," he replied, "that between a Man and a Woman, who are both young and both endowed with Heart and Soul and Temperament, there may be Enmity or Love, Hatred or Passion; but Friendship, never."

"You talk vaguely, Sir," she rejoined coldly. "I pray You, give me my cloak."

"Not," he retorted, "before I have caused your Ladyship to cast one short Glance back over the past few months."

"With what purpose, I pray You?"

"So that You might recognize, as You gaze along their vista, the man who since he first beheld you hath madly worshipped You."

She stood before him, still facing him, tall and of a truth divinely fair. Nay! this no one could gainsay. For the moment I found it in my Heart to sympathize with his Infatuation. You, dear Mistress, were not there to show him how much lovelier still a Woman could be, and the Lady Barbara had all the subtle flavour, too, of forbidden fruit. Mr. Betterton sank on one knee before her; his mellow Voice sounded exquisitely tender and caressing. Oh! had I been a Woman, how gladly would I have listened to his words.

There never was such a Voice as that of Mr. Betterton. No wonder that he can sway the hearts of thousands by its Magic; no wonder that thousands remain entranced while he speaks. Now, I assure You, Mistress, that tears gathered in my eyes, there was such true Passion, such depth of feeling in his tone. But Lady Barbara's heart was not touched. In truth, she loved another Man, and her whole outlook on Life and Men was distorted by the Environment amidst which she had been brought up.

The exquisite, insinuating Voice with its note of tender Appeal only aroused her contempt. She jumped to her feet with an angry exclamation. What she said, I do not quite remember; but it was a Remark which must have stung him to the quick, for I can assure You, dear Mistress, that Mr. Betterton's pride is at least equal to that of the greatest Nobleman in the land. But all that he did say was:

"Nay, Madam; an Artist's love is not an insult, even to a Queen."

"Possibly, Sir," she riposted coldly. "But I at least cannot listen to You. So I pray You let me rejoin my Servants."

"And I pray You," he pleaded, without rising, "humbly on my knees, to hear me just this once!"

She protested, and would have left him there, kneeling, while she ran out of the room; but he had succeeded in getting hold of her Hand and was clinging to it with both his own, whilst from his lips there came a torrent of passionate pleading such as I could not have thought any Woman capable of resisting for long.

"I am not a young Dandy," he urged; "nor yet a lank-haired, crazy Poet who grows hysterical over a Woman's eyebrow. I am a Man, and an Artist, rich with an inheritance such as even your Ancestors would have envied me. Mine inheritance is the Mind and Memory of cultured England and a Name which by mine Art I have rendered immortal."

"I honour your Genius, Sir," she rejoined coolly; "and because of it, I try to excuse your folly."

"Nay!" he continued with passionate insistence. "There are Passions so sweet that they excuse all the Follies they provoke. Oh! I pray You listen ... I have waited in silence for months, not daring to approach You. You seemed immeasurably above me, as distant as the Stars; but whilst I, poor and lowly-born, waited and worshipped silently, success forged for me a Name, so covered with Glory that I dare at last place it at your feet."

"I am touched, Sir, and honoured, I assure You," she said somewhat impatiently. "But all this is naught but folly, and reason should teach you that the Daughter of the Marquis of Sidbury can be nothing to You."

But by this time it was evident that the great and distinguished Actor had allowed his Folly to conquer his Reason. I closed my eyes, for I could not bear to see a Man whom I so greatly respected kneeling in such abject humiliation before a Woman who had nothing for him but disdain. Ah! Women can be very cruel when they do not love. In truth, Lady Barbara, with all her Rank and Wealth, could not really have felt contempt for a Man whom the King himself and the highest in the land delighted to honour; yet I assure You, Mistress, that some of the things she said made me blush for the sake of the high-minded Man who honours me with his Friendship.

"Short of reason, Sir," she said, with unmeasured hauteur at one time, "I pray you recall your far-famed sense of humour. Let it show you Thomas Betterton, the son of a Scullion, asking the hand of the Lady Barbara Wychwoode in marriage."

This was meant for a Slap in the Face, and was naught but a studied insult; for we all know that the story of Mr. Betterton's Father having been a menial is utterly without foundation. But I assure You that by this time he was blind and deaf to all save to the insistent call of his own overwhelming passion. He did not resent the insult, as I thought he would do; but merely rejoined fervently:

"I strive to conjure the picture; but only see Tom Betterton, the world-famed Artist, wooing the Woman he loves."

But what need is there for me to recapitulate here all the fond and foolish things which were spoken by a truly great Man to a chit of a Girl, who was too self-centred and egotistical to appreciate the great Honour which he was conferring on her by his Wooing. I was holding my breath, fearful lest I should be seen. To both of these proud People before me, my known Presence would have been an added humiliation. Already Lady Barbara, impatient of Mr. Betterton's importunity, was raising her Voice and curtly bidding him to leave her in peace. I thought every moment that she would call out to her Brother, when Heaven alone would know what would happen next.

"Your importunity becomes an insult, Sir," she said at last. "I command You to release my hand."

She tried to wrench it from his Grasp, but I imagine that his hold on her wrist was so strong that she could not free herself. She looked around her now with a look of Helplessness, which would have gone to my Heart if I had any feeling of sympathy left after I had poured out its full measure for my stricken Friend. He was not himself then, I assure You, Mistress. I know that the evil tongue of those who hate and envy him have poured insidious poison in your ears, that they told you that Mr. Betterton had insulted the Lady Barbara past forgiveness and had behaved towards her like a Cad and a Bully. But this I swear to be untrue. I was there all the time, and I saw it all. He was on his knees, and never attempted to touch her beyond clinging to her Hand and covering it with kisses. He was an humbled and a stricken Man, who saw his Love rejected, his Passion flouted, his Suffering mocked.

I tell you that all he did was to cling to her hand.

7

Then, all at once, I suppose something frightened her, and she called loudly:

"Douglas! Douglas!"

I don't think that she meant to call, and I am sure that the very next moment she had already regretted what she had done.

Mr. Betterton jumped to his feet, sobered in the instant; and she stood alone in the middle of the room, gazing somewhat wild-eyed in the direction of the door, which had already been violently flung open and through which my Lord Stour and Lord Douglas now hurriedly stepped forward.

"What is it, Babs?" Lord Douglas queried roughly. "Why are You still here? ... And what...?"

He got no further. His glance had alighted on Mr. Betterton, and I never saw quite so much concentrated Fury and Hatred in any one's eyes as now appeared in those of Lord Douglas Wychwoode.

But already the Lady Barbara had recovered herself. No doubt she realized the Mischief which her involuntary call had occasioned. The Quarrel which had been slowly smouldering the whole Afternoon was ready to burst into living flame at this moment. Even so, she tried to stem its outburst, protesting that she had been misunderstood. She even tried to laugh; but the laugh sounded pitiably forced.

"But it's nothing, Douglas, dear," she said. "I protest. Did I really call? I do not remember. As a matter of fact, Mr. Betterton was good enough to recite some verses for my delectation ... My Enthusiasm must have run away with me ... and, unwittingly, I must have called out..."

Obviously the Explanation was a lame one. I felt myself that it would not be believed. On the face of my Lord Stour thunderclouds of Wrath were fast gathering, and though Mr. Betterton had recovered his presence of mind with all the Art at his command, yet there was a glitter in his eyes which he was powerless to veil, whilst the tremor of her Ladyship's lips while she strove to speak calmly aroused my Lord Stour's ever-wakeful Jealousy.

Lord Douglas, as was his wont apparently whenever he was deeply moved, was pacing up and down the room; his hands were clasped behind his back and from time to time I could see their convulsive twitching. Lord Stour now silently helped her Ladyship on with her cloak. I was thankful that Mr. Baggs and Mistress Euphrosine were keeping in the background, else I verily believe that their obsequious Snivellings would have caused my quivering Nerves to play me an unpleasant trick.

Mr. Betterton had retired to the nearest window recess, so that I could not see him. All that I did see were the two Gentlemen and the threatening Clouds which continued to gather upon their Brows. I also heard my Lord Stour whisper hurriedly in Lord Douglas' ear:

"In the name of our Friendship, Man, let me deal with this."

I felt as if an icy hand had gripped my Heart. I could not conjecture what that ominous Speech could portend. Lady Barbara now looked very pale and troubled; her hands as they fumbled with her cloak trembled visibly. Lord Stour, with a masterful gesture, took one of them and held it firmly under his arm.

He then led her towards the door. Just before she went with him, however, her Ladyship turned, and I imagine sought to attract Mr. Betterton's attention.

"I must thank you, Sir," she said, with a final pathetic attempt at Conciliation, "for your beautiful Recitation. I shall be greatly envied, methinks, by those who have only heard Mr. Betterton declaim upon the Stage."

Lord Douglas had gone to the door. He opened it and stood grimly by whilst my Lord Stour walked out, with her Ladyship upon his arm.

CHAPTER V

THE OUTRAGE

1

A great Sadness descends upon my Soul, dear Mistress, even as I write. Cold shivers course up and down the length of my spine and mine eyes feel hot with tears still unshed—tears of Sorrow and of Shame, aye! and of a just Anger that it should have been in the power of two empty-headed Coxcombs to wreak an irreparable Injury upon one who is as much above them as are the Stars above the grovelling Worms.

I use the words "irreparable Injury" advisedly, dear Lady, because what happened on that late September afternoon will for ever be graven upon the Heart and Memory of a great and noble Man, to the exclusion of many a gentle feeling which was wont to hold full sway over his Temperament before then. Time, mayhap, and the triumph of a great Soul over overwhelming temptation, have no doubt somewhat softened the tearing ache of that cruel brand; but only your Hand, fair Mistress, can complete the healing, only your Voice can, with its tender gentleness, drown the insistent call of Pride still smarting for further Revenge.

2

Lord Douglas Wychwoode did not speak to Mr. Betterton after her Ladyship and my Lord Stour had gone out of the room, but continued his restless pacing up and down. I thought his Silence ominous.

Half consciously, I kept my attention fixed upon the street below, and presently saw the Lady Barbara get into her chair and bid adieu to his Lordship, who remained standing on our doorstep until the Sedan was borne away up the street and out of sight. Then, to my astonishment, he walked down as far as the Spread Eagle tavern and disappeared within its doors.

The Silence in our parlour was getting on my nerves. I could not see Mr. Betterton, only Lord Douglas from time to time, when in his ceaseless tramping his short, burly figure crossed the line of my vision.

Anon I once more thought of my Work. There were a couple more copies of the Manifesto to be done, and I set to, determined to finish them. Time went on, and the afternoon light was now rapidly growing dim. Outside, the weather had not improved. A thin rain was coming down, which turned the traffic-way of our street to sticky mud. I remember, just after I had completed my Work and tidied up my papers, looking out of the window and seeing, in the now fast-gathering gloom, the young Lord of Stour on the doorstep of the Spread Eagle tavern, in close conversation with half a dozen ill-clad and ill-conditioned Ruffians. But I gave the matter no further thought just then, for my mind happened to be engrossed with doubts as to how I should convey the Copies I had made to my Employer without revealing my presence to Lord Douglas Wychwoode.

His Lordship himself, however, soon relieved me of this perplexity, for presently he came to a halt by the door which led to the inner office and quite unceremoniously pushed it open and walked through. I heard his peremptory demands for the Copies, and Mr. Baggs' muttered explanations. But I did not wait a moment longer. This was obviously my best opportunity for reappearing upon the Scene without his Lordship realizing that I had been in the parlour all the time. I slipped out from my hiding place and carefully rearranged the screen in its former position, then I tiptoed across the room.

In the gloom, I caught sight of Mr. Betterton standing in one of the Recesses, his slender white hands, which were so characteristic of his refined, artistic Personality, were clasped behind his back. I would have given a year or two of my humdrum life for the privilege of speaking to him then and of expressing to him some of that Sympathy with which my heart was overflowing. But no one knows better than I how proud a Man he is, and how he would have resented the thought that any one else had witnessed his Humiliation.

So I executed the Manoeuvre which I had in my mind without further delay. I opened the door which gave on the stairs noiselessly, then closed it again with a bang, as if I had just come in. Then I strode as heavily as I could across the room to the door of the inner office, against which I then rapped with my knuckles.

"Who's that?" Mr. Baggs' voice queried immediately.

"The Copies, Sir, which you ordered," I replied in a firm voice. "I have finished them."

"Come in! come in!" then broke in Lord Douglas impatiently. "I have waited in this accursed hole quite long enough."

The whole thing went off splendidly, and even Mr. Baggs did subsequently compliment me on my clever Ruse. Lord Douglas never suspected the fact that I had not been out of the Parlour for a moment, but had heard from the safe shelter of the window-recess everything that had been going on.

3

When, a few moments later, I returned to the Parlour, eager to have a few minutes' speech with Mr. Betterton, I saw that he had gone. Anon, Kathleen, the maid, brought in the candles and closed the shutters. I once more took my place at my desk, but this time made no use of the screen. After awhile, Lord Douglas came in, followed by the ever-obsequious Mr. Baggs, and almost directly after that, my Lord Stour came back.

His clothes were very wet and he shook the rain out from the brim of his hat.

"What a time You have been!" Lord Douglas said to him. "I was for going away without seeing You."

"I wanted to find out what had happened in here," my Lord Stour gave reply, speaking in a whisper.

"What do you mean?"

"The Fellow had the audacity to pay his addresses to Lady Barbara," my Lord Stour went on, still speaking below his breath. "I guessed as much, but wanted to make sure."

Lord Douglas uttered an angry Oath, and Lord Stour continued hurriedly:

"Such Insolence had to be severely punished, of course; and I saw to it."

"How?" queried the other eagerly.

"I have hired half a dozen Ruffians from the tavern yonder, to waylay him with sticks on his way from here, and to give him the sound thrashing he deserves."

It was with the most terrific effort at self-control that I succeeded in smothering the Cry of Horror which had risen to my lips. As it was, I jumped to my feet and both my chair and the candle from my desk fell with a clatter to the floor. I think that Mr. Baggs hurled a Volley of abuse upon me for my clumsiness and chided me

57

in that the grease from the candle was getting wasted by dripping on the floor. But the Gentlemen paid no heed to me. They were still engaged in their abominable conversation. While I stooped to pick up the chair and the candle, I heard my Lord Stour saying to his Friend:

"Come with me and see the Deed accomplished. The Mountebank must be made to know whose Hand is dealing him the well-merited punishment. My Hirelings meant to waylay him at the corner of Spreadeagle Court, a quiet place which is not far from here, and which leads into a blind Alley. Quickly, now," he added; "or we shall be too late."

More I did not hear; for, believe me, dear Mistress, I felt like one possessed. For the nonce, I did not care whether I was seen or not, whether Mr. Baggs guessed my purpose or not. I did not care if he abused me or even punished me later for my strange behaviour. All that I knew and felt just then was that I must run to the corner of Spreadeagle Court, where one of the most abominable Outrages ever devised by one Man against Another was even then being perpetrated. I tore across the room, through the door and down the stairs, hatless, my coat tails flying behind me, like some Maniac escaping from his Warders.

I ran up Chancery Lane faster, I think, than any man ever ran before. Already my ears were ringing with the sound of distant shouts and scuffling. My God! grant that I may not come too late. I, poor, weak, feeble of body, could of course do nothing against six paid and armed Ruffians; but at least I could be there to ward off or receive some of the blows which the arms of the sacrilegious Miscreants were dealing, at the instance of miserable Coxcombs, to a man whose Genius and Glory should have rendered him almost sacred in their sight.

4

As long as I live will that awful picture haunt me as I saw it then.

You know the Blind Alley on the left-hand side of Spreadeagle Court, with, at the end of it, the great double doorway which gives on the back premises of Mr. Brooks' silk warehouse. It was against that doorway that Mr. Betterton had apparently sought some semblance of refuge when first he was set upon by the Ruffians. By the time that I reached the corner of the Blind Alley, he had fallen against the door; for at first I could not see him. All that I saw was a group of burly backs, and arms waving sticks about in the air. All that I heard, oh, my God! were ribald cries and laughter, and sounds such as wild animals must make when they fall, hungry, upon their Prey. The Ruffians, I make no doubt, had no grudge against their Victim; but they had been well instructed and would be well paid if their foul deed was conscientiously accomplished.

My Wrath and Anxiety gave me the strength which I otherwise lack. Pushing, jostling, crawling, I contrived to work my way through the hideous Barrier which seethed and moved and shouted betwixt me and the Man whom I love.

When I at last kneeled beside him, I saw and heard nothing more. I did not feel the blows which one or two of the Ruffians thought fit to deal to Me. I only saw him, lying there against the door, panting, bleeding from forehead and hands, his clothes torn, his noble Face of a deathly Pallor. I drew his handkerchief from his coat pocket and staunched the wounds upon his face; I pillowed his head against my Shoulder; I helped him to struggle to his feet. He was in mortal pain and too weak to speak; but a ray of kindliness and of gratitude flashed through his eyes when he recognised me.

The Ruffians were apparently satisfied with their hideous work; but they still stood about at the top of the Alley, laughing and talking, waiting no doubt for their Blood Money. Oh! if wishes could have struck those Miscreants dumb or blind or palsied, my feeble voice would have been raised to Heaven, crying for Vengeance on such an infamous Deed. Hot tears came coursing down my cheeks, my temples throbbed with pain and Misery, as my arm stole round the trembling figure of my Friend.

Then all at once those tears were dried, the throbbing of my temples was stilled. I felt no longer like a Man, but like a petrified Statue of Indignation and of Hate. The sound of my Lord Stour's Voice had just struck upon mine ear. Vaguely through the gloom I could see him and Lord Douglas Wychwoode parleying with those abominable Ruffians.... I heard the jingle of Money ... Blood Money ... the ring of ribald laughter, snatches of a bibulous song.

These sounds and the clang of the Gentlemen's footsteps upon the cobble-stones also reached Mr. Betterton's fast-fading Senses. I felt a tremor coursing right through his limbs. With an almost superhuman Effort, he pulled himself together and drew himself erect, still clinging with both hands to my arms. By the time that the two young Cavaliers had reached the end of the blind Alley, the outraged Man was ready to confront them. Their presence there, those sounds of jingling money and of laughter, had told him the whole abominable tale. He fought against his Weakness, against Pain and against an impending Swoon. He was still livid, but it was with Rage. His eyes had assumed an unnatural Fire; his whole appearance as he stood there against the solid background of the massive door, was sublime in its forceful Expression of towering Wrath and of bitter, deadly Humiliation.

Even those two miserable Coxcombs paused for an instant, silenced and awed by what they saw. The laughter died upon their lips; the studied sneer upon their Face gave place to a transient expression of fear.

Mr. Betterton's arm was now extended and with trembling hand he pointed at Lord Stour.

"'Tis You——" he murmured hoarsely. "You—who have done—this thing?"

"At your service," replied the young Man, with a lightness of manner which was obviously forced and a great show of Haughtiness and of Insolence. "My friend Lord Douglas here, has allowed me the privilege of chastising a common Mountebank for daring to raise his eyes to the Lady Barbara Wychwoode——"

At mention of the Lady's name, I felt Mr. Betterton's clutch on my arm tighten convulsively.

"Does she——" he queried, "does she—know?"

"I forbid You," interposed Lord Douglas curtly, "to mention my Sister's name in the matter."

"'Tis to my Lord Stour I am speaking," rejoined Mr. Betterton more firmly. Then he added: "You will give me satisfaction for this outrage, my Lord——"

"Satisfaction?" riposted his Lordship coolly. "What do you mean?"

"One of us has got to die because of this," Mr. Betterton said loudly.

Whereupon my Lord Stour burst into a fit of hilarious laughter, which sounded as callous as it was forced.

"A Duel?" he almost shrieked, in a rasping voice. "Ha! ha! ha! a Duel!!!—a duel with You? ... With Tom Betterton, the Son of a Scullion.... By my faith! 'tis the best joke you ever made, Sir Actor ... 'tis worth repeating upon the Stage!"

But the injured Man waited unmoved until his Lordship's laughter died down in a savage Oath. Then he said calmly:

"The day and hour, my Lord Stour?"

"This is folly, Sir," rejoined the young Cavalier coldly. "The Earl of Stour can only cross swords with an Equal."

"In that case, my lord," was Mr. Betterton's calm reply, "you can only cross swords henceforth with a Coward and a Liar."

"Damned, insolent cur!" cried Lord Stour, maddened with rage no doubt at the other's calm contempt. He advanced towards us with arm uplifted—then perhaps felt ashamed, or frightened—I know not which. Certain it is that Lord Douglas succeeded in dragging him back a step or two, whilst he said with well-studied contempt:

"Pay no further heed to the fellow, my Friend. He has had his Punishment—do not bandy further Words with him."

He was for dragging Lord Stour away quickly now. I do believe that he was ashamed of the abominable Deed. At any rate, he could not bear to look upon the Man who had been so diabolically wronged.

"Come away, Man!" he kept reiterating at intervals. "Leave him alone!"

"One moment, my Lord," Mr. Betterton called out in a strangely powerful tone of Voice. "I wish to hear your last Word."

By now we could hardly see one another. The Blind Alley was in almost total gloom. Only against the fast-gathering dusk I could still see the hated figures of the two young Cavaliers, their outlines blurred by the evening haze. Lord Stour was certainly on the point of going; but at Mr. Betterton's loudly spoken Challenge, he paused once more, then came a step or two back towards us.

"My last Word?" he said coldly. Then he looked Mr. Betterton up and down, his every Movement, his whole Attitude, a deadly Insult. "One does not fight with such as You," he said, laughed, and would have turned away immediately, only that Mr. Betterton, with a quick and unforeseen Movement, suddenly reached forward and gripped him by the Wrist.

"Insolent puppy!" he said in a whisper, so hoarse and yet so distinct that not an Intonation, not a syllable of it was lost, "that knows not the Giant it has awakened by its puny bark. You refuse to cross swords with Tom Betterton, the son of a Menial, as you choose to say? Very well, then, 'tis Thomas Betterton, the Artist of undying renown, who now declares war against You. For every Jeer to-day, for every Insult and for every Blow, he will be even with You; for he will launch against You the irresistible Thunderbolt that kills worse than death and which is called Dishonour! ... Aye! I will fight You, my Lord; not to your death, but to your undying Shame. And now," he added more feebly, as he threw his Lordship's arm away from him with a gesture of supreme contempt, "go, I pray You, go! I'll not detain You any longer. You and your friend are free to laugh for the last time to-day at the name which I, with my Genius, have rendered immortal. Beware, my Lord! The Ridicule that kills, the Obloquy which smirches worse than the impious hands of paid Lacqueys.

This is the Word of Tom Betterton, my Lord; the first of his name, as you, please God, will be the last of yours!"

Then, without a groan, he fell, swooning, upon my shoulder. When consciousness of my surroundings once more returned to me, I realized that the two Gentlemen had gone.

CHAPTER VI

THE GATHERING STORM

1

It was after that never-to-be-forgotten Episode that Mr. Betterton honoured me with his full and entire Confidence. At the moment that he clung so pathetically to my feeble arms, he realized, I think for the first time, what a devoted Friend he would always find in me. Something of the powerful magical Fluid of my devotion must have emanated from my Heart and reached his sensitive Perceptions. He knew from that hour that, while I lived and had Health and Strength, I should never fail him in Loyalty and willing Service.

Soon afterwards, if you remember, Mr. Betterton went again to Paris, by command of His Majesty this time, there to study and to master the whole Question of Scenery and scenic Effects upon the Stage, such as is practised at the Theatre de Molière in the great City. That he acquitted himself of his task with Honour and Understanding goes without saying. The rousing Welcome which the public of London gave him on his return testified not only to his Worth but also to his Popularity.

The scenic Innovations, though daring and at times crudely realistic, did, in the opinion of Experts, set off the art of Mr. Betterton to the greatest possible Advantage. No doubt that his overwhelming Success at that time was in a great measure due to his familiarity with all those authentic-looking doors and trees and distant skies which at first bewildered such old-fashioned actors as Mr. Harris or the two Messrs. Noakes.

Never indeed had Mr. Betterton been so great as he was now. Never had his Talents stood so high in the estimation of the cultured

World. His success as Alvaro in "Love and Honour," as Solyman in the "Siege of Rhodes," as Hamlett or Pericles, stand before me as veritable Triumphs. Bouquets and Handkerchiefs, scented Notes and Love-tokens, were showered upon the brilliant Actor as he stood upon the Stage, proudly receiving the adulation of the Audience whom he had conquered by the Magic of his Art.

His Majesty hardly ever missed a Performance at the new Duke's Theatre when Mr. Betterton was acting, nor did my Lady Castlemaine, who was shamelessly vowing about that time that she was prepared to bestow upon the great Man any Favour he might ask of her.

2

But outwardly at any rate, Mr. Betterton had become a changed Man. His robust Constitution and splendid Vitality did in truth overcome the physical after-effects of the abominable Outrage of which he had been the Victim; but the moral consequences upon his entire character and demeanour were indeed incalculable. Of extraordinary purity in his mode of living, it had been difficult, before that Episode, for evil Gossip to besmirch his fair name, even in these lax and scandalous times. But after that grim September afternoon it seemed as if he took pride in emulating the least estimable characteristics of his Contemporaries. His Majesty's avowed predilection for the great Actor brought the latter into daily contact with all those noble and beautiful Ladies who graced the Court and Society, more by virtue of their outward appearance than of their inner worth. Scarce ever was a banquet or fête given at While Hall now but Mr. Betterton was not one of the most conspicuous guests; never a Supper party at my Lady Castlemaine's or my Lady Shrewsbury's but the famous Actor was present there. He was constantly in the company of His Grace of Buckingham, of my Lord Rochester and others of those noble young Rakes; his name was constantly before the Public; he was daily to be seen on the Mall, or in St. James's Park, or at the more ceremonious parade in Hyde Park. His elegant clothes were the talk of every young Gallant that haunted Fop's Corner; his sallies were quoted by every Cavalier who strove for a reputation as a wit. In fact, dear Lady, You know just as well as I do, that for that brief period of his life Mr. Betterton became just one of the gay, idle, modish young Men about town, one of that hard-drinking, gambling, scandal-mongering crowd of Idlers, who were none of them fit to tie the lacets of his shoes.

I, who saw more and more of him in those days, knew, however, that all that gay, butterfly Existence which he led was only on the surface. To me he was like some poor Animal stricken by a mortal wound, who, nevertheless, capers and gyrates before a grinning Public with mechanical movements of the body that have nothing in common with the mind.

3

Of the beautiful Lady Barbara I saw but little during the autumn.

There was much talk in the Town about her forthcoming Marriage to my Lord of Stour, which was to take place soon after the New Year. Many were the conjectures as to why so suitable a Marriage did not take place immediately, and it seemed strange that so humble and insignificant a Person as I was could even then have supplied the key to the riddle which was puzzling so many noble Ladies and Gentlemen. I knew, in my humble capacity as Spectator of great events, that the Marriage would only take place after the vast and treasonable projects which had originated in my Lord Douglas Wychwoode's turbulent mind had come to a successful issue.

I often confided to You, dear Mistress, in those days that Mr. Betterton, in the kindness of his Heart, had made me many an offer to leave my present humdrum employment and to allow myself to be attached to his Person as his private Secretary and personal Friend. For a long time I refused his offers—tempting and generous though they were—chiefly because if I had gone then to live with Mr. Betterton, I should have been irretrievably separated from You. But in my Heart I knew that, though the great Man was not in pressing need of a Secretary, his soul did even long and yearn for a Friend. A more devoted one, I vow, did not exist than my humble self; and when, during the early part of the autumn, You, dear Mistress, finally decided to leave your present uncomfortable quarters for lodgings more befitting your growing Fame and your Talents, there was nothing more to keep me tied to my dour and unsympathetic Employer, and to his no less unpleasant Spouse.

I therefore gave Mr. Theophilus Baggs notice that I had

resolved to quit his Employ, hoping that my Decision would meet with his Convenience.

I could not help laughing to myself when I saw the manner in which he received this Announcement. To say that he was surprised and indignant would be to put it mildly; indeed, he used every Mode of persuasion to try and make me alter my decision. He began by chiding me for an Ingrate, vowing that he had taught me all I knew and had lavished Money and Luxuries upon me, and that I was proposing to leave him just when the time had come for him to see some slight return for his Expenditure and for his pains, in my growing Efficiency. He went on to persuade, to cajole and to bribe, Mistress Euphrosine joining him both in Vituperation and in Unctuousness. But, as You know, I was adamant. I knew the value of all this soft-sawder and mouth-honour. I had suffered too many Hardships and too many Indignities at the hands of these selfish Sycophants, to turn a deaf ear now that friendship and mine own future happiness called to me so insistently.

Finally, however, I yielded to the extent of agreeing to stay a further three months in the service of Mr. Baggs, whilst he took steps to find another Clerk who would suit his purpose. But I only agreed to this on the condition that I was to be allowed a fuller amount of personal Freedom than I had enjoyed hitherto; that I should not be set any longer to do menial tasks, which properly pertained to a Scullion; and that, whenever my clerical work for the day was done, I should be at liberty to employ my time as seemed best to me.

Thus it was that I had a certain amount of leisure, and after You left us, fair Mistress, I was able to take my walks abroad, there where I was fairly certain of meeting You, or of having a glimpse of Mr. Betterton, surrounded by his brilliant Friends.

Often, dear Mistress, did You lavish some of your precious time and company upon the seedy Attorney's Clerk, who of a truth was not worthy to be seen walking in the Park or in Mulberry Gardens beside the beautiful and famous Mistress Saunderson, who by this time had quite as many Followers and Adorers as any virtuous Woman could wish for. You never mentioned Mr. Betterton to me in those days, even though I knew that You must often have been thrown in his Company, both in the Theatre and in Society. That your love for him had not died in your Heart, I knew from the wistful look which was wont to come into your eyes whenever You chanced to meet him in the course of a Promenade. You always returned his respectful and elaborate bow on those occasions with cool Composure; but as soon as he had passed by and his rich, mellow Voice, so easily distinguishable amongst others, had died away in the distance, I, who knew every line of your lovely face, saw the familiar look of Sorrow and of bitter Disappointment once more mar its perfect serenity.

4

We had an unusually mild and prolonged autumn this past year, if you remember, fair Mistress; and towards the end of October there were a few sunny days which were the veritable aftermath of Summer. The London Parks and Gardens were crowded day after day with Ladies and Gallants, decked in their gayest attire, for the time to don winter clothing still appeared remote.

I used to be fond of watching all these fair Ladies and dazzling Cavaliers, and did so many a time on those bright mornings whilst waiting to see You pass. On one occasion I saw the Lady Barbara Wychwoode, in company with my Lord Stour.

Heaven knows I have no cause to think kindly of her; but truth compels me to say that she appeared to me more beautiful than ever before. She and his Lordship had found two chairs, up against a tree, somewhat apart from the rest of the glittering throng. I, as a Spectator, could see that they were supremely happy in one another's company.

"How sweet the air is!" she was sighing contentedly. "More like spring than late autumn. Ah, me! How happily one could dream!"

She threw him a witching glance, which no doubt sent him straight to Heaven, for I heard him say with passionate earnestness:

"Of what do Angels dream, my beloved?"

They continued to whisper, and I of course did not catch all that they said. My Lord Stour was obviously very deeply enamoured of the Lady Barbara. Because of this I seemed to hate and despise him all the more. Oh! when the whole World smiled on him, when Fortune and Destiny showered their most precious gifts into his lap, what right had he to mar the soul which God had given him with such base Passions as Jealousy and Cruelty? With his monstrous Act of unwarrantable violence he had ruined the happiness of a Man greater, finer than himself; he had warped a noble disposition, soured a gentle and kindly spirit. Oh! I hated him! I hated him! God forgive me, but I had not one spark of Christian spirit for him within

66

my heart. If it lay in my power, I knew that I was ready to do him an Injury.

From time to time I heard snatches of his impassioned speeches. "Barbara, my beloved! Oh, God! how I love You!" Or else: "'Tis unspeakable joy to look into your eyes, joyous madness to hold your little hand!" And more of such stuff, as Lovers know how to use.

And she, too, looked supremely happy. There was a sparkle in her eyes which spoke of a Soul intoxicated with delight. She listened to him as if every word from his lips was heaven-sent Manna to her hungering heart. And I marvelled why this should be; why she should listen to this self-sufficient, empty-headed young Coxcomb and have rejected with such bitter scorn the suit of a Man worthy in every sense to be the Mate of a Queen. And I thought then of Mr. Betterton kneeling humbly before her, his proud Head bent before this ignorant and wilful Girl, who had naught but cruel words for him on her lips. And a great wrath possessed me, greater than it ever had been before. I suppose that I am very wicked and that the Devil of Revenge had really possessed himself of my Soul; but then and there, under the trees, with the translucent Dome of blue above me, I vowed bitter hatred against those two, vowed that Fate should be even with them if I, the humble Clerk, could have a say in her decrees.

5

Just now, they were like two Children playing at love. He was insistent and bold, tried to draw her to him, to kiss her in sight of the fashionable throng that promenaded up and down the Avenue less than fifty yards away.

"A murrain on the Conventions!" he said with a light laugh, as she chided him for his ardour. "I want the whole Universe to be witness of my joy."

She placed her pretty hand playfully across his mouth.

"Hush, my dear Lord," she said with wonderful tenderness. "Heaven itself, they say, is oft times jealous to see such Happiness as ours.... And I am so happy..." she continued with a deep sigh, "so happy that sometimes a horrible presentiment seems to grip my heart..."

"Presentiment of what, dear love?" he queried lightly.

I did not catch what she said in reply, for just at that moment I caught sight of Mr. Betterton walking at a distant point of the Avenue, in the Company of a number of admiring Friends.

They were hanging round him, evidently vastly amused by some witty sallies of his. Never had I seen him look more striking and more brilliant. He wore a magnificent coat of steel-grey velvet with richly embroidered waistcoat, and a cravat and frills of diaphanous lace, whilst the satin breeches, silk stockings and be-ribboned shoes set off his shapely limbs to perfection. His Grace of Buckingham was walking beside him, and he had my Lady Shrewsbury upon his arm, whilst among his Friends I recognised my Lords Orrery and Buckhurst, and the Lord Chancellor himself.

The Lady Barbara caught sight of Mr. Betterton, too, I imagine, for as I moved away, I heard her say in a curiously constrained voice:

"That man—my Lord—he is your deadly Enemy."

"Bah!" he retorted with a careless shrug of the shoulders. "Actors are like toothless, ill-tempered curs. They bark, but they are powerless to bite!"

Oh, I hated him! Heavens above! how I hated him!

How puny and insignificant he was beside his unsuccessful Rival should of a surety have been apparent even to the Lady Barbara. Even now, Mr. Betterton, with a veritable crowd of Courtiers around him, had come to a halt not very far from where those two were sitting; and it was very characteristic of him that, even whilst the Duke of Buckingham was whispering in his ear and the Countess of Shrewsbury was smiling archly at him, his eyes having found me, he nodded and waved his hand to me.

6

A minute or two later, another group of Ladies and Gallants, amongst whom Her Grace the Duchess of York was conspicuous by her elegance and the richness of her attire, literally swooped down upon Mr. Betterton and his Friends, and Her Grace's somewhat high-pitched voice came ringing shrilly to mine ear.

"Ah, Mr. Betterton!" she exclaimed. "Where have you hid yourself since yesterday, you wicked, adorable Man? And I, who wished to tell you how entirely splendid was your performance in that supremely dull play you call 'Love and Honour.' You were superb, Sir, positively superb! ... I was telling His Grace a moment ago that every Actor in the world is a mere Mountebank when compared with Mr. Betterton's Genius."

And long did she continue in the same strain, most of the Ladies and Gentlemen agreeing with her and engaging in a chorus of Eulogy, all delivered in high falsetto voices, which in the olden days, when first I knew him, would have set Mr. Betterton's very teeth on edge. But now he took up the ball of airy talk, tossed it back to the Ladies, bowed low and kissed Her Grace's hand—I could see that she gave his a significant pressure—gave wit for wit and flattery for flattery.

He had of a truth made a great success the day before in a play called "Love and Honour," writ by Sir William Davenant, when His Majesty himself lent his own Coronation Suit to the great Actor, so that he might worthily represent the part of Prince Alvaro. This Success put the crowning Glory to his reputation, although in my humble opinion it was unworthy of so great an Artist as Mr. Betterton to speak the Epilogue which he had himself written in eulogy of the Countess of Castlemaine, and which he delivered with such magnificent Diction at the end of the Play, that His Majesty waxed quite enthusiastic in his applause.

7

Standing somewhat apart from that dazzling group, I noticed my Lord Douglas Wychwoode, in close conversation with my Lord Teammouth and another Gentleman, who was in clerical attire. After awhile, my Lord Stour joined them, the Lady Barbara having apparently slipped away unobserved.

My Lord Stour was greeted by his friends with every mark of cordiality.

"Ah!" the Cleric exclaimed, and extended both his hands—which were white and plump—to my Lord. "Here is the truant at last!" Then he waxed playful, put up an accusing finger and added with a smirking laugh: "Meseems I caught sight of a petticoat just behind those trees, where his Lordship himself had been apparently communing with Nature, eh?"

Whereupon my Lord Teammouth went on, not unkindly and in that dogmatic way which he was pleased to affect: "Youth will ever smile, even in the midst of dangers; and my Lord Stour is a great favourite with the Ladies."

Lord Douglas Wychwoode was as usual petulant and impatient, and rejoined angrily:

"Even the Castlemaine has tried to cast her nets around him."

My Lord Stour demurred, but did not try to deny the soft impeachment.

"Only because I am new at Court," he said, "and have no eyes for her beauty."

This, of course, was News to me. I am so little versed in Court and Society gossip and had not heard the latest piece of scandal, which attributed to the Lady Castlemaine a distinct penchant for the young Nobleman. Not that it surprised me altogether. The newly created Countess of Castlemaine, who was receiving favours from His Majesty the King with both hands, never hesitated to deceive him, and even to render him ridiculous by flaunting her predilections for this or that young Gallant who happened to have captured her wayward fancy. My Lord Sandwich, Colonel Hamilton, the handsome Mr. Wycherley, and even such a vulgar churl as Jacob Hill, the rope dancer, had all, at one time or another, been favoured with the lady's fitful smiles, and while responding to her advances with the Ardour born of Cupidity or of a desire for self-advancement rather than of true love, they had for the most part lost some shreds of their Reputation and almost all of their Self-respect.

But at the moment I paid no heed to Lord Douglas' taunt levelled at his Friend, nor at the latter's somewhat careless way of Retort. In fact, the whole Episode did not then impress itself upon my mind, and it was only in face of later events that I was presently to be reminded of it all.

8

For the moment I was made happy by renewed kindly glances from Mr. Betterton. It seemed as if his eyes had actually beckoned to me, so I made bold to advance nearer to the dazzling group of Ladies and Gentlemen that stood about, talking—jabbering, I might say, like a number of gay-plumaged birds, for they seemed to me irresponsible and unintellectual in their talk.

Of course, I could not hear everything, and I had to try and make my unfashionably attired Person as inconspicuous as possible. So I drew a book from my pocket, one that looked something like a Greek Lexicon, though in truth it was a collection of Plays writ by the late Mr. William Shakespeare, in one or two of which—notably in one called "Hamlett"—Mr. Betterton had scored some of his most conspicuous Triumphs.

The book, and my seeming absorption in it, gave me the countenance of an earnest young Student intent on the perusal of Classics, even whilst it enabled me to draw quite near to the brilliant Throng of Distinguished People, who, if they paid any heed to me at all, would find excuses for my Presumption in my obvious earnest Studiousness. I was also able to keep some of my attention fixed upon Mr. Betterton, who was surrounded by admiring Friends; whilst at some little distance close by, I could see Mr. Harris—also of the Duke's Theatre—who was holding forth in a didactic manner before a group of Ladies and gay young Sparks, even though they were inclined to mock him because of his Conceit in pitting his talent against that of Mr. Betterton.

There was no doubt that a couple of years ago Mr. Harris could be, and was considered, the greatest Actor of his time; but since Mr. Betterton had consolidated his own triumph by playing the parts of Pericles, of Hamlett and of Prince Alvaro in "Love and Honour," the older Actor's reputation had undoubtedly suffered by comparison with the Genius of his younger Rival, at which of course he was greatly incensed. I caught sight now and then of his florid face, so different in expression to Mr. Betterton's more spiritual-looking countenance, and from time to time his pompous, raucous voice reached my ears, as did the more strident, high-pitched voices of the Ladies. I heard one young Lady say, to the accompaniment of some pretty, mincing gestures:

"Mr. Betterton was positively rapturous last night ... enchanting! You, Mr. Harris, will in truth have to look to your laurels."

And an elderly Lady, a Dowager of obvious consideration and dignity, added in tones which brooked of no contradiction:

"My opinion is that there never has been or ever will be a Player equal to Mr. Betterton in Purity of Diction and Elegance of Gesture. He hath indeed raised our English Drama to the level of High Art."

I could have bowed low before her and kissed her hand for this; aye! and have paid homage, too, to all these gaily-dressed Butterflies who, in truth, had more Intellectuality in them than I had given them credit for. Every word of Eulogy of my beloved Friend was a delight to my soul. I felt mine eyes glowing with enthusiasm and had grave difficulty in keeping them fixed upon my book.

I had never liked Mr. Harris personally, for I was wont to

think his conceit quite overweening beside the unalterable modesty of Mr. Betterton, who was so incomparably his Superior; and I was indeed pleased to see that both the Dowager Lady—who, I understood, was the Marchioness of Badlesmere—and the younger Ladies and Gentlemen felt mischievously inclined to torment him.

"What is your opinion, Mr. Harris?" my Lady Badlesmere was saying to the discomfited Actor. "It would be interesting to know one Player's opinion of another."

She had a spy-glass, through which she regarded him quizzically, whilst a mocking smile played around her thin lips. This, no doubt, caused poor Mr. Harris to lose countenance, for as a rule he is very glib of tongue. But just now he mouthed and stammered, appeared unable to find his words.

"It cannot be denied, your Ladyship," he began sententiously enough, "that Mr. Betterton's gestures are smooth and pleasant, though they perhaps lack the rhythmic grandeur ... the dignified sweep ... of ... of ... the..."

He was obviously floundering, and the old Lady broke in with a rasping laugh and a tone of somewhat acid sarcasm.

"Of the gestures of Mr. Harris, you mean, eh?"

"No, Madam," he retorted testily, and distinctly nettled. "I was about to say 'of the gestures of our greatest Actors.'"

"Surely the same thing, dear Mr. Harris," a young Lady rejoined with well-assumed demureness, and dropped him a pert little curtsey.

I might have been sorry for the Man—for of a truth these small pin-pricks must have been very irritating to his Vanity, already sorely wounded by a younger Rival's triumph—but for the fact that he then waxed malicious, angered no doubt by hearing a veritable Chorus of Eulogy proceeding from that other group of Ladies and Gentlemen of which Mr. Betterton was the centre.

I do not know, as a matter of fact, who it was who first gave a spiteful turning to the bantering, mocking Conversation of awhile ago; but in my mind I attributed this malice to Lord Douglas Wychwoode, who came up with his clerical friend just about this time, in order to pay his respects to the Marchioness of Badlesmere, who, I believe, is a near Relative of his. Certain it is that very soon after his arrival upon the scene, I found that every one around him was talking about the abominable Episode, the very thought of which sent my blood into a Fever and my thoughts running a veritable riot of Revenge and of Hate. Of course, Mr. Harris was to the fore with pointed Allusions to the grave Insult done to an eminent Artist, and which, to my thinking, should have been condemned by every right-minded Man or Woman who had a spark of lofty feeling in his or her heart.

"Ah, yes!" one of the Ladies was saying; "I heard about it at the time ... a vastly diverting story...."

"Which went the round of the Court," added another.

"Mr. Betterton's shoulders," a gay young Spark went on airily, "are said to be still very sore."

"And his usually equable Temper the sorer of the two."

Lord Douglas did not say much, but I felt his spiteful Influence running as an undercurrent through all that flippant talk.

"Faith!" concluded one of the young Gallants, "were I my Lord Stour, I would not care to have Mr. Betterton for an enemy."

"An Actor can hit with great accuracy and harshness from the Stage," Mr. Harris went on pompously. "He speaks words which a vast Public hears and goes on to repeat ad infinitum. Thus a man's— aye! or a Lady's—reputation can be made or marred by an Epilogue spoken by a popular Player at the end of a Drama. We all remember the case of Sir William Liscard, after he had quarrelled with Mr. Kynaston."

Whereupon that old story was raked up, how Mr. Kynaston had revenged himself for an insult upon him by Sir William Liscard by making pointed Allusions from the Stage to the latter's secret intrigue with some low-class wench, and to the Punishment which was administered to him by the wench's vulgar lover. The Allusions were unmistakable, because that punishment had taken the form of a slit nose, and old Sir William had appeared in Society one day with a piece of sticking plaster across the middle of his face.

Well, we all know what happened after that. Sir William, covered with Ridicule, had to leave London for awhile and bury himself in the depths of the Country, for, in Town he could not show his face in the streets but he was greeted with some vulgar lampoon or ribald song, hurled at him by passing roisterers. It all ended in a Tragedy, for Lady Liscard got to hear of it, and there was talk of Divorce proceedings, which would have put Sir William wholly out of Court—His Majesty being entirely averse to the dissolution of any legal Marriage.

But all this hath naught to do with my story, and I only recount the matter to You to show You how, in an instant, the temper of all these great Ladies and Gentlemen can be swayed by the judicious handling of an evil-minded Person.

All these Ladies and young Rakes, who awhile ago were loud in their praises of a truly great Man, now found pleasure in throwing mud at him, ridiculing and mocking him shamefully, seeing that, had he been amongst them, he would soon have confounded them with his Wit and brought them back to Allegiance by his magic Personality.

Once again I heard a distinct Allusion to the Countess of Castlemaine's avowed predilection for Lord Stour. It came from one of the Cavaliers, who said to Lord Douglas, with an affected little laugh:

"Perhaps my Lord Stour would do well to place himself unreservedly under the protection of Lady Castlemaine! 'Tis said that she is more than willing to extend her Favours to him."

"Nay! Stour hath nothing to fear," Lord Douglas replied curtly. "He stands far above a mere Mountebank's spiteful pin-pricks."

Oh! had but God given me the power to strike such a Malapert dumb! I looked around me, marvelling if there was not one sane Person here who would stand up in the defence of a great and talented Artist against this jabbering of irresponsible Monkeys.

9

I must admit, however, that directly Mr. Betterton appeared upon the scene the tables were quickly turned once more on Mr. Harris, and even on Lord Douglas, for Mr. Betterton is past Master in the art of wordy Warfare, and, moreover, has this great Advantage, that he never loses control over his Temper. No malicious shaft aimed at him will ever ruffle his Equanimity, and whilst his Wit is most caustic, he invariably retains every semblance of perfect courtesy.

He now had the Duchess of York on his arm, and His Grace of Buckingham had not left his side. His Friends were unanimously chaffing him about that Epilogue which he had spoken last night, and which had so delighted the Countess of Castlemaine. My Lord Buckhurst and Sir William Davenant were quoting pieces out of it, whilst I could only feel sorry that so great a Man had lent himself to such unworthy Flattery.

"'Divinity, radiant as the stars!'" Lord Buckhurst quoted with a laugh. "By gad, you Rogue, you did not spare your words."

Mr. Betterton frowned almost imperceptibly, and I, his devoted Admirer, guessed that he was not a little ashamed of the fulsome Adulation which he had bestowed on so unworthy an Object, and I was left to marvel whether some hidden purpose as yet unknown to me had actuated so high-minded an Artist thus to debase the Art which he held so dear. It was evident, however, that the whole Company thought that great things would come from that apparently trivial incident.

"My Lady Castlemaine," said Sir William Davenant, "hath been wreathed in smiles ever since you spoke that Epilogue. She vows that there is nothing she would not do for You. And, as already You are such a favourite with His Majesty, why, Man! there is no end to your good fortune."

And I, who watched Mr. Betterton's face again, thought to detect a strange, mysterious look in his eyes—something hidden and brooding was going on behind that noble brow, something that was altogether strange to the usually simple, unaffected and sunny temperament of the great Artist, and which I, his intimate Confidant and Friend, had not yet been able to fathom.

Whenever I looked at him these days, I was conscious as of a sultry Summer's day, when nature is outwardly calm and every leaf on every tree is still. It is only to those who are initiated in the mysteries of the Skies that the distant oncoming Storm is revealed by a mere speck of cloud or a tiny haze upon the Bosom of the Firmament, which hath no meaning to the unseeing eye, but which foretells that the great forces of Nature are gathering up their strength for the striking of a prodigious blow.

CHAPTER VII

AN ASSEMBLY OF TRAITORS

1

I, in the meanwhile, had relegated the remembrance of Lord Douglas Wychwoode and his treasonable Undertakings to a distant cell of my mind. I had not altogether forgotten them, but had merely ceased to think upon the Subject.

I was still nominally in the employ of Mr. Baggs, but he had engaged a new Clerk—a wretched, puny creature, whom Mistress

Euphrosine already held in bondage—and I was to leave his Service definitely at the end of the month.

In the meanwhile, my chief task consisted in initiating the aforesaid wretched and puny Clerk into the intricacies of Mr. Theophilus Baggs' business. The boy was slow-witted and slow to learn, and Mr. Baggs, who would have liked to prove to me mine own Worthlessness, was nevertheless driven into putting some of his more important work still in my charge.

Thus it came to pass that all his Correspondence with Lord Douglas Wychwoode went through my Hands, whereby I was made aware that the Traitors—for such in truth they were—were only waiting for a favourable opportunity to accomplish their damnable Purpose.

They meant to kidnap His Majesty's sacred Person, to force him to sign an Abdication in favour of the son of Mistress Barlow— now styled the Duke of Monmouth—with the Prince of Orange as Regent during the Duke's minority.

A more abominable and treasonable Project it were impossible to conceive, and many a wrestling match did I have with mine own Conscience, whilst debating whether it were my Duty or no to betray the confidence which had been reposed in me, and to divulge the terrible Secret of that execrable plot, which threatened the very life of His Majesty the King.

I understood that the Manifestos which it had been my task to multiplicate, had met with some success. Several Gentlemen, who held rigidly Protestant views, had promised their support to a project which ostensibly aimed at the overthrow of the last vestiges of Popery in the Country. My Lord Stour, who had also become a firm Adherent of the nefarious scheme, in deference, I presume, to the Lady Barbara's wishes in the matter, had, it seems, rendered valuable service to the cause, by travelling all over the Country, seeing these proposed Adherents in person and distributing the fiery Manifestos which were to rally the Waverers to the cause.

I imagined, however, that the whole project was in abeyance for the moment, for I had heard but little of it of late; until one day I happened to be present when the Conspirators met in the house of Mr. Theophilus Baggs.

How it came to pass that these Gentlemen—who were literally playing with their lives in their nefarious undertaking—talked thus openly of their Plans and Projects in my hearing, I do not pretend to say. It is certain that they did not suspect me; thought me one of themselves, no doubt, since I had written out the Manifestos and was Clerk to Mr. Baggs, who was with them Body and Soul. No doubt, had Mr. Baggs been on the spot on that day, he would have

76

warned the Traitors of my presence, and much of what happened subsequently would never have occurred.

Thus doth Fate at times use simple tools to gain her own ends, and it was given to an insignificant Attorney's Clerk to rule, for this one day, the future Destinies of England.

2

My Lord Stour was present on that memorable afternoon. I am betraying no Secret nor doing him an injury by saying that, because his connection with the Affair is of public knowledge, as is that of Lord Douglas Wychwoode. The names of the other Gentlemen whom I saw in Mr. Baggs' room that day I will, by your leave, keep hidden behind the veil of Anonymity, contenting myself by calling the most important among them my Lord S., and another Sir J., whilst there was also present on that occasion the gentleman in clerical Attire whom I had seen of late in Lord Douglas' Company, and who was none other than the Lord Bishop of D.

My Lord Stour was in great favour amongst them all. Every one was praising him and shaking him by the hand. His Lordship the Bishop took it upon himself to say, as he did most incisively:

"Gentlemen! I am proud and happy to affirm that it is to the Earl of Stour that we shall owe to-night the Success of our Cause. It is he who has distributed our Appeal and helped to rally round us some of our most loyal Friends!"

Lord Stour demurred, deprecated his own efforts. His Attitude was both modest and firm; I had not thought him capable of so much Nobility of Manner.

But, believe me, dear Mistress, that I felt literally confounded by what I heard. Mr. Baggs, who had pressing business in town that day, had commanded me to remain at home in order to receive certain Gentlemen who were coming to visit him. I had introduced some half-dozen of them, and they had all gone into the inner office, but left the communicating door between that room and the parlour wide open, apparently quite acquiescing in my presence there. In fact, they had all nodded very familiarly to me as they entered; evidently they felt absolutely certain of my Discretion. This, as you will readily understand, placed me in a terrible Predicament. Where lay my duty, I did not know; for, in truth, to betray the Confidence of those who trust in You is a mean and low trick, unworthy of a right-minded Christian. At the same time, there was His Majesty the

77

King's own sacred Person in peril, and that, as far as I could gather, on this very night; and surely it became equally the duty of every loyal Subject in the land to try and protect his Sovereign from the nefarious attacks of Traitors!

Be that as it may, however, I do verily believe that if my Lord—Stour whom I hated with so deadly a hatred, and who had done my dear, dear Friend such an irreparable injury—if he, I say, had not been mixed up in the Affair, I should have done my duty as a Christian rather than as a subject of the State.

But You, dear Mistress, shall be judge of mine actions, for they have a direct bearing upon those subsequent events which have brought Mr. Betterton once again to your feet.

I have said that my Lord Stour received his Friends' congratulations and gratitude with becoming Modesty; but his Lordship the Bishop and also Lord S. insisted.

"It is thanks to your efforts, my dear Stour," Lord S. said, "that at last success is assured."

"But for you," added the Bishop, "our plan to-night might have miscarried."

My God! I thought, then it is for to-night! And I felt physically sick, whilst wondering what I should do. Even then, Lord Douglas Wychwoode's harsh Voice came quite clearly to mine ear.

"The day is ours!" he said, with a note of triumph in his tone. "Ere the sun rises again over our downtrodden Country, her dissolute King and his Minions will be in our hands!"

"Pray God it may be so!" assented one of the others piously.

"It shall and will be so," protested Lord Douglas with firm emphasis. "I know for a fact that the King sups with the Castlemaine to-night. Well! we are quite ready. By ten o'clock we shall have taken up our Positions. These have all been most carefully thought out. Some of us will be in hiding in the Long Avenue in the Privy Garden; others under the shadow of the Wall of the Bowling Green; whilst others again have secured excellent points of vantage in King Street. I am in command of the Party, and I give you my word that my Company is made up of young Enthusiasts. They, like ourselves, have had enough of this corrupt and dissolute Monarch, who ought never to have been allowed to ascend the Throne which his Father had already debased."

"You will have to be careful of the Night Watchmen about the Gardens, and of the Bodyguard at the Gate," one of the Gentlemen broke in.

"Of course we'll be careful," Lord Douglas riposted impatiently. "We have minimized our risks as far as we are able. But the King, when he sups with the Castlemaine, usually goes across to

78

her House unattended. Sometimes he takes a Man with him across the Privy Gardens, but dismisses him at the back door of Her Ladyship's House. As for the City Watchmen over in King Street, they will give us no trouble. If they do, we can easily overpower them. The whole thing is really perfectly simple," he added finally; "and the only reason why we have delayed execution is because we wanted as many Sympathizers here in London as possible."

"Now," here interposed His Lordship the Bishop, "thanks to my Lord Stour's efforts, a number of our Adherents have come up from the country and have obtained lodgings in various Quarters of the town, so that to-morrow morning, when we proclaim the Duke of Monmouth King and the Prince of Orange Regent of the Realm, we shall be in sufficient numbers to give to our successful Coup the appearance of a national movement."

"Personally," rejoined Lord Douglas, with something of a sneer, "I think that the Populace will be very easily swayed. The Castlemaine is not popular. The King is; but it is a factitious Popularity, and one easily blown upon, once we have his Person safely out of the way. And we must remember that the 'No Popery' cry is still a very safe card to play with the mob," he added with a dry laugh.

Then they all fell to and discussed their abominable Plans all over again; whilst I, bewildered, wretched, indignant, fell on my knees and marvelled, pondered what I should do. My pulses were throbbing, my head was on fire; I had not the faculty for clear thinking. And there, in the next room, not ten paces away from where I knelt in mute and agonized Prayer, six Men were planning an outrage against their King; amidst sneers and mirthless laughter and protestations of loyalty to their Country, they planned the work of Traitors. They drew their Swords and there was talk of invoking God's blessing upon their nefarious Work.

God's blessing! Methought 'twas Blasphemy, and I put my hands up to mine ears lest I should hear those solemn words spoken by a consecrated Bishop of our Church, and which called for the Almighty's help to accomplish a second Regicide.

Aye! A Regicide! What else was it? as all those fine Gentlemen knew well enough in their hearts. Would not the King resist? He was young and vigorous. Would he not call for help? Had not my Lady Castlemaine Servants who would rush to His Majesty's assistance? What then? Was there to be murder once more, and bloodshed and rioting—fighting such as we poor Citizens of this tortured land had hoped was behind us forever?

And if it came to a hand-to-hand scuffle with the King's most

Sacred Majesty? My God! I shuddered to think what would happen then!

There was a mighty humming in my ears, like the swarm of myriads of bees; a red veil gradually spread before my eyes, which obscured the familiar Surroundings about me. Through the haze which gradually o'er-clouded my brain, I heard the voices of those Traitors droning out their blasphemous Oaths.

"Swear only to draw your swords in this just cause, and not to shed unnecessary blood!"

And then a chorus which to my ears sounded like the howling of Evil Spirits let loose from hell:

"We swear!"

"Then may God's blessing rest upon You. May His Angels guard and protect You and give You the strength to accomplish what You purpose to do!"

There was a loud and prolonged "Amen!" But I waited no longer. I rose from my knees, suddenly calm and resolved. Do not laugh at me, dear Mistress, for my conceit and my presumption when I say that I felt that the destinies of England rested in my hands.

Another Regicide! Oh, my God! Another era of civil Strife and military Dictatorship such as we had endured in the past decade! Another era of Suspicions and Jealousies and Intrigues between the many Factions who would wish to profit by this abominable crime! It was unthinkable. Whether the King was God's Anointed or not, I, for one, am too ignorant to decide; but this I know, that the Stuart Prince was chosen little more than a year ago by the will of his People, that he returned to England acclaimed and beloved by this same Populace which was now to be egged on to treason against him by a handful of ambitious Malcontents, who did not themselves know what it was they wanted.

No! It should not be! Not while there existed an humble and puny subject of this Realm who had it in his power to put a spoke in the wheel of that Chariot of Traitors.

Ah! there was no more wavering in my heart now! no more doubts and hesitation! I would not be betraying the confidence of a trusting Man; merely disposing of a secret which Chance had tossed carelessly in my path—a Secret which pertained to abominable Miscreants, one of whom was the man whom I detested more than any one or anything on God's earth—a flippant, arrogant young Reprobate who had dared to level a deadly insult against a Man infinitely his superior in Intellect and in Worth, and before whom now he should be made to lick the dust of Ignominy.

I was now perfectly calm. From my desk I took a copy of the

80

Manifesto which had remained in my possession all this while. I read the contents through very carefully, so as to refresh my memory. Then I took up my pen and, at the foot of the treasonable document, I wrote the word: "To-night." Having done that, I took a sheet of notepaper and carefully wrote down the names of all the Gentlemen who were even now in the next room, and of several others whom I had heard mentioned by the Traitors in the course of their Conversation. The two papers I folded carefully and closed them down with sealing wax.

My hand did not shake whilst I did all this. I was perfectly deliberate, for my mind was irrevocably made up. When I had completed these preparations, I slipped the precious Documents into my pocket, took up my hat and cloak, and went out to accomplish the Errand which I had set myself to do.

CHAPTER VIII

THE LION'S WRATH

1

His Majesty the King was, of course, inaccessible to such as I. And the time was short.

Did I say that the hour was even then after six? The streets were very dark, for overhead the sky was overcast, and as I walked rapidly down the Lane to the Temple Stairs, a thin, penetrating drizzle began to fall.

My first thought had been to take boat to Westminster and to go to the house of Mr. Betterton in Tothill Street, there to consult with him as to what would be my best course to pursue. But I feel sure that You, dear Mistress, will understand me when I say that I felt a certain pride in keeping my present Project to myself.

I was not egotistical enough to persuade myself that love of Country and loyalty to my King were the sole motive powers of my Resolve. My innermost Heart, my Conscience perhaps, told me that an ugly Desire for Revenge had helped to stimulate my patriotic

Ardour. I had realized that it lay in my power to avenge upon an impious Malapert the hideous Outrage which he had perpetrated against the Man whom I loved best in all the World.

I had realized, in fact, that I could become the instrument of Mr. Betterton's revenge.

That my Denunciation of the abominable Conspiracy would involve the Disgrace—probably the Death—of others who were nothing to me, I did not pause to consider. They were all Traitors, anyhow, and all of them deserving of punishment.

So, on the whole, I decided to act for myself. When I had seen the Countess of Castlemaine and had put her on her guard, I would go to Mr. Betterton and tell him what I had done.

I beg you to believe, however, dear Mistress, that no thought of any reward had entered my mind, other than a Word of Appreciation from my Friend.

2

I had, as perhaps you know, a slight acquaintance with Mistress Floid, who is one of my Lady Castlemaine's tire-women. Through her, I obtained speech with her Ladyship.

It was not very difficult. I sent in the two Documents through Mistress Floid's hands. Five minutes later I was told that my Lady desired speech with me.

I was a little bewildered and somewhat dazzled to be in the presence of so great a lady. The richness of the House, the liveries of the Servants, the superciliousness of the Lacqueys, all tended to discompose me; whilst the subtle Scent of Spice and Perfumes which hung in the air and the chorus of bird-song which came from an unseen Aviary, helped to numb my Senses. I was thankful that I had not trusted to Speech and Memory, but had set documentary Evidence forward to prove what I had to say.

Of my interview with her Ladyship I have only a confused memory. I know that she asked many questions and listened to my stammering replies with obvious impatience; but I have only a very vague recollection of her flashing Eyes, of her Face, flaming with anger, of her jewelled Hand clutching the documents which I had brought, and of the torrent of vituperative abuse which she poured upon the Traitors, who she vowed would pay with their lives for their Infamy. I know that, in the end, I was allowed to kiss her hand and that she thanked me in her own Name and that of His Majesty for my Loyalty and my Discretion.

I went out of the room and out of the house like a Man in a dream. A whirl of conflicting Emotions was rending my heart and my brain, until sheer physical nausea caused me nigh to swoon.

Truly it was a terrible Experience for a simple-minded Clerk to go through, and it is a marvel to me that my brain did not give way under the Strain.

But my instinct—like that of a faithful dog seeking shelter—led me to the lodgings of Mr. Betterton in Tothill Street, the very house in which his father had lived before him.

He had not yet returned from the Theatre, where he was at Rehearsal; but his Servant knew me well and allowed me to go up into the parlour and to lie down upon the sofa for a moment's rest.

It was then nearing seven, and I knew that Mr. Betterton would soon be coming home. I now felt infinitely weary; numbness of body and brain had followed the conflicting Emotions of the past hours, and I was only conscious of an overwhelming desire to rest.

I closed my eyes. The place was warm and still; a veritable Haven of Quietude. And it was the place where dwelt the Man for whose sake I had just done so much. For awhile I watched the play of the firelight upon the various articles of furniture in the room; but soon a pleasing Torpor invaded my tired Brain, and I fell asleep.

3

The sound of Voices upon the landing outside, the opening and closing of one door and then another, recalled me to myself. The familiar sound of my Friend's footsteps gave me an infinity of Pleasure.

The next moment Mr. Betterton came into the room. He was preceded by his Servant, who brought in a couple of Candles which he placed upon the table. Apparently he had said nothing to his Master about my presence here, for Mr. Betterton seemed vastly surprised when he saw me. I had just jumped to my feet when I heard him entering the room, and I suppose that I must have looked somewhat wild and dishevelled, for he expressed great astonishment at my Appearance.

83

Astonishment, and also Pleasure.

"Why, friend Honeywood!" he exclaimed, and came to greet me with both hands outstretched. "What favourable Wind hath blown you to this port?"

He looked tired and very much aged, methought. He, a young Man, then in the prime of Life, looked harassed and weary; all the Elasticity seemed to have gone out of his Movements, all the Springiness from his Footstep. He sat down and rested his elbows on his knees, clasped his slender hands together and stared moodily into the fire.

I watched him for awhile. His clear-cut Profile was outlined like an Italian Cameo against the dark angle of the room; the firelight gave a strange glow to his expressive Eyes and to the sensitive Mouth with the firm lips pressed closely together, as if they would hold some Secret which was even then threatening to escape.

That look of dark and introspective Brooding sat more apparent now than ever upon his mobile face, and I marvelled if the News which I was about to impart would tend to dissipate that restless, searching glance, which seemed for ever to be probing into the future decrees of Fate.

"I have come to tell you news, Sir," I said after a while.

He started as from a Reverie, and said half-absently:

"News? What news, friend? Good, I hope."

"Yes," I replied very quietly, even though I felt that my heart was beating fast within my breast with excitement. "Good news of the Man You hate."

He made no reply for the moment, and even by the dim, uncertain light of the fire I could see the quick change in his face. I cannot explain it exactly, but it seemed as if something Evil had swept over it, changing every noble line into something that was almost repellent.

My heart beat faster still. I was beginning to feel afraid and a queer, choking Sensation gripped me by the throat and silenced the Words which were struggling to come to my lips.

"Well?" queried Mr. Betterton a second or two later, in a calm, dull, unemotional Voice. "What is thy news, friend Honeywood?"

"There is a plot," I replied, still speaking with an effort, "against His Majesty and the Countess of Castlemaine."

"I knew that," he rejoined. "'Tis no news. There is more than one plot, in fact, against the King and the Castlemaine. You surely haven't come out on this wet night," he added with a mirthless laugh, "in order to tell me that!"

After all that I had gone through, after my tussle with my conscience and my fight against myself, I felt nettled by his flippant tone.

"I know not," I said firmly, "if there is more than one plot against His Majesty the King. But I do know that there is one which aims at striking at his sacred Person to-night."

"That also is possible," he retorted, with still that same air of flippant Carelessness. "But even so, I do not see, my dear Friend, what You can do in the matter."

"I can denounce the Plot," I riposted warmly, "and help to save the life of His Majesty the King."

"So you can, my dear Honeywood," he said with a smile, amused at my vehemence. "So you can! And upon the King's gratitude you may lay the foundations of your future Fortune."

"I was not thinking of a Fortune," I retorted gruffly; "only of Revenge."

At this he looked up suddenly, leaned forward and in the firelight tried to read my face.

"Revenge?" he queried curtly. "What do you mean?"

"I mean," I replied earnestly, "that the Plot of which I speak is real, tangible and damnable. That a set of young Gallants have arranged between themselves to waylay His Majesty the King this night in the house of the Countess of Castlemaine, to kidnap his sacred person, force him to abdicate, then proclaim the Duke of Monmouth King and the Prince of Orange Regent of the Realm."

"How do you know all this, Honeywood?" Mr. Betterton rejoined quietly, dragged, meseemed, out of his former Cynicism by the earnestness of my manner.

"I was one of the first to know of it," I replied, "because on a certain day in September I was employed in copying the Manifesto wherewith that pack of Traitors hoped to rally distant Friends around their Standard. For awhile I heard nothing more of the Affair, thought the whole thing had sizzled out like a fire devoid of fuel; until to-day, when the Conspirators once more met in the house of Mr. Theophilus Baggs and arranged to carry their execrable Project through to-night. Careless of my presence, they planned and discussed their Affairs in my hearing. They thought, I suppose, that I, like Mr. Baggs, was one of their Gang."

Gradually, while I spoke, I could see the Dawn of Comprehension illumining Mr. Betterton's face. He still was silent, and let me speak on to the end. He was once more gazing into the fire; his arms were resting on his knees, but his hands were beating

85

one against the other, fist to palm, with a violent, intermittent Gesture, which proclaimed his growing Impatience.

Then suddenly he raised his head, looked me once more straight in the eyes, and said slowly, reiterating some of my words:

"The Conspirators met in the house of Mr. Theophilus Baggs—then—he——"

I nodded.

"My Lord Stour," I said, deliberately measuring my words, "is up to his neck in the damnable Conspiracy."

Still his searching gaze was fixed upon me; and now he put out his hand and clutched my forearm. But he did not speak.

"I was burning with rage," I said, "at the insult put upon you by my Lord Stour ... I longed to be revenged..."

His clutch upon my arm tightened till it felt like a Vice of Steel, and his Voice came to my ear, hoarse and almost unrecognizable.

"Honeywood," he murmured, "what do You mean? What have You done?"

I tried to return his gaze, but it seemed to sear my very Soul. Terror held me now. I scarce could speak. My voice came out in a husky whisper.

"I had the copy of the Manifesto," I said, "and I knew the names of the Conspirators. I wrote these out and placed them with the Manifesto in the hands of my Lady Castlemaine."

Dear Mistress, you know the beautiful picture by the great Italian artist Michael Angelo which represents Jove hurling his thunderbolt at some puny human Creature who hath dared to defy him. The flash of Anger expressed by the Artist in the mighty god's eyes is truly terrifying. Well! that same Expression of unbounded and prodigious Wrath flashed out in one instant from the great Actor's eyes. He jumped to his feet, towered above me like some Giant whom I, in my presumption, had dared to defy. The flickering candle light, warring with the fireglow, and its play of ruddy Lights and deep phantasmagoric Shadows, lent size and weirdness to Mr. Betterton's figure and enhanced the dignity and magnitude of his Presence. His lips were working, and I could see that he had the greatest difficulty in forcing himself to speak coherently.

"You have done that?" he stammered. "You...?"

"To avenge the deadly insult——" I murmured, frightened to death now by his violence.

"Silence, you fool!" he riposted hoarsely. "Is it given to the Mouse to avenge the hurt done to the Lion?"

I guessed how deeply he was moved by these Words which he spoke, more even than by his Attitude. Never, had he been in his normal frame of mind, would he have said them, knowing how their cruel intent would hurt and wound me.

He was angry with me. Very angry. And I, as yet, was too ignorant, too unsophisticated, to know in what way I had injured him. God knows it had been done unwittingly. And I could not understand what went on in that noble and obviously tortured Brain. I could only sit there and gaze upon him in helpless Bewilderment, as he now started to pace up and down the narrow room in very truth like a caged Lion that hath been teased till it can endure the irritation no longer.

"You are angry with me?" I contrived to stammer at last; and indeed I found much difficulty in keeping the tears which were welling up to mine eyes.

But my timid query only appeared to have the effect of bringing his Exasperation to its highest pitch. He did in truth turn on me as if he were ready to strike me, and I slid down on my Knees, for I felt now really frightened, as his fine voice smote mine ears in thunderous Accents of unbridled Wrath.

"Angry?" he exclaimed. "Angry...? I..."

Then he paused abruptly, for he had caught sight of me, kneeling there, an humble and, I doubt not, a pathetic Figure; and, as you know, Mr. Betterton's heart is ever full of Pity for the Lowly and the Weak. By the flickering candle light I could distinguish his noble Features, a moment ago almost distorted with Passion, but now, all of a sudden, illumined by tender Sympathy.

He pulled himself together. I almost could see the Effort of Will wherewith he curbed that turbulent Passion which had threatened to overmaster him. He passed his hand once or twice across his brow, as if he strove to chase away, by sheer physical Force, the last vestige of his own Anger.

"No—no——," he murmured gently, bent down to me and helped me to my feet. "No, my dear Friend; I am not angry with You ... I—I forgot myself just now ... something seemed to snap in my Brain when you told me that ... When you told me that——" he reiterated slowly; then threw back his head and broke into a laugh. Oh! such a laugh as I never wish to hear again. It was not only mirthless, but the Sound of it did rend my heart until the tears came back to mine eyes; but this time through an overwhelming feeling of Pity.

And yet I did not understand. Neither his Anger nor his obvious Despair were clear to my Comprehension. I hoped he would soon explain, feeling that if he spoke of it, it would ease his heartache. Mine was almost unendurable. I felt that I could cry like a child, Remorse warring with Anxiety in my heart.

Then suddenly Mr. Betterton came close to me, sat down on the sofa beside me and said, with a Recrudescence of his former Vehemence:

"Friend Honeywood, you must go straightway back to my Lady Castlemaine."

"Yes," I replied meekly, for I was ready to do anything that he desired.

"Either to my Lady Castlemaine," he went on, his voice trembling with agitation, "or to her menial first, but ultimately to my Lady Castlemaine. Go on your hands and knees, Honeywood; crawl, supplicate, lick the dust, swear that the Conspiracy had no existence save in your own disordered brain ... that the Manifesto is a forgery ... the list of Conspirators a fictitious one ... swear above all that my Lord Stour had no part in the murderous Plot——"

I would, dear Lady, that mine was the pen of a ready Writer, so that I might give you a clear idea of Mr. Betterton's strange aspect at that moment. His face was close to mine, yet he did not seem like himself. You know how serene and calm is the Glance of his Eyes as a rule. Well! just then they were strangely luminous and restless; there was a glitter in them, a weird, pale Light that I cannot describe, but which struck me as coming from a Brain that, for the moment, was almost bereft of Reason.

That he was not thinking coherently was obvious to me from what he said. I, who was ready and prepared to do anything that might atone for the Injury, as yet inexplicable, which I had so unwittingly done to him, felt, nevertheless, the entire Futility of his Suggestion. Indeed, was it likely that my Lady Castlemaine's Suspicions, once roused, could so easily be allayed? Whatever I told her now, she would of a surety warn the King—had done so, no doubt, already. Measures would be taken—had already been taken—to trap the infamous Plotters, to catch them red-handed in the Act; if indeed they were guilty. Nay! I could not very well imagine how such great Personages would act under the Circumstances that had come about. But this much I did know; that not one of them would be swayed by the Vagaries of a puny Clerk, who had taken it upon himself to denounce a number of noble Gentlemen for Treason one moment and endeavoured to exonerate them the next. So I could only shake my head and murmur:

"Alas, Sir! all that now would be too late."

He looked at me searchingly for a second or two. The strange glitter died out from his eyes, and he gave a deep sigh of weariness and of disappointment.

"Aye!" he said. "True! true! It is all too late!"

Imagine, dear Mistress, how puzzled I was. What would You have thought of it all, yourself, had your sweet Spirit been present then at that hour, when a truly good, yet deeply injured Man bared his Soul before his Friend?

Just for a second or two the Suspicion flashed through my mind that Mr. Betterton himself was in some secret and unaccountable manner mixed up with the abominable Conspiracy. But almost at once my saner Judgment rejected this villainous Suggestion; for of a truth it had no foundation save in Foolishness engendered by a bewildered brain. In truth, I had never seen Mr. Betterton in the Company of any of those Traitors whose names were indelibly graven upon the tablets of my Memory, save on that one occasion—that unforgettable afternoon in September, when he entered the house of Mr. Theophilus Baggs at the hour when Lord Douglas Wychwoode had just entrusted his Manifesto to me. What was said then and what happened afterwards should, God help me! have convinced me that no sort of intimate Connection, political or otherwise, could ever exist between my Lord Stour, Lord Douglas Wychwoode or their Friends, and Mr. Betterton.

4

Even while all these Thoughts and Conjectures were coursing through my brain, my innermost Consciousness kept my attention fixed upon my friend.

He had once more resumed his restless pacing up and down the narrow room. His slender hands were closely linked together behind his back, and at times he strode quite close to me, so close that the skirts of his fashionably cut coat brushed against my knee. From time to time disconnected Phrases came to his lips. He was talking to himself, a thing which I had never known him do before.

"I, who wished to return Taunt for Taunt and Infamy for Infamy!" he said at one time. And at another: "To-day ... in a few hours perhaps, that young Coxcomb will be in the Tower ... and then the Scaffold!"

I listened as attentively as I could, without seeming to do so, thinking that, if I only caught more of these confused Mutterings, the Puzzle, such as it was, would become more clear to me. Picture the two of us then, dear Mistress, in the semi-darkness, with only fitful candle light to bring into occasional bold relief the fine Figure of the great Actor pacing up and down like a restless and tortured Beast; and mine own meagre Form cowering in an angle of the sofa, straining mine ears to catch every syllable that came from my Friend's lips, and mine eyes to note every Change of his Countenance.

"She will think 'twas I who spied upon him," I heard him say quite distinctly through his clenched teeth. "I who betrayed him, her Friends, her Brother."

"He will die a Martyr to the cause she loves," he murmured a few moments later. "A Hero to his friends—to her a demi-god whose Memory she will worship."

Then he paused, and added in a loud and firm voice, apostrophizing, God knows what Spirits of Hate and of Vengeance whom he had summoned:

"And that is to be my Revenge for the deadliest Insult Man ever put upon Man! ... Ha! ha! ha! ha!" he laughed, with weird Incontinence. "God above us, save me from my Friends and let me deal alone with mine Enemies!"

He fell back into the nearest chair and, resting his elbows on his knees, he pressed his forehead against his clenched fists. I stared at him, mute, dumbfounded. For now I understood. I knew what I had done, knew what he desired, what he had striven for and planned all these past weary weeks. His Hopes, his Desires, I had frustrated. I, his Friend, who would have given my Life for his welfare!

I had been heart-broken before. I was doubly so now. I slid from the sofa once more on my knees and, not daring to touch him, I just remained there, sobbing and moaning in helpless Dejection and Remorse.

"What can I do?—what can I do?"

He looked at me, obviously dazed, had apparently become quite oblivious of my presence. Once more that look of tender Commiseration came into his eyes, and he said with a gently ironical smile:

"You? Poor little, feeble Mouse, who has gnawed at the Giant's prey—what can you do? ... Why, nothing. Go back to our mutual Friend, Mr. Theophilus Baggs, and tell him to make his way—and quickly too—to some obscure corner of the Country, for he also is up to the neck in that damnable Conspiracy."

This set my mind to a fresh train of thought.

"Shall I to my Lord Stour by the same token?" I asked eagerly.

"To my Lord Stour?" he queried, with a puzzled frown. "What for?"

"To warn him," I replied. "Give him a chance of escape. I could tell him you sent me," I added tentatively.

He laughed.

"No, no, my Friend," he said drily. "We'll not quite go to that length. Give him a chance of Escape?" he reiterated. "And tell him I sent You? No, no! He would only look upon my supposed Magnanimity as a sign of cringing Humility, Obsequiousness and Terror of further Reprisals. No, no, my Friend; I'll not give the gay young Spark another chance of insulting me.... But let me think ... let me think ... Oh, if only I had a few days before me, instead of a mere few hours! ... And if only my Lady Castlemaine..."

He paused, and I broke in on the impulse of the moment.

"Oh, Sir! hath not the Countess of Castlemaine vowed often of late that she would grant any Favour that the great Mr. Betterton would ask of her?"

No sooner were the words out of my mouth than I regretted them. It must have been Instinct, for they seemed innocent enough at the time. My only thought in uttering them was to suggest that at Mr. Betterton's request the Traitors would be pardoned. My Lady Castlemaine in those days held the King wholly under her Domination. And I still believed that my Friend desired nothing so much at this moment than that my Lord Stour should not die a Hero's death—a Martyr to the cause which the beautiful Lady Barbara had at heart.

But since that hour, whenever I have looked back upon the Sequence of Events which followed on my impulsive Utterance, I could not help but think that Destiny had put the words into my mouth. She had need of me as her tool. What had to be, had to be. You, dear Mistress, can now judge whether Mr. Betterton is still worthy of your Love, whether he is still worthy to be taken back into your heart. For verily my words did make the turning point in the workings of his Soul. But I should never have dared to tell you all that happened, face to face, and I desired to speak of the matter impartially. Therefore I chose the medium of a pen, so that I might make You understand and, understanding, be ready to forgive.

CHAPTER IX

A LAST CHANCE

1

Of course, what happened subsequently, I can only tell for the most part from what Mr. Betterton told me himself, and also from one or two facts revealed to me by Mistress Floid.

At the moment, Mr. Betterton commended me for my Suggestion, rested his hand with all his former affectionate Manner upon my shoulder, and said quite simply:

"I thank you, friend, for reminding me of this. My Lady Castlemaine did indeed last night intimate to me that she felt ready to grant any Favour I might ask of her. Well! I will not put her Magnanimity to an over severe test. Come with me, friend Honeywood. We'll to her Ladyship. There will be plenty of time after that to go and warn that worthy Mr. Baggs and my equally worthy Sister. I should not like them to end their days upon the Scaffold. So heroic an ending doth not seem suitable to their drabby Existence, and would war with all preconceived Dramatic Values."

He then called to his man and ordered a couple of linkmen to be in readiness to guide us through the Streets, as these were far from safe for peaceful Pedestrians after dark! Then he demanded his hat and cloak, and a minute or so later he bade me follow him, and together we went out of the house.

2

It was now raining heavily, and we wrapped our Cloaks tightly round our Shoulders, speeding along as fast as we could. The streets were almost deserted and as dreary as London streets alone can be on a November evening. Only from the closed Windows of an occasional Tavern or Coffee-house did a few rays of bright light fall across the road, throwing a vivid bar of brilliance athwart our way, and turning the hundreds of Puddles into shining reflections, like so many glimmering Stars.

For the rest, we were dependent on the linkmen, who walked ahead of us, swinging their Lanterns for Guidance on our path.

Being somewhat timid by nature, I had noted with satisfaction that they both carried stout Cudgels, for of a truth there were many Marauders about on dark nights such as this, Footpads and Highway Robbers, not to mention those bands of young Rakes, who found pleasure in "scouring" the streets o' nights and molesting the belated Wayfarer.

Mr. Betterton, too, carried a weighted stick, and he was a Man whom clean, sturdy living had rendered both athletic and powerful. We were soon, both of us, wet to the Skin, but Mr. Betterton appeared quite oblivious of discomfort. He walked with a quick step, and I perforce had to keep up with him as best I could.

He had told me, before we started out, that he was bent for my Lady Castlemaine's House, the rear of which looks down upon the Gardens of White Hall. I knew the way thither just as well as he did. Great was my astonishment, therefore, when having reached the bottom of King Street, when we should have turned our steps northwards, Mr. Betterton suddenly ordered the linkmen to proceed through Palace Yard in the direction of Westminster Stairs.

I thought that he was suffering from a fit of absent-mindedness, which was easily understandable on account of his agitated Frame of Mind; and presently I called his attention to his mistake. He paid no heed to me, however, and continued to walk on until we were some way up Canon's Row.

Here he called to his linkmen to halt, and himself paused; then caught hold of my cloak, and dragged me under the shelter of a great gateway belonging to one of those noble Mansions which front the River. And he said to me, in a strange and peremptory Voice, hardly raised above a Whisper:

"Do You know where we are, Honeywood?"

"Yes," I said, not a little surprised at the question. "We are at the South End of Canon's Row. I know this part very well, having often——"

"Very well, then," he broke in, still in the same imperious Manner. "You know that we are under the gateway belonging to the Town Mansion of the Earl of Stour, and that the house is some twenty yards up the fore-court."

"I know the house," I replied, "now you mention it."

"Then you will go to my Lord Stour now, Honeywood," my Friend went on.

"To warn him?" I queried eagerly, for of a truth I was struck with Admiration at this excess of Magnanimity on the part of an injured Man.

"No," Mr. Betterton replied curtly. "You will go to my Lord Stour as my Friend and Intermediary. You will tell him that I sent

You, because I desire to know if he hath changed his mind, and if he is ready to give me Satisfaction for the Insult, which he put upon me nigh on two months ago."

I could not restrain a gasp of surprise.

"But——" I stammered.

"You are not going to play me false, Honeywood," he said simply.

That I swore I would not do. Indeed, he knew well enough that if he commanded me to go to the outermost ends of the Earth on his errand, or to hold parley with the Devil on his behalf, I would have been eager and ready to do it.

But I must confess that at this moment I would sooner have parleyed with the Devil than with the Earl of Stour. The Man whom I had denounced, You understand. I felt that the shadow of Death—conjured by me, menacing and unevasive—would perhaps lie 'twixt him and me whilst I spoke with him. Yet how could I demur when my Friend besought me?—my Friend, who was gravely troubled because of me.

I promised that I would do as he wished. Whereupon he gave me full instructions. Never had so strange a task been put upon a simple-minded Plebeian: for these were matters pertaining to Gentlemen. I knew less than nothing of Duels, Affairs of Honour, or such like; yet here was I—John Honeywood, an humble Attorney's Clerk—sent to convey a challenge for a Duel to a high and noble Lord, in the manner most approved by Tradition.

I was ready to swoon with Fright; for, in truth, I am naught but a timid Rustic. In spite of the cold and the rain I felt a rush of hot blood coursing up and down my Spine. But I learned my Lesson from end to end, and having mastered it, I did not waver.

Leaving Mr. Betterton under the shelter of the gateway, I boldly crossed the fore-court and mounted the couple of steps which led up to the front door of the Mansion. The fore-court and the front of the House were very dark, and I was not a little afraid of Night Prowlers, who, they do say, haunt the immediate Purlieus of these stately Abodes of the Nobility, ready to fall upon any belated Visitor who might be foolish enough to venture out alone.

Indeed, everything around me was so still and seemed so desolate that an Access of Fear seized me, whilst I vainly tried to grope for the bell-handle in the Darkness. I very nearly gave way to my Cowardice then and there, and would have run back to my Friend or called out to the Linkmen for their Company, only that at the very moment my Hand came in contact with the iron bell pull, and fastened itself instinctively upon it.

Whereupon the clang of the Bell broke the solemn Silence which reigned around.

3

I had grave Difficulty in obtaining access to my Lord Stour, his Servant telling me in the first instance that his Lordship was not at home, and in the second that he was in any event too busy to receive Visitors at this hour. But I have oft been told that I possess the Obstinacy of the Weak, and I was determined that, having come so far, I would not return to Mr. Betterton without having accomplished mine Errand. So, seeing that the Servant, with the Officiousness and Insolence of his kind, was about to slam the door in my face, an Inspiration seized me, and taking on a haughty Air, I stepped boldly across the Threshold and then commanded the Menial to go to his Lordship at once and announce the visit of Mr. Theophilus Baggs' Clerk on a matter of the utmost Urgency.

I suppose that now I looked both determined and fierce, and after a good deal of hem-ming and hawing, the Varlet apparently felt that non-compliance with my Desire might bring contumely upon himself; so he went, leaving me most unceremoniously to cool my heels in the Hall, and returned but a very few minutes later looking distinctly crestfallen and not a little astonished.

His Lordship would see me at once, he announced. Then bade me follow him up the stairs.

To say that my Heart was beating furiously within my Breast would be but a bald Statement of my Frame of Mind. I fully expected that his Lordship, directly he knew that it was not Mr. Baggs who had sent me, would have me ignominiously turned out of the House. However, I was not given much time to indulge in my Conjectures and my Fears, for presently I was ushered into a large room, dimly lighted by a couple of wax candles and the Walls of which, I noticed, were entirely lined with Books.

After the Menial had closed the door behind me, a Voice bade me curtly to come forward and to state mine Errand. Then I saw that my Lord Stour was not alone. He was sitting in a chair in front of the fire, and opposite to him sat the beautiful Lady Barbara, whilst standing in front of the hearth, with legs apart and hands thrust in the pockets of his breeches, was Lord Douglas Wychwoode.

What Courage was left in me now went down into my shoes. I felt like a Man faced with three Enemies where he had only expected to meet one. My Throat felt very dry and my Tongue seemed to cleave to my Palate. Nevertheless, in response to a reiterated curt Command to state mine Errand, I did so unfalteringly.

"Mr. Thomas Betterton, one of His Majesty's Well-Beloved Servants," I said, "hath sent me to his Lordship the Earl of Stour."

My Words were greeted with an angry Oath from Lord Douglas, an ironical Laugh from my Lord Stour and a strange little Gasp, half of Terror, wholly of Surprise, from the Lady Barbara.

"Methought You came from Mr. Baggs," my Lord Stour remarked haughtily. "So at least You gave my Servant to understand, else You would not have been admitted."

"Your Lordship's Servant misunderstood me," I rejoined quite quietly. "I gave my name as Clerk to Mr. Baggs; but mine Errand concerns Mr. Thomas Betterton, and he honours me with his Friendship."

"And as Mr. Betterton's Affairs do not concern me in any way——" his Lordship began coldly, and would no doubt have dismissed me then and there, but that the Lady Barbara interposed gently yet with great Firmness.

"I pray You, my Lord," she said, "do not be over-hasty. We might at least listen to what Mr. Betterton's Messenger has to say."

"Yes," added Lord Douglas in his habitual brusque Manner. "Let us hear what the Fellow wants."

This was not encouraging, you will admit; but, like many over-timid People, there are times when I am conscious of unwonted Calm and Determination. So even now I confronted these two supercilious Gentlemen with as much Dignity as I could command, and said, addressing myself directly to the Earl of Stour:

"Mr. Betterton hath sent me to You, my Lord, to demand Satisfaction for the abominable Outrage which You perpetrated upon his Person nigh on two months ago."

Lord Stour shrugged his Shoulders and riposted coldly:

"That tune is stale, my Man. Mr.—er—Betterton has had mine Answer."

"Since then, my Lord," I insisted firmly, "Time hath no doubt brought saner Reflection. Mr. Betterton's Fame and his Genius have raised him to a level far above that conferred by mere Birth."

"Have made a Gentleman of him, You mean?" Lord Stour rejoined with a sarcastic curl of the lip.

"More noble far than any Gentleman in the Land," I retorted proudly.

He gave a harsh laugh.

96

"In that case, my Man," he said tartly, "you can inform your worthy Friend that two hundred years hence my Descendants might fight him on a comparatively equal Footing. But until then," he added firmly and conclusively, "I must repeat for the last time what I have already told Mr.—er—Betterton: the Earl of Stour cannot cross Swords with a Mountebank."

"Take care, my Lord, take care——"

The Exclamation had burst quite involuntarily from my Lips. The next moment I felt ashamed to have uttered it, for my Lord Stour looked me up and down as he would an importunate Menial, and Lord Douglas Wychwoode strode towards me and pointed to the door.

"Get out!" he commanded curtly.

There was nothing more to be done—nothing more to be said, if I desired to retain one last Shred of Dignity both for myself and for the great Artist who—in my Person this time—had once again been so profoundly humiliated.

My wet cloak I had left down in the Hall, but I still held my hat in my hands. I now bowed with as much Grace as I could muster. Lord Douglas still pointed a peremptory finger towards the door, making it clear that I was not going of mine own Accord, like the Intermediary of any Gentleman might be, but that I was being kicked out like some insolent Varlet.

Oh! the shame of it! The shame!

My ears were tingling, my temples throbbing. A crimson Veil, thrust before mine eyes by invisible Hands, caused my footsteps to falter. Oh! if only I had had the strength, I should even then have turned upon those aristocratic Miscreants and, with my hands upon their throats, have forced them to eat their impious Words.

But even as I crossed the Threshold of that Room where I had suffered such bitter Humiliation, I heard loud and mocking Laughter behind me; and words such as: "Insolence!" "Mountebank!" "Rogue!" and "Vagabond!" still reached my ears.

I suppose that the door did not close quite fully behind me, for even as I crossed the landing meseemed that I heard the Lady Barbara's voice raised in a kind of terrified Appeal.

"Would to God, my dear Lord," she appeared to plead with passionate Earnestness, "You had not incurred the Enmity of that Man. Ever since that awful day I have felt as if You were encompassed by Spirits of Hate and of Vengeance which threaten our Happiness."

Her Voice broke in a sob. And, indeed, I found it in my heart to pity her, for she seemed deeply grieved. I still could hear him—

97

her Lover and mine Enemy, since he was the Enemy of my Friend—trying to laugh away her fears.

"Nay, sweetheart," he was saying tenderly. "A Man like that can do us no harm. Mine own Conscience is clear—my Life honourable—and to-night will see the triumph of your Cause, to which I have given willing help. That Man's Malice cannot touch me, any more than the snarling of a toothless cur. So do not waste these precious moments, my Beloved, by thinking of him."

After which the door behind me was closed to, and I heard nothing more. I hurried down the Stairs, snatched up my cloak and hurried out of the House.

Never should I have believed that a human Heart could contain so much Hatred as mine held for my Lord Stour at that moment.

4

I found Mr. Betterton waiting for me under the Gateway where I had left him a quarter of an hour ago.

As soon as he heard my footsteps upon the uneven pavement of the fore-court, he came forward to meet me, took hold of my cloak and dragged me back into shelter.

He only said the one word: "Well?" but it is not in my power, dear Mistress, to render adequately all that there was of Anxiety, Impatience and of Passion in that one brief Query.

I suppose that I hesitated. Of a truth the Message which I was bringing was choking me. And he who is so sensitive, so understanding, learned everything, and at once, from my Silence.

"He hath refused?" he said simply.

I nodded.

"He will not fight me?"

And my Silence gave reply. A curious, hoarse Cry, like that of a wounded Animal, escaped his Throat and for a moment we were both silent—so silent that the patter of the rain appeared like some thunderous Noise: and the divers sounds of the great City wrapped in the Cloak of Evening came to us with sharp and eerie Distinctness. Far away, a dog barked; some belated Chairman called: "Make room, there!"; a couple of Watchmen passed close by, clinking their halberts against the ground, and from one of the noble Mansions nigh to us there came the sound of Revelry and of Laughter.

I felt like in a Dream, conscious only that the Finger of Destiny was pointing to the Dial of a Clock, and that I was set here to count the Seconds and the Minutes until that ghostly Finger had completed its task and registered the final Hour when the Decrees of God would inevitably be fulfilled.

CHAPTER X

THE HOUR

1

A quarter of an hour—perhaps less—later, we were speeding back, Mr. Betterton and I, down Canon's Row on our way to Westminster Stairs, intending to take boat for the City.

In the terrible mental upheaval which had followed on the renewed Outrage that had been put upon my beloved Friend, I had well-nigh forgotten that secret conspiracy which was even now threatening the stability of our Country, and in which my former Employer and his Spouse were so deeply involved.

The striking of Church Bells far and near, chiming the hour of eight, recalled me to the danger which threatened Mr. Baggs along with his more aristocratic co-traitors. And, strangely enough, Mr. Betterton thought of this at the very same time. He had been sunk in moody Reverie ever since my Silence had told him the grim tale of my unsuccessful Embassy to the Earl of Stour, and through the darkness it was impossible even for my devoted eyes to watch the Play of Emotions upon his tell-tale face, or to read in his eyes the dark thoughts which I knew must be coursing through his Brain.

In myself, I could not help but be satisfied at the turn of Events. The Conspirators, denounced by me to the Countess of Castlemaine, would of a certainty meet the Punishment which they so fully deserved. Lord Stour was one of them, so was Lord Douglas Wychwoode. The Scaffold, or at least, Banishment, would be their lot, and how could I grieve—I, who hated them so!—that the Earth would presently be rid of two arrogant and supercilious Coxcombs, Traitors to their King, vainglorious and self-seeking. True, the Lady Barbara would weep. But when I remembered the many bitter tears which you, dear Mistress, have shed these past months because she had enchained the fancy of the Man whom you loved, then had scorned his Ardour and left him a Prey to Humiliation and Shame at the hands of Men unworthy to lick the dust at his feet; when I remembered all that, I could find no Pity in my heart for the Lady Barbara, but rather a Hope that one so exquisitely fair would pass through Sorrow and Adversity the purer and softer for the Ordeal.

True again, that for some reason still unexplained Mr. Betterton appeared to desire with an almost passionate intensity that his successful Rival should escape the fate of his fellow-Conspirators. Such Magnanimity was beyond my Comprehension, and I felt that the Sentiment which engendered it could not be a lasting one. Mr. Betterton was for the moment angry with me—very angry—for what I had done; but his Anger I knew would soon melt in the Warmth of his own kindly Heart. He would forgive me, and anon forget the insolent Enemy after the latter had expiated his Treachery and his Arrogance upon the Scaffold. The whole of this hideous past Episode would then become a mere Memory, like unto a nightmare which the healthful freshness of the newly-born Day so quickly dispels.

2

So on the whole it was with a lightened heart that I stepped into the boat in the wake of Mr. Betterton. I thanked the Lord that the Rain had ceased for the moment, for truly I was chilled to the Marrow and could not have borne another wetting.

Every Angle and Stone and Stair and Landing Stage along the Embankment was of course familiar to me; and I could not help falling into a Reverie at sight of those great houses which were the City homes of some of the noblest Families in the Land. How many of these stately walls, thought I, sheltered a nest of Conspirators as vile and as disloyal as were Lord Douglas Wychwoode and his friends? Suffolk House and Yorke House, Salisbury House and Worster House, to mention but a few. How did the mere honest Citizen know what went on behind their Portals, what deadly secrets were whispered within their doors?

I had been taught all my life to respect those who are above me in Station and to reverence our titled Nobility; but truly my short Experience of these high-born Sparks was not calculated to enhance my Respect for their Integrity or my Admiration for their Intellect. Some older Gentlemen there were, such as the Lord Chancellor himself, who were worthy of Everybody's regard; but I must confess that the Behaviour of the younger Fops was oft blameworthy.

I might even instance our Experience this dark night after we had landed at the Temple Stairs, and were hurrying along our way up Middle Temple Lane in the wake of our linkmen. We were speeding on, treading carefully so as to avoid as much as was possible the mud which lay ankle-deep in the Lane, when we suddenly spied ahead of us a party of "Scourers"—young Gentlemen of high Rank, very much the worse for drink, who, being at their wits' end to know how to spend their evenings, did it in prowling about the Streets, insulting or maltreating peaceable Passers-by, molesting Women, breaking Tavern windows, stealing Signboards and otherwise rendering themselves noxious to honest Citizens, and helping to make the Streets of our great City an object of terror by night, in emulation of highway Robbers and other foul Marauders.

No doubt Mr. Betterton and I would—despite the aid of our two linkmen and of their stout Cudgels—have fallen a victim to these odious Miscreants, and the great Actor would of a surety have been very rudely treated, since he had so often denounced these Mal-practices from the Stage and held up to public Ridicule not only the young Rakes who took part in the riotous Orgies, but also our Nightwatchmen, who were too stupid or too cowardly to cope with them. But, knowing our danger, we avoided it, and hearing the young Mohocks coming our way we slipped up Hare Alley and bided our time until the noise of Revels and Riotings were well behind us.

I heard afterwards that those Abominable Debauchees—who surely should have known better, seeing that they were all Scions of great and noble Families—had indeed "scoured" that night with some purpose. They broke into Simond's Inn in Fleet Street, smashed every Piece of Crockery they could find there, assaulted the Landlord, beat the Customers about, broke open the money-box, stole some five pounds in hard cash and insulted the waiting-maids. Finally they set a seal to their Revels by falling on the Nightwatchmen who had come to disperse them, beating them with their own halberts and with sticks, and wounding one so severely that he ultimately died in Hospital, while the Miscreants themselves got off scot-free.

Truly a terrible state of Affairs in such a noble City as London!

As for Mr. Betterton and myself, we reached the corner of Chancery Lane without serious Adventure. As we neared the house of Mr. Theophilus Baggs, however, I felt my Courage oozing down into my shoes. Truly I could not then have faced my former Employer, whom I had just betrayed, and the mean side of my Action in the Matter came upon me with a shaming force.

I begged Mr. Betterton, therefore, to go and speak with Mr. Baggs whilst I remained waiting outside upon the doorstep.

Of all that miserable day, this was perhaps to me the most painful moment. From the instant that Mr. Betterton was admitted into the house until he returned to me some twenty minutes later, I was in a cold sweat, devoured with Apprehension and fighting against Remorse. I could not forget that Mr. Baggs had been my Master and Employer—if not too kind an one—for years, and if he had been sent to the Tower and accompanied his fellow Conspirators upon the Scaffold, I verily believe that I should have felt like Judas Iscariot and, like him, would have been unable to endure my life after such a base Betrayal.

Fortunately, however, Mr. Betterton was soon able to reassure me. He had, he said, immediately warned Mr. Baggs that something of the Secret of the Conspiracy had come to the ears of the Countess of Castlemaine, and that all those who were in any way mixed up in the Affair would be wise to lie low as far as possible, at any rate for a while.

Mr. Baggs, it seems, was at first terrified, and was on the point of losing his Head and committing some act of Folly through sheer fright. But Mr. Betterton's quieting Influence soon prevailed. The worthy Attorney, on thinking the matter over, realized that if he destroyed certain Documents which might prove incriminating to himself, he would have little else to fear. He himself had never written a compromising Letter—he was far too shrewd to have thus committed himself—and there was not a scrap of paper in any one else's possession which bore his Name or might mark his Identity, whilst he had not the slightest fear that the other Conspirators—who were all of them Gentlemen—would betray the Complicity of an humble Attorney who had rendered them loyal Service.

Strangely enough, Mr. Baggs never suspected me of having betrayed the whole thing; or, if he did, he never said so. So many People plotted these days, so many Conspiracies were hatched then blown upon, that I for one imagine that Mr. Baggs had a hand in several of these and was paid high Fees for his share in them. Then, when anything untoward happened, when mere Chance, or else a Traitor among the Traitors, caused the Conspiracy to abort, the worthy Attorney would metaphorically shake the dust of political Intrigue from his shabby shoes, and make a bonfire of every compromising Document that might land him in the Tower and further. After which, he was no doubt ready to begin all over again.

So it had occurred in this instance. Mr. Betterton did not wait to see the bonfire, which was just beginning to blaze merrily in the old-fashioned hearth. He told me all about it when he joined me once more upon the doorstep, and for the first time that day I heard him laugh quite naturally and spontaneously while he recounted to me Mr. Baggs' Terrors and Mistress Euphrosine's dignified Fussiness.

"She would have liked to find some Pretext," he said quite gaily, "for blaming me in the Matter. But on the whole, I think that they were both thankful for my timely Warning."

4

But, as far as I was concerned, this ended once and for all my Connection with the house of Mr. Theophilus Baggs, and since that memorable night I have never once slept under his roof.

I went back with Mr. Betterton to his House in Tothill Street. By the time we reached it, it was close on ten o'clock. Already he had intimated to me that henceforth I was to make my home with him; and as soon as we entered the House he ordered his Servant to make my room and bed ready for me. My Heart was filled with inexpressible gratitude at his Kindness. Though I had, in an altogether inexplicable manner, run counter to his Plans, he was ready to forgive me and did not withdraw his Friendship from me.

As time went on, I was able to tell him something of the Emotions which coursed through my Heart in recognition of his measureless Kindness to me; but on that first evening I could not speak of it. When I first beheld the cosy room which he had assigned to me, with its clean and comfortable bed and substantial furniture, I could only bow my Head, take his Hand and kiss it reverently. He withdrew it as if he had been stung.

"Keep such expressions of Respect," he said almost roughly, "for one who is worthy."

"You," I riposted simply, "are infinitely worthy, because You are good."

Then once again his harsh, mirthless Laugh—so unlike his usual light-hearted Merriment—grated upon mine ear.

"Good!" he exclaimed. "Nay, friend Honeywood, You are not, meseems, a master of intuition. Few Hearts in London this night," he added earnestly, "harbour such evil Desires as mine."

But in spite of what he said, in spite of that strange look in his eyes, that Laugh which proclaimed a perturbed Soul, I could not bring myself to believe that his noble Heart was a Prey to aught but noble Desires, and that those awful and subtle Schemes of deadly Revenge which have subsequently threatened to ruin his own Life were even now seething in his Brain.

For the moment, I only remembered that when first he had requested me to accompany him on his evening Peregrinations, it had been with a view to visiting the Countess of Castlemaine, and I now reminded him of his Purpose, thinking that his desire had been to beg for my Lord Stour's pardon. I did so, still insisting upon her Ladyship's avowed Predilection for himself, and I noticed that while I spoke thus he smiled grimly to himself and presently said with slow Deliberation:

"Aye! Her Ladyship hath vowed that out of Gratitude for his public Eulogy of her Virtue and her Beauty, she would grant Mr. Thomas Betterton any Favour he might ask of her."

"Aye! and her Ladyship is not like to go back on her word," I assented eagerly.

"Therefore," he continued, not heeding me, "the Countess of Castlemaine, who in her turn can obtain any Favour she desires from His Majesty the King, will at my request obtain a full and gracious Pardon for the Earl of Stour."

"She will indeed!" I exclaimed, puzzled once more at this strange trait of Magnanimity—Weakness, I called it—on the part of a Man who had on two occasions been so monstrously outraged. "You are a hero, Sir," I added in an awed whisper, "to think of a pardon for your most deadly Enemy."

He turned and looked me full in the eyes. I could scarce bear his Glance, for there seemed to dwell within its glowing depths such a World of Misery, of Hatred and of thwarted Passion, that my Soul was filled with dread at the sight. And he said very slowly:

"You are wrong there, my Friend. I was not thinking of a pardon for mine Enemy, but of Revenge for a deadly Insult, which it seems cannot be wiped out in Blood."

I would have said something more after that, for in truth my Heart was full of Sympathy and of Love for my Friend and I longed to soothe and console him, as I felt I could do, humble and unsophisticated though I was. Thoughts of You, dear Mistress, were running riot in my Brain. I longed at this momentous hour, when the Fate of many Men whom I knew was trembling in the balance, to throw myself at Mr. Betterton's feet and to conjure him in the name of all his most noble Instincts to give up all thoughts of the proud Lady who had disdained him and spurned his Affections, and to turn once more to the early and pure Love of his Life—to You, dear Mistress, whose Devotion had been so severely tried and yet had not been found wanting, and whose influence had always been one of Gentleness and of Purity.

But, seeing him sitting there brooding, obviously a Prey to Thoughts both deep and dark, I did not dare speak, and remained silent in the hope that, now that I was settled under his roof, an Opportunity would occur for me to tell him what weighed so heavily on my Heart.

Presently the Servant came in and brought Supper, and Mr. Betterton sat down to it, bidding me with perfect Grace and Hospitality to sit opposite to him. But we neither of us felt greatly inclined to eat. I was hungry, it is true; yet every Morsel which I conveyed to my mouth cost me an effort to swallow. This was all the more remarkable as at the moment my whole Being was revelling in the Succulence of the fare spread out before me, the Excellence of the Wine, the snowy Whiteness of the Cloths, the Beauty of Crystal and of Silver, all of which bore testimony to the fastidious Taste and the Refinement of the great Artist.

Of the great Events which were even then shaping themselves in White Hall, we did not speak. We each knew that the Other's mind was full of what might be going on even at this hour. But Mr. Betterton made not a single Reference to it, and I too, therefore, held my tongue. In fact, we spoke but little during Supper, and as I watched my dearly loved Friend toying with his food, and I myself felt as if the next mouthful would choke me, I knew his Mind was far away.

It was fixed upon White Hall and its stately Purlieus and upon the house of the Countess of Castlemaine, which overlooked the Privy Gardens, and of His Majesty the King. His senses, I knew, were strained to catch the sound of distant Murmurs, of running Footsteps, of the grinding of Arms or of pistol shots.

But not a Sound came to disturb the peaceful Silence of this comfortable Abode. The Servant came and went, bringing food, then clearing it away, pouring Wine into our glasses, setting and removing the silver Utensils.

Anon Mr. Betterton and I both started and furtively caught one another's Glance. The tower clock of Westminster was striking eleven.

"For Good or for Evil, all is over by now," Mr. Betterton said quietly. "Come, friend Honeywood; let's to bed."

I went to bed, but not to sleep. For hours I lay awake, wondering what had happened. Had the Conspirators succeeded and was His Majesty a Prisoner in their hands? or were they themselves Captives in that frowning Edifice by the Water, which had witnessed so many Deaths and such grim Tragedies, and from which the only Egress led straight to the Scaffold?

CHAPTER XI

RUMOURS AND CONJECTURES

1

Very little of what had actually occurred came to the ear of the Public. In fact, not one Man in ten in the whole of the Cities of London and Westminster knew that a couple of hours before midnight, when most simple and honest Citizens were retiring to their beds, a batch of dangerous Conspirators had been arrested even within the Precincts of White Hall.

I heard all that there was to know from Mr. Betterton, who went out early the following Morning and returned fully informed of the events of the preceding Night. Subsequently too, I gleaned a good deal of information through the instrumentality of Mistress Floid. As far as I could gather, the Conspirators did carry out their Project just as they had decided on it in my Presence. They did assemble in King Street and in the by-lanes leading out of it,

106

keeping my Lady Castlemaine's House in sight, whilst others succeeded in Concealing themselves about the Gardens of White Hall, no doubt with the Aid of treacherous and suborned Watchmen.

The striking of the hour of ten was to be the signal for immediate and concerted Action. Those in the Gardens stood by on the watch, until after His Majesty the King had walked across from his Palace to Her Ladyship's House. His Majesty, as was his wont when supping with Lady Castlemaine, entered her house by the back door, and his Servants followed him into the house.

Then the Conspirators waited for the Hour to strike. Directly the last clang of church bells had ceased to reverberate through the humid evening air, they advanced both from the Back and the Front of the House simultaneously, when they were set upon on the one side by a Company of His Majesty's Body Guard under the Command of Major Sachvrell, who had remained concealed inside the Palace, and on the other by a Company of Halberdiers under the Command of Colonel Powick.

When the Traitors were thus confronted by loyal Troops, they tried to put up a Fight, not realizing that such measures had been taken by Major Sachvrell and Colonel Powick that they could not possibly hope to escape.

A scuffle ensued, but the Conspirators were very soon overpowered, as indeed they were greatly outnumbered. The Neighbourhood—even then slumbering peacefully—did no more than turn over in bed, marvelling perhaps if a party of Mohocks on mischief bent had come in conflict with a Posse of Night-watchmen. The Prisoners were at once marched to the Tower, despite the Rain which had once more begun to fall heavily; and during the long, wearisome Tramp through the City, their Ardour for Conspiracies and Intrigues must have cooled down considerably.

The Lieutenant of the Tower had everything ready for the Reception of such exalted Guests; for in truth my Lady Castlemaine had not allowed things to be done by halves. Incensed against her Enemies in a manner in which only an adulated and spoilt Woman can be, she was going to see to it that those who had plotted against her should be as severely dealt with as the Law permitted.

Later on, I had it from my friend, Mistress Floid, that the Lady Barbara Wychwoode visited the Countess of Castlemaine during the course of the morning. She arrived at her Ladyship's House dressed in black and with a Veil, as if of mourning, over her fair Hair.

Mistress Floid hath oft told me that the Interview between the two Ladies was truly pitiable, and that the Lady Barbara presented a heart-rending Spectacle. She begged and implored her Ladyship to exercise Mercy over a few young Hotheads, who had been misled into Wrong-doing by inflammatory Speeches from Agitators, these being naught but paid Agents of the Dutch Government, she averred, set to create Discontent and if possible Civil War once again in England, so that Holland might embark upon a War of Revenge with some Certainty of Success.

But the Countess of Castlemaine would not listen to the Petition at all, and proud Lady Barbara Wychwoode then flung herself at the other Woman's feet and begged and implored for Pardon for her Brother, her Lover and her Friends. Mistress Floid avers that my Lady Castlemaine did nothing but laugh at the poor Girl's pleadings, saying in a haughty, supercilious Manner:

"Beauty in tears? 'Tis a pretty sight, forsooth! But had your Friends succeeded in their damnable Plot, would You have shed tears of sympathy for Me, I wonder?"

And I could not find it in me to be astonished at my Lady Castlemaine's Spitefulness, for in truth the Lady Barbara's Friends had plotted her Disgrace and Ruin. Not only that, they had taken every opportunity of vilifying her Character and making her appear as odious in the Eyes of the People as they very well could.

You must not infer from this, dear Mistress, that I am upholding my Lady Castlemaine in any way. Her mode of life is abhorrent to me and I deeply regret her Influence over His Majesty and over the public Morals of the Court Circle, not to say of the entire Aristocracy and Gentry. I am merely noting the fact that human Nature being what it is, it is not to be wondered at that when the Lady had a Chance of hitting back, she did so with all her Might, determined to lose nothing of this stupendous Revenge.

However secret the actual Arrest of the Conspirators was kept from public Knowledge, it soon transpired that such great and noble Gentlemen as Lord Teammouth, Lord Douglas Wychwoode, the Earl of Stour, not to mention others, were in the Tower, and that a sensational Trial for Conspiracy and High Treason was pending.

Gradually the History of the Plot had leaked out, and how it had become abortive owing to an anonymous Denunciation (for so it was called). The Conspiracy became the talk of the Town. Several Ladies and Gentlemen, though not directly implicated in the Affair, but of known ultra-Protestant views, thought it best to retire to their Country Estates, ostensibly for the benefit of their Health.

Sinister Rumours were afloat that the Conspirators would be executed without Trial—had already suffered the extreme Penalty of the Law; that the Marquis of Sidbury, Father of Lord Douglas Wychwoode, had suddenly died of Grief; that Torture would be applied to the proletarian Accomplices of the noble Lords—of whom there were many—so as to extract further Information and Denunciations from them. In fact, the Town seethed with Conjectures; People talked in Whispers and dispersed at sight of any one who was known to belong to the Court Circle. The Theatres played to empty Benches, the Exchanges and Shops were deserted, for no one liked to be abroad when Arrests and Prosecutions were in the Air.

Through it all, very great Sympathy was evinced for the Lady Barbara Wychwoode, whose pretty Face was so well-known in Town and whose Charm of Manner and kindly Disposition had endeared her to many who had had the privilege of her Acquaintance. Public Opinion is a strange and unaccountable Factor in the Affairs of Men, and Public Opinion found it terribly hard that so young and adulated a Girl as was the Lady Barbara should at one fell swoop lose Brother, Lover and Friends. And I may truly say that Satisfaction was absolutely genuine and universal when it became known presently that the young Earl of Stour had received a full and gracious Pardon for his supposed Share in the abominable Plot.

Whether, on closer Investigation, he had been proved innocent or whether the Pardon was due to exalted or other powerful Influences, no one knew as yet: all that was a Certainty was that my Lord Stour presently left the Tower a free Man even whilst his Friends were one and all brought to Trial, and subsequently most of them executed for High Treason, or otherwise severely punished.

Lord Teammouth suffered Death upon the Scaffold, so did Sir James Campsfield and Mr. Andrew Kinver; and there were others, whose Names escape me for the moment. Lord Douglas Wychwoode succeeded in fleeing to Scotland and thence to Holland; most people averred owing to the marvellous Pluck and Ingenuity of his Sister. A number of Persons of meaner degree were hanged; in fact, a Reign of Terror swept over the country, and many thought that the Judges had been unduly harsh and over free with their Pronouncements of Death Sentences.

But it was obvious that His Majesty himself meant to make an Example of such abominable Traitors, before political Intrigues and Rebellion spread over the Country once again.

It was all the more strange, therefore, that one of the Conspirators—the Earl of Stour, in fact, whose name had been most conspicuous in connection with the Affair—should thus have been the only one to enjoy Immunity. But, as I said before, nothing but Satisfaction was expressed at first for this one small Ray of Sunshine which came to brighten poor Lady Barbara Wychwoode's Misery.

As for me, I did not know what to think. Surely my heart should have been filled with Admiration for the noble Revenge which a great Artist had taken upon a hot-headed young Coxcomb. Such Magnanimity was indeed unbelievable; nay, I felt that it showed a Weakness of Character of which in my innermost Heart I did not believe Mr. Betterton capable.

To say that I was much rejoiced over the Clemency shown to my Lord Stour would be to deviate from the Truth. Looking back upon the Motives which had actuated me when I denounced the infamous Plot to the Countess of Castlemaine, I could not help but admit to myself that Hatred of a young Jackanapes and a Desire for Vengeance upon his impudent Head had greatly influenced my Course of Action. Now that I imagined him once more kneeling at the Lady Barbara's feet, an accepted Lover, triumphant over Destiny, all the Sympathy which I may have felt for him momentarily in the hour of his Adversity, died out completely from my Heart, and I felt that I hated him even more virulently than before.

His Image, as he had last stood before me in the dimly-lighted room of his noble Mansion, surrounded by Books, costly Furniture, and all the Appurtenances of a rich and independent Gentleman, was constantly before my Mind. I could, just by closing mine eyes, see him sitting beside the hearth, with the lovely Lady Barbara beaming at him from the place opposite, and his Friend standing by, backing him up with Word and Deed in all his Arrogance and Overbearing.

"The Earl of Stour cannot cross swords with a Mountebank."

I seemed to hear those Words reverberating across the street like the clank of some ghostly Bell; and whenever mine ears rang to their sound I felt the hot Blood of a just Wrath surge up to my cheeks and my feeble Hands would close in a Clutch, that was fierce as it was impotent.

110

The reported Death from grief of the Marquis of Sidbury proved to be a false Rumour. But the aged Peer did suffer severely from the Shame put upon him by his Son's Treachery. The Wychwoodes had always been loyal Subjects of their King. At the time of the late lamented Monarch's most crying Adversity, he knew that he could always count on the Devotion of that noble Family, the Members of which had jeopardized their entire Fortune, their very Existence, in the royal Cause.

Of course, the present Marquis's two Children were scarce out of the Nursery when the bitter Conflict raged between the King and his People; but it must have been terribly hard for a proud Man to bear the thought that his only Son, as soon as he had reached Man's Estate, should have raised his Hand against his Sovereign.

No doubt owing to the disturbed State of many influential Circles of Society that Winter, and the number of noble Families who were in mourning after the aborted Conspiracy and the wholesale Executions that ensued, the Marriage between the Lady Barbara Wychwoode and the Earl of Stour was postponed until the Spring, and then it would take place very quietly at the Bride's home in Sussex, whither she had gone of late with her Father, both living there for a while in strict Retirement.

Lord Douglas Wychwoode, so it was understood, had succeeded in reaching Holland, where, I doubt not, he continued to carry on those political Intrigues against his lawful Sovereign which would of a surety one day bring him to an ignominious End.

I was now living in the greatest Comfort and was supremely happy, in the House of Mr. Betterton. He employed me as his Secretary, and in truth my place was no sinecure, for I never could have believed that there were so many foolish Persons in the World who spent their time in writing Letters—laudatory or otherwise—to such great Men as were in the public Eye. I myself, though I have always been a wholehearted Admirer of Men of Talent and Erudition, would never have taken it upon myself to trouble them with Effusions from my Pen. And yet Letter after Letter would come to the house in Tothill Street, addressed to Mr. Thomas Betterton. Some written by great and noble Ladies whose Names would surprise You, dear Mistress, were I to mention them; others were from Men of position and of learning who desired to express to the great Artist all the Pleasure that they had derived from his rendering of noble Characters.

Mr. Pepys, a Gentleman of great knowledge and a Clerk in the Admiralty, wrote quite frequently to Mr. Betterton, sometimes to express unstinted Praise for the great Actor's Performance in one of his favourite Plays, or sometimes venturing on Criticism, which was often shrewd and never disdained.

But, after all, am I not wasting time by telling You that which You, dear Mistress, know well enough from your own personal Experience? I doubt not but you receive many such Letters, both from Admirers and from Friends, not to mention Enemies, who are always to the fore when a Man or Woman rises by Talent or Learning above the dead level of the rest of Humanity.

It was then my duty to read those Letters and to reply to them, which I did at Mr. Betterton's Dictation, and in my choicest Caligraphy with many Embellishments such as I had learned whilst I was Clerk to Mr. Baggs. Thus it was that I obtained Confirmation of the Fact which was still agitating my Mind: namely, Mr. Betterton's share in the Events which led to His Majesty's gracious Pardon being extended to the Earl of Stour. I had, of course, more than suspected all along that it was my Friend who had approached the Countess of Castlemaine on the Subject, yet could not imagine how any Man, who was smarting under such a terrible Insult, as Mr. Betterton had suffered at the hands of my Lord Stour, could find it in his Heart thus to return Good for Evil, and with such splendid Magnanimity.

But here I had Chapter and Verse for the whole Affair, because my Lady Castlemaine wrote to Mr. Betterton more than once upon the Subject, and always in the same bantering tone, chaffing him for his Chivalry and his Heroism, saying very much what I should myself, if I had had the Courage or the Presumption to do so. She kept him well informed of her Endeavours on behalf of Lord Stour, referring to the King's Severity and Obstinacy in the matter in no measured Language, but almost invariably closing her Epistles with a reiteration of her promise to the great Artist to grant him any Favour he might ask of her.

"I do work most strenuously on your behalf, You adorably wicked Man," her Ladyship wrote in one of her Letters; "but I could wish that You would ask something of me which more closely concerned Yourself."

On another occasion she said:

"For the first time yester evening I wrung a half Promise from His Majesty; but You cannot conceive in what a Predicament You have placed me, for His Majesty hath shown signs of Suspicion since I plead so earnestly on behalf of Lord Stour. If my Insistence were really to arouse his Jealousy your Protégé would certainly lose his Head and I probably my Place in the King's Affections."

And then again:

"It greatly puzzles me why You should thus favour my Lord Stour. Is it not a fact that he hath insulted You beyond the Hope of Pardon? And yet, not only do You plead for your Enemy with passionate insistence, but You enjoin me at the same time to keep your noble purpose a Secret from him. Truly, but for my promise to You, I would throw up the Sponge, and that for your own good.... I did not know that Artists were Altruists. Methought that Egotism was their most usual Foible."

Thus I could no longer remain in doubt as to who the Benefactor was, whom my Lord of Stour had to thank for his very life. Yet, withal, the Secret was so well kept that, even in this era of ceaseless Gossip and Chatter, every one, even in the most intimate Court Circle, was ignorant of the subtle Intrigue which had been set in motion on behalf of the young Gallant.

CHAPTER XII

POISONED ARROWS

1

Do you remember, dear Mistress, those lovely days we had in February this year? They were more like days of Spring than of Winter. For a fortnight we revelled in sunshine and a temperature more fitting for May than for one of the Winter months.

In London, Rich and Poor alike came out into the Air like flies; the public Gardens and other Places of common resort were alive with Promenaders; the Walks and Arbours in the Gray's Inn Walks or the Mulberry Garden were astir with brilliant Company. All day, whether you sauntered in Hyde Park, refreshed yourself with a collation in Spring Gardens or strolled into the New Exchange, you would find such a crowd of Men and Women of Mode, such a Galaxy of Beauty and Bevy of fair Maids and gallant Gentlemen as had not been seen in the Town since that merry month of May, nigh on two years ago now, when our beloved King returned from Exile and all vied one with the other to give him a cheerful Welcome.

To say that this period was one of unexampled Triumph for Mr. Betterton would be but to repeat what You know just as well as I do. He made some truly remarkable hits in certain Plays of the late Mr. William Shakespeare, notably in "Macbeth," in "King Lear," and in "Hamlett." Whether I like these Plays myself or not is beside the point; whatever I thought of them I kept to myself, but was loud in my Admiration of the great Actor, who indeed had by now conquered all Hearts, put every other Performer in the Shade and raised the Status of the Duke's Company of Players to a level far transcending that ever attained by Mr. Killigrew's old Company.

This Opinion, at any rate, I have the Honour of sharing with all the younger generation of Play-goers who flock to the Theatre in Lincoln's Inn Fields, even while the King's House in Vere Street is receiving but scanty Patronage. Of course my Judgment may not be altogether impartial, seeing that in addition to Mr. Betterton, who is the finest Actor our English Stage has ever known, the Duke's House also boasts of the loveliest Actress that ever walked before the Curtain.

You, dear Mistress, were already then, as You are now, at the zenith of your Beauty and Fame, and your damask Cheeks would blush, I know, if you were to read for yourself some of the Eulogies which the aforementioned Mr. Samuel Pepys in his Letters to Mr. Betterton bestows upon the exquisite Mistress Saunderson— "Ianthe," as he has been wont to call you ever since he saw You play that part in Sir William Davenant's "The Siege of Rhodes."

Of course I know that of late no other sentimental tie hath existed outwardly between Mr. Betterton and Yourself save that of Comradeship and friendly Intercourse; but often when sitting in the Pit of the Theatre I watched You and Him standing together before the curtain, and receiving the Plaudits of an enthusiastic Audience, I prayed to God in my Heart to dissipate the Cloud of Misunderstanding which had arisen between You; aye! and I cursed fervently the Lady Barbara and her noble Lover, who helped to make that Cloud more sombre and impenetrable.

I naturally heard a great deal more of Society Gossip these days than I was wont to do during the time that I was a mere Clerk in the Employ of Mr. Theophilus Baggs. My kind Employer treated me more as a Friend than a Servant. I had fine Clothes to wear, accompanied him on several Occasions when he appeared in Public, and was constantly in his tiring-room at the Theatre, where he received and entertained a never-ending Stream of Friends.

Thus, towards the end of the Month, I gathered from the Conversation of Gentlemen around me that the Marquess of Sidbury had come up to Town in the Company of his beautiful Daughter. He had, they said, taken advantage of the fine Weather to make the Journey to London, as he desired to consult the Court Physician on the Matter of his Health.

I shall never forget the strange Look that came into Mr. Betterton's face when first the Subject was mentioned. He and some Friends—Ladies as well as Gentlemen—were assembled in the small Reception Room which hath lately been fitted up behind the Stage. Upholstered and curtained with a pleasing Shade of Green, the Room is much frequented by Artists and their Friends, and it is always crowded during the Performance of those Plays wherein one of the leading Actors or Actresses has a part.

We have taken to calling the place the Green Room, and here on the occasion of a performance of Mr. Webster's "Duchess of Malfy," in which You, dear Mistress, had no part, a very brilliant Company was assembled. Sir William Davenant was there, as a matter of course, so was Sir George Etherege, and that brilliant young dramatist Mr. Wycherley. In addition to that, there were one or two very great Gentlemen there, members of the Court Circle and enthusiastic Playgoers, who were also intimate Friends of Mr. Betterton. I am referring particularly to the Duke of Buckingham, to my Lord Rochester, Lord Orrery and others. A brilliant Assembly forsooth, which testified to the high Esteem in which the great Artist is held by all those who have the privilege of knowing him.

I told You that when first the Name of the Lady Barbara was mentioned in the Green Room, a strange Glance, which I was unable to interpret, shot out of Mr. Betterton's eyes, and as I gazed upon that subtle, impalpable Change which suddenly transformed his serene Expression of Countenance into one that was almost Evil, I felt a curious sinking of the Heart—a dread Premonition of what was to come. You know how his lips are ever ready to smile: now they appeared thin and set, while the sensitive Nostrils quivered almost like those of the wild Beasts which we have all of us frequently watched in the Zoological Gardens, when the Attendants bring along the food for the day and they, eager and hungry, know that the Hour of Satisfaction is nigh.

"The fair Lady Babs," one of the young Gallants was saying with studied Flippancy, "is more beautiful than ever, methinks; even though she goes about garbed in the Robes of Sorrow."

"Poor young thing!" commented His Grace of Buckingham kindly. "She has been hard hit in that last Affair."

"I wonder what has happened to Wychwoode," added Lord Rochester, who had been a known Friend of Lord Douglas.

"Oh! he reached Holland safely enough," another Gentleman whom I did not know averred. "I suppose he thinks that it will all blow over presently and that he will obtain a free pardon——"

"Like my Lord Stour," commented Mr. Betterton drily.

"Oh! that's hardly likely," interposed Sir George Etherege. "Wychwoode was up to the neck in the Conspiracy, whilst Stour was proved to be innocent of the whole affair."

"How do you know that?" Mr. Betterton asked quietly.

"How do I know it?" retorted Sir George. "Why? ... How do we all know it?"

"I was wondering," was Mr. Betterton's calm Rejoinder.

"I imagine," broke in another Gentleman, "that at the Trial—"

"Stour never stood his trial, now you come to think of it," here interposed my Lord of Rochester.

"He was granted a free Pardon," asserted His Grace of Buckingham, "two days after his Arrest."

"At the Instance of the Countess of Castlemaine, so I am told," concluded Mr. Betterton.

You see, he only put in a Word here and there, but always to some purpose; and oh! that Purpose I simply dared not guess. I was watching him, remember, watching him as only a devoted Friend or a fond Mother know how to watch; and I saw that set look on his Face grow harder and harder and a steely, glittering Light flash out of his Eyes.

My God! how I suffered! For with that Intuition which comes to us at times when those whom we love are in deadly peril, I had suddenly beheld the Abyss of Evil into which my Friend was about to plunge headlong. Yes! I understood now why Mr. Betterton had pleaded with my Lady Castlemaine for his Enemy's Life. It was not in order to confer upon him a lasting benefit and thus shame him by his Magnanimity; but rather in order to do him an Injury so irreparable that even Death could not wipe it away.

116

But you shall judge, dear Mistress; and thus judging You will understand much that has been so obscure in my dear Friend's Character and in his Actions of late. And to understand All is to forgive All. One thing you must remember, however, and that is that no Man of Mr. Betterton's Worth hath ever suffered in his Pride and his innermost Sensibilities as he hath done at the Hands of that young Jackanapes whom he hated—as I had good cause to know now—with an Intensity which was both cruel and relentless. He meant to be even with him, to fight him with his own Weapons, which were those of Contempt and of Ridicule. He meant to wound there, where he himself had suffered most, in Reputation and in Self-Respect.

I saw it all, and was powerless to do aught save to gaze in mute Heart-Agony on the marring of a noble Soul. Nay! I am not ashamed to own it: I did in my Heart condemn my Friend for what he had set out to do. I too hated Lord Stour, God forgive me! but two months ago I would gladly have seen his arrogant Head fall upon the Scaffold; but this subtle and calculating Revenge, this cold Intrigue to ruin a Man's Reputation and to besmirch his Honour, was beyond my ken, and I could have wept to see the great Soul of the Man, whom I admired most in all the World, a prey to such an evil Purpose.

"We all know," one of the young Sparks was saying even now, "that my Lady Castlemaine showed Stour marked favour from the very moment he appeared at Court."

"We also know," added Mr. Betterton with quiet Irony, "that the whisper of a beautiful Woman often drowns the loudest call of Honour."

"But surely you do not think——?" riposted Lord Rochester indignantly, "that—that——"

"That what, my lord?" queried Mr. Betterton calmly.

"Why, demme, that Stour did anything dishonourable?"

"Why should I not think that?" retorted Mr. Betterton, with a slight Elevation of the Eyebrows.

"Because he is a Stourcliffe of Stour, Sir," broke in Sir George Etherege in that loud, blustering way he hath at times; "and bears one of the greatest Names in the Land."

"A great Name is hereditary, Sir," rejoined the great Actor quietly. "Honesty is not."

"But what does Lady Castlemaine say about it all?" interposed Lord Orrery.

"Lady Castlemaine hath not been questioned on the subject, I imagine," interposed Sir William Davenant drily.

"Ah!" rejoined His Grace of Buckingham. "There you are

117

wrong, Davenant. I remember speaking to her Ladyship about Stour one day—saying how glad I was that he, at any rate, had had nothing to do with that abominable Affair."

"Well?" came eagerly from every one. "What did she say?"

His Grace remained thoughtful for a time, as if trying to recollect Something that was eluding his Memory. Then he said, turning to Mr. Betterton:

"Why, Tom, you were there at the time. Do You recollect? It was at one of Her Ladyship's Supper Parties. His Majesty was present. We all fell to talking about the Conspiracy, and the King said some very bitter things. Then I thought I would say something about Stour. You remember?"

"Oh, yes!" replied Mr. Betterton.

"What did Lady Castlemaine say?"

"I don't think she said anything. Methinks she only laughed."

"So she did!" assented His Grace; "and winked at You, you Rogue! I recollect the Circumstance perfectly now, though I attached no importance to it at the time. But I can see it all before me. His Majesty frowned and continued to look glum, whilst the Countess of Castlemaine vowed with a laugh that, anyway, my lord Stour was the handsomest Gentleman in London, and that 'twere a pity to allow such a beautiful Head to fall on the Scaffold."

"It certainly sounds very strange," mused my Lord Rochester, and fell to talking in Whispers with Sir George Etherege, whilst His Grace of Buckingham went and sat down beside Mr. Betterton, and obviously started to discuss the Incident of the Supper Party all over again with the great Actor. Other isolated Groups also formed themselves, and I knew that my Lord Stour's Name was on every one's lips.

Traducement and Gossip is Meat and Drink to all these noble and distinguished Gentlemen, and here they had something to talk about, which would transcend in Scandal anything that had gone before. The story about my Lord Stour would spread with the Rapidity which only evil-loving Tongues can give. Alas! my poor Friend knew that well enough when he shot his poisoned Arrows into the Air. I was watching him whilst His Grace of Buckingham conversed with him: I saw the feverishly keen look in his eyes as he, in his turn, watched the Ball of Slander and Gossip being tossed about from one Group to another. He said but little, hardly gave Answer to His Grace; but I could see that he was on the alert, ready with other little poisoned Darts whenever he saw Signs of weakening in the Volume of Backbiting, which he had so deliberately set going.

"I liked Stour and I admired him," Lord Rochester said at one time. "I could have sworn that Nature herself had written 'honest man' on his face."

"Ah!——" interposed Mr. Betterton, with that quiet Sarcasm which I had learned to dread. "Nature sometimes writes with a very bad Pen."

3

It was not to be wondered at that the Scandal against my Lord Stour, which was started in the Green Room of the Theatre, grew in Magnitude with amazing Rapidity. I could not tell you, dear Mistress, what my innermost feelings were in regard to the Matter: being an humble and ignorant Clerk and devoted to the one Man to whom I owe everything that makes life pleasing. I had neither the Wish nor the mental Power to tear my Heart to Pieces, in order to find out whether it beat in Sympathy with my Friend, or with the Victim of such a complete and deadly Revenge.

My Lord Stour was not then in London. He too, like many of his Friends—notably the Marquis of Sidbury and others not directly accused of Participation in the aborted Plot—had retired to his Country Estate, probably unwilling to witness the gaieties of City Life, while those he cared for most were in such dire Sorrow. But now that the Lady Barbara and her Father were once more in Town, there was little doubt that he too would return there presently. Since he was a free Man, and Lord Douglas Wychwoode had succeeded in evading the Law, there was no doubt that the natural Elasticity of Youth coupled with the prospect of the happy future which lay before him, would soon enable him to pick up the Threads of Life, there where they had been so unexpectedly and ruthlessly entangled.

I imagine that when his Lordship first arrived in Town and once more established himself in the magnificent Mansion in Canon's Row which I had bitter cause to know so well, he did not truly visualize the Atmosphere of brooding Suspicion which encompassed him where e'er he went. If he did notice that one or two of his former Friends did give him something of a cold shoulder, I believe that he would attribute this more to political than to personal Reasons. He had undoubtedly been implicated in a Conspiracy which was universally condemned for its Treachery and Disloyalty, and no doubt for a time he would have to bear the brunt of public Condemnation, even though the free Pardon, which had so unexpectedly been granted him, proved that he had been more misguided than really guilty.

His Arrival in London, his Appearance in Public Places, his obvious ignorance of the Cloud which was hanging over his fair Name, were the subject of constant Discussion and Comment in the Green Room of the Theatre as well as elsewhere. And I take it that his very Insouciance, the proud Carelessness wherewith he met the cold Reception which had been granted him, would soon have got over the scandalous tale which constant Gossip alone kept alive, except that one tongue—and one alone—never allowed that Gossip to rest.

And that Tongue was an eloquent as well as a bitter one, and more cunning than even I could ever have believed.

How oft in the Green Room, in the midst of a brilliant Company, have I listened to the flippant talk of gay young Sparks, only to hear it drifting inevitably toward the Subject of my Lord Stour, and of that wholly unexplainable Pardon, which had left him a free Man, whilst all his former Associates had either perished as Traitors, or were forced to lead the miserable life of an Exile, far from Home, Kindred and Friends.

Drifting, did I say? Nay, the Talk was invariably guided in that direction by the unerring Voice of a deeply outraged Man who, at last, was taking his Revenge. A word here, an Insinuation there, a witty Remark or a shrug of the shoulders, and that volatile sprite, Public Opinion, would veer back from any possible doubt or leniency to the eternally unanswered Riddle: "When so many of his Friends perished upon the Scaffold, how was it that my Lord Stour was free?"

How it had come about I know not, but it is certain that very soon it became generally known that his Lordship had been entrusted by his Friends with the distribution of Manifestos which were to rally certain Waverers to the cause of the Conspirators. And it was solemnly averred that it was in consequence of a Copy of this same Manifesto, together with a list of prominent Names, coming into the hands of my Lady Castlemaine, that so many Gentlemen were arrested and executed, and my Lord Stour had been allowed to go scot-free.

How could I help knowing that this last Slander had emanated from the Green Room, with the object of laying the final stone to the edifice of Calumnies, which was to crush an Enemy's Reputation and fair Fame beyond the hope of Retrieval?

4

A day or two later my Lord Stour, walking with a Friend in St. James's Park, came face to face with Mr. Betterton, who had Sir William Davenant and the Duke of Albemarle with him as well as one or two other Gentlemen, whilst he leaned with his wonted kindness and familiarity on my arm. Mr. Betterton would, I think, have passed by; but my Lord Stour, ignoring him as if he were dirt under aristocratic feet, stopped with ostentatious good-will to speak with the General.

But his Grace did in truth give the young Lord a very cold shoulder and Sir William Davenant, equally ostentatiously, started to relate piquant Anecdotes to young Mr. Harry Wordsley, who was just up from the country.

I saw my Lord Stour's handsome face darken with an angry frown. For awhile he appeared to hesitate as to what he should do, then with scant Ceremony he took the Duke of Albemarle by the coat-sleeve and said hastily:

"My Lord Duke, You and my Father fought side by side on many occasions. Now, I like not your Attitude towards me. Will you be pleased to explain?"

The General tried to evade him, endeavoured to disengage his coat-sleeve, but my Lord Stour was tenacious. A kind of brooding Obstinacy sat upon his good-looking face, and after awhile he reiterated with almost fierce Insistence:

"No! no! you shall not go, my Lord, until You have explained. I am tired," he added roughly, "of suspicious looks and covert smiles, an atmosphere of ill-will which greets me at every turn. Politically, many may differ from Me, but I have yet to learn that a Gentleman hath not the right to his own Opinions without being cold-shouldered by his Friends."

The Duke of Albemarle allowed him to talk on for awhile. His Grace obviously was making up his mind to take a decisive step in the matter. After a while he did succeed in disengaging his coat-sleeve from the persistent Clutch of his young Friend, and then, looking the latter straight between the eyes, he said firmly:

"My Lord, as You say, your Father and I were Friends and Comrades in Arms. Therefore You must forgive an old Man and a plain Soldier a pertinent question. Will you do that?"

"Certainly," was my Lord Stour's quiet Reply.

"Very well then," continued His Grace, while all of us who were there held our breath, feeling that this Colloquy threatened to have a grave issue. "Very well. I am glad that You have given me this opportunity of hearing some sort of Explanation from You, for in truth, Rumour of late hath been over busy with your Name."

"An Explanation, my Lord?" the young Man said, with an added frown.

"Aye!" replied His Grace. "That's just the Word. An Explanation. For I, my Lord, as your Father's Friend, will ask You this: how is it that while Teammouth, Campsfield and so many of your Associates perished upon the Scaffold, You alone, of those implicated in that infamous Plot, did obtain an unconditional Pardon?"

Lord Stour stepped back as if he had been hit in the face. Boundless Astonishment was expressed in the Gaze which he fixed upon the General, as well as wrathful indignation.

"My Lord!" he exclaimed, "that Question is an insult!"

"Make me swallow mine own Words," retorted His Grace imperturbably, "by giving me a straight Answer."

"Mine Answer must be straight," rejoined Lord Stour firmly, "since it is based on Truth. I do not know."

The Duke shrugged his Shoulders, and there came a sarcastic laugh from more than one of the Gentlemen there.

"I give your Lordship my Word of Honour," Lord Stour insisted haughtily. Then, as His Grace remained silent, with those deep-set eyes of his fixed searchingly upon the young Man, the latter added vehemently: "Is then mine Honour in question?"

Whereupon Mr. Betterton, who hitherto had remained silent, interposed very quietly:

"The honour of some Gentlemen, my Lord, is like the Manifestation of Ghosts—much talked of ... but always difficult to prove!"

You know his Voice, dear Mistress, and that subtle carrying Power which it has, although he never seems to raise it. After he had spoken You could have heard the stirring of every little twig in the trees above us, for no one said another Word for a moment or two. We all stood there, a compact little Group: Lord Stour facing the Duke of Albemarle and Mr. Betterton standing a step or two behind His Grace, his fine, expressive Face set in a mask of cruel Irony. Sir William Davenant and the other Gentlemen had closed in around those three. They must have felt that some strange Storm of Passions was brewing, and instinctively they tried to hide its lowering Clouds from public gaze.

Fortunately there were not many Passers-by just then, and the little Scene remained unnoted by the idly curious, who are ever wont to collect in Crowds whenever anything strange to them happens to attract their Attention.

My Lord Stour was the first to recover Speech. He turned on Mr. Betterton with unbridled Fury.

"What!" he cried, "another sting from that venomous Wasp? I might have guessed that so miserable a Calumny came from such a vile Caitiff as this!"

"Abuse is not Explanation, my Lord," interposed the Duke of Albemarle firmly. "And I must remind you that you have left my Question unanswered."

"Put it more intelligibly, my Lord," retorted Lord Stour haughtily. "I might then know how to reply."

"Very well," riposted His Grace, still apparently unmoved. "I will put it differently. I understand that your Associates entrusted their treasonable Manifestos to you. Is that a fact?"

"I'll not deny it."

"You cannot," rejoined the Duke drily. "Sir James Campsfield, in the course of his Trial, admitted that he had received his Summons through You. But a Copy of that Manifesto came into the hands of my Lady Castlemaine just in time to cause the Conspiracy to abort. How was that?"

"Some Traitor," replied Lord Stour hotly, "of whom I have no Cognizance."

"Yet it was You," riposted the General quietly, "who received a free Pardon ... no one else. How was that?" he reiterated more sternly.

"I have sworn to You that I do not know," protested my Lord Stour fiercely.

He looked now like a Man at Bay, trapped in a Net which was closing in around him and from which he was striving desperately to escape. His face was flushed, his eyes glowed with an unnatural fire. And always his restless gaze came back to Mr. Betterton, who stood by, calm and impassive, apparently disinterested in this Colloquy wherein a man's Honour was being tossed about to the Winds of Slander and of Infamy. Now Lord Stour gazed around him, striving to find one line of genuine Sympathy on the stern Faces which were confronting him.

"My word of Honour, Gentlemen," he exclaimed with passionate Earnestness, "that I do not know."

Honestly, I think that one or two of them did feel for him and were inclined to give him Credence. After all, these young Fops are not wicked; they are only mischievous, as Children or young Puppies are wont to be, ready to snarl at one another, to yap and to tear to pieces anything that happens to come in their way.

123

Moreover, there was the great bond of Caste between these People. They were, in their innermost Hearts, loth to believe that one of themselves—a Gentleman, one bearing a great Name—could be guilty of this type of foul Crime which was more easily attributable to a Plebeian. It was only their Love of Scandal-monging and of Backbiting that had kept the Story alive all these weeks. Even now there were one or two sympathetic Murmurs amongst those present when my Lord Stour swore by his Honour.

But just then Mr. Betterton's voice was heard quite distinctly above that Murmur:

"Honour is a strangely difficult word to pronounce on the Stage," he was saying to Sir William Davenant, apparently á propos of something the latter had remarked just before. "You try and say it, Davenant; you will see how it always dislocates your Jaw, yet produces no effect."

"Therefore, Mr. Actor," Lord Stour broke in roughly, "it should only be spoken by those who have a glorious Ancestry behind them to teach them its true Significance."

"Well spoken, my Lord," Mr. Betterton rejoined placidly. "But you must remember that but few of His Majesty's Servants have a line of glorious Ancestry behind them. In that way they differ from many Gentlemen who, having nothing but their Ancestry to boast of, are very like a Turnip—the best of them is under the ground."

This Sally was greeted with loud Laughter, and by a subtle process which I could not possibly define, the wave of Sympathy which was setting in the direction of my Lord Stour, once more receded from him, leaving him wrathful and obstinate, His Grace of Albemarle stern, and the young Fops flippant and long-tongued as before.

"My Lord Stour," the General now broke in once more firmly, "'tis You sought this Explanation, not I. Now You have left my Question unanswered. Your Friends entrusted their Manifestos to You. How came one of these in Lady Castlemaine's hands?"

And the young Man, driven to bay, facing half a dozen pairs of eyes that held both Contempt and Enmity in their glance, reiterated hoarsely:

"I have sworn to You that I do not know." Then he added: "Hath Loyalty then left this unfortunate Land, that You can all believe such a vile thing of me?"

And in the silence that ensued, Mr. Betterton's perfectly modulated Voice was again raised in quietly sarcastic accents:

"As You say, my Lord," he remarked. "Loyalty hath left this unfortunate Country. Perhaps," he added with a light shrug of the shoulders, "to take Refuge with your glorious Ancestry."

This last Gibe, however, brought my Lord Stour's exasperation to a raging Fury. Pushing unceremoniously past His Grace of Albemarle, who stood before him, he took a step forward and confronted Mr. Betterton eye to eye and, drawing himself up to his full Height, he literally glowered down upon the great Artist, who stood his Ground, placid and unmoved.

"Insolent Varlet!" came in raucous tones from the young Lord's quivering lips. "If you had a spark of chivalry or of honour in You——"

At the arrogant Insult every one drew their breath. A keen Excitement flashed in every eye. Here was at last a Quarrel, one that must end in bloodshed. Just what was required—so thought these young Rakes, I feel sure—to clear the Atmosphere and to bring abstruse questions of Suspicion and of Honour to a level which they could all of them understand. Only the Duke of Albemarle, who, like a true and great Soldier, hath the greatest possible Abhorrence for the gentlemanly Pastime of Duelling, tried to interpose. But Mr. Betterton, having provoked the Quarrel, required no interference from any one. You know his way, dear Mistress, as well as I do—that quiet Attitude which he is wont to assume, that fraction of a second's absolute Silence just before he begins to speak. I know of no Elocutionist's trick more telling than that. It seems to rivet the Attention, and at the same time to key up Excitement and Curiosity to its greatest strain.

"By your leave, my Lord," he said slowly, and his splendid Voice rose just to a sufficient pitch of Loudness to be distinctly heard by those immediately near him, but not one yard beyond. "By your leave, let us leave the word 'honour' out of our talk. It hath become ridiculous and obsolete, now that every Traitor doth use it for his own ends."

But in truth my Lord Stour now was beside himself with Fury.

"By gad!" he exclaimed with a harsh laugh. "I might have guessed that it was your pestilential Tongue which stirred up this Treason against me. Liar!—Scoundrel!——"

He was for heaping up one Insult upon the other, lashing himself as it were into greater Fury still, when Mr. Betterton's quietly ironical laugh broke in upon his senseless ebullitions.

"Liar?—Scoundrel, am I?" he said lightly, and, still laughing, he turned to the Gentlemen who stood beside him. "Nay! if the sight of a Scoundrel offends his Lordship, he should shut himself up in his own Room ... and break his Mirror!"

At this, my Lord Stour lost the last vestige of his self-control, seized Mr. Betterton by the Shoulder and verily, I thought, made as if he would strike him.

125

"You shall pay for this Insolence!" he cried.

But already, with perfect sang-froid, the great Artist had arrested his Lordship's uplifted hand and wrenched it away from his shoulder.

"By your leave, my Lord," he said, and with delicate Fingers flicked the dust from off his coat. "This coat was fashioned by an honest tailor, and hath never been touched by a Traitor's hand."

I thought then that I could see Murder writ plainly on My Lord's face, which was suddenly become positively livid. The Excitement around us was immense. In truth I am convinced that every Gentleman there present at the moment, felt that something more deep and more intensely bitter lay at the Root of this Quarrel, between the young Lord and the great and popular Artist. Even now some of them would have liked to interfere, whilst the younger ones undoubtedly enjoyed the Spectacle and were laying, I doubt not, imaginary Wagers as to which of the two Disputants would remain Master of the Situation.

His Grace of Albemarle tried once more to interpose with all the Authority of his years and of his distinguished Position, for indeed there was something almost awesome in Lord Stour's Wrath by now. But Mr. Betterton took the Words at once out of the great General's mouth.

"Nay, my Lord," he said with quiet Firmness, "I pray You, do not interfere. I am in no danger, I assure You. My Lord Stour would wish to kill me, no doubt. But, believe me, Fate did not ordain that Tom Betterton should die by such a hand ... the fickle Jade hath too keen a Sense of Humour."

Whereupon he made a movement, as if to walk away. I felt the drag upon my arm where his slender hand was still resting. The Others were silent. What could they say? Senseless Numskulls though they were for the most part, they had enough Perception to realize that between these two Men there was Hatred so bitter that no mere Gentlemanly Bloodshed could ever wipe it away.

But ere Mr. Betterton finally turned to go, my Lord of Stour stepped out in front of him. All the Rage appeared to have died out of him. He was outwardly quite calm, only a weird twitching of his lips testified to the Storm of Passion which he had momentarily succeeded in keeping under control.

"Mr. Actor," he said slowly, "but a few Weeks ago You asked me to cross swords with You.... I refused then, for up to this hour I have never fought a Duel save with an Equal. But now, I accept," he added forcefully, even while the Words came veiled and husky from his throat. "I accept. Do You hear me? ... for the laws of England do

126

not permit a Murder, and as sure as there's a Heaven above me, I am going to kill You."

Mr. Betterton listened to him until the end. You know that Power which he hath of seeming to tower above every one who stands nigh him? Well! he exercised that Power now. He stepped quite close to my Lord Stour, and though the latter is of more than average height, Mr. Betterton literally appeared to soar above him, with the sublime Magnificence of an outraged Man coming into his own at last.

"My Lord of Stour," he said, with perfect quietude, "a few weeks ago you insulted me as Man never dared to insult Man before. With every blow dealt upon my shoulders by your Lacqueys, You outraged the Majesty of Genius ... yes! its Majesty! ... its Godhead! ... You raised your insolent hand against me—against me, the Artist, whom God Himself hath crowned with Immortality. For a moment then, my outraged Manhood clamoured for satisfaction. I asked You to cross swords with me, for You seemed to me ... then ... worthy of that Honour. But to-day, my Lord of Stour," he continued, whilst every Word he spoke seemed to strike upon the ear like Blows from a relentless Hammer; "Traitor to your Friends, Liar and Informer!!!! Bah! His Majesty's Well-Beloved Servant cannot fight with such as You!"

In truth I do not remember what happened after that. The unutterable Contempt, the Disgust, the Loathing expressed in my Friend's whole Attitude, seemed to hit even me between the eyes. I felt as if some giant Hands had thrown a kind of filmy grey veil over my Head, for I heard and saw nothing save a blurred and dim Vision of uplifted Arms, of clenched Fists and of a general Scrimmage, of which my Lord Stour appeared to be the Centre, whilst my ears only caught the veiled Echo of Words flung hoarsely into the air:

"Let me go! Let me go! I must kill him! I must!"

Mr. Betterton, on the other hand, remained perfectly calm. I felt a slight pressure on my arm and presently realized that he and I had turned and were walking away down the Avenue of the Park, and leaving some way already behind us, a seething mass of excited Gentlemen, all intent on preventing Murder being committed then and there.

What the outcome of it all would be, I could not visualize. Mr. Betterton had indeed been able to give Insult for Insult and Outrage for Outrage at last. For this he had schemed and worked and planned all these weeks. Whether God and Justice were on his side in this terrible Revenge, I dared not ask myself, nor yet if the Weapon which he had chosen were worthy of his noble Character and of his Integrity. That public Opinion was on his side, I concluded from the fact that the Duke of Albemarle and Sir William Davenant both walked a few yards with him after he had turned his back on my Lord, and that His Grace constituting himself Spokesman for himself and Sir William, offered their joint Services to Mr. Betterton in case he changed his mind and agreed to fight my Lord Stour in duel.

"I thank your Grace," was Mr. Betterton's courteous reply; "but I am not like to change my Mind on that Score."

CHAPTER XIII

THE LADY PLEADS

1

I am not able quite to determine in my own mind whether the Lady Barbara Wychwoode did hear and see something of the violent Scene which I have just attempted to describe.

I told You, dear Mistress, that fortunately for us all, this part of the Park where the Scene occurred was for the moment practically deserted. At any rate, no Crowd collected around us, for which, methinks, we were, every one of us, thankful. If a few of the Passers-by heard anything of the altercation, they merely hurried past, thinking no doubt, that it was only one or two young City Sparks, none too sober even at this morning hour, who were quarrelling among themselves.

When we walked away down the Avenue which leads in the direction of Knight's Bridge, Mr. Betterton's well-known, elegant figure was remarked by a few Pedestrians on their way to and fro, as was also the familiar one of the Duke of Albemarle, and some People raised their hats to the great Artist, whilst others saluted the distinguished General.

Presently His Grace and Sir William Davenant took leave of Mr. Betterton, and a few moments later the latter suggested that we should also begin to wend our way homewards.

We retraced our steps and turned back in the direction of

Westminster. Mr. Betterton was silent; he walked quite calmly, with head bent and firm footsteps, and I, knowing his humour, walked along in silence by his side.

Then suddenly we came upon the Lady Barbara.

That she had sought this meeting I could not doubt for a moment. Else, how should a Lady of her Rank and Distinction be abroad, and in a public Park, unattended? Indeed, I was quite sure that she had only dismissed her maid when she saw Mr. Betterton coming along, and that the Wench was lurking somewhere behind one of the shrubberies, ready to accompany her Ladyship home when the interview was at an end.

I said that I am even now doubtful as to whether the Lady Barbara saw and heard something of the violent Altercation which had taken place a quarter of an hour ago between her Lover and the great Actor. If not, she certainly displayed on that occasion that marvellous intuition which is said to be the prerogative of every Woman when she is in love.

She was walking on the further side of Rosamond Pond when first I caught sight of her, and when she reached the Bridge, she came deliberately to a halt. There is no other way across the Pond save by the Bridge, so Mr. Betterton could not have escaped the meeting even if he would. Seeing the Lady, he raised his hat and made a deep bow of respectful salutation. He then crossed the Bridge and made as if he would pass by, but she held her Ground, in the very centre of the Path, and when he was quite near her, she said abruptly:

"Mr. Betterton, I desire a word with you."

He came at once to a halt, and replied with perfect deference:

"I await your Ladyship's commands."

2

I was for hurrying away, thinking that my Presence would be irksome both to the Lady and to my Friend; but an unmistakable pressure of Mr. Betterton's hand on my arm caused me to stay where I was. As for the Lady, she appeared not to care whether I stayed or went, for immediately she retorted:

"My commands, Sir Actor? They are, that you at once and completely do Reparation for the wrong which you are trying to do to an innocent Man."

She looked proud and commanding as a Queen, looking through the veil of her lashes at Mr. Betterton as if he were a supplicating Slave rather than the great Artist whom cultured Europe delighted to honour. Never did I admire my Friend so much as I did then. His self-possession was perfect: his attitude just the right balance 'twixt deference due to a beautiful Woman and the self-assurance which comes of conscious Worth. He looked splendid, too—dressed in the latest fashion and with unerring taste. The fantastic cut of his modish clothes became his artistic Personality to perfection: the soft shade of mulberry of which his coat was fashioned made an harmonious note of colour in the soft grey mist of this late winter's morning. The lace at his throat and wrists was of unspeakable value, filmy and gossamer-like in texture as a cobweb; and in his cravat glittered a diamond, a priceless gift to the great English Artist from the King of France.

Indeed, the Lady Barbara Wychwoode might look the world-famous Actor up and down with well-studied superciliousness; she might issue her commands to him as if she were his royal Mistress and he but a Menial set there to obey her behest; but, whatever she did, she could not dwarf his Personality. He had become too great for disdain or sneers ever to touch him again; and the shafts of scorn aimed at him by those who would set mere Birth above the claims of Genius, would only find their points broken or blunted against the impenetrable armour of his Glory and his Fame.

For the nonce, I think that he was ready enough to parley with the Lady Barbara. He had not to my knowledge spoken with her since that never forgotten day last September; and I, not understanding the complex workings of an Artist's heart, knew not if his Love for her had outlived the crying outrage, or had since then turned to Hate.

In answer to her peremptory command, he assumed an air of innocent surprise.

"I?" he queried. "Your Ladyship is pleased to speak in riddles."

"Nay!" she retorted. "'Tis you, Sir, who choose not to understand. But I'll speak more plainly, an you wish. I am a woman, Mr. Actor, and I love the Earl of Stour. Now, you know just as well as I do, that his Lordship's honour has of late been impugned in a manner that is most mysterious. His Friends accuse him of treachery; even mere Acquaintances prefer to give him the cold shoulder. And this without any definite Indictment being levelled against him. Many there are who will tell You that they have not the faintest conception of what crime my Lord Stour stands accused. Others aver that they'll not believe any Slander that may be levelled against so high-souled a Gentleman. Nevertheless, the Slander continues. Nay! it gathers volume as it worms its way from one house to another, shedding poison in its wake as it drifts by; and more and more People now affect to look another way when the Earl of Stour comes nigh them, and to be otherwise engaged when he desires to shake them by the hand."

She paused for a moment, obviously to regain her Composure, which was threatening to leave her. Her cheeks were pale as ashes, her breath came and went in quick, short gasps. The Picture which she herself had drawn of her Lover's plight caused her heart to ache with bitterness. She seemed for the moment to expect something—a mere comment, perhaps, or a word of Sympathy, from Mr. Betterton. But none came. He stood there, silent and deferential, with lips firmly set, his slender Hand clutched upon the gold knob of his stick, till the knuckles shone creamy-white, like ivory. He regarded her with an air of Detachment rather than Sympathy, and though by her silence she appeared to challenge him now, he did not speak, and after awhile she resumed more calmly:

"My Lord of Stour himself is at his wits' ends to interpret the attitude of his Friends. Nothing tangible in the way of a spoken Calumny hath as yet reached his ears. And his life has been rendered all the more bitter that he feels that he is being struck by a persistent but mysterious Foe in what he holds dearer than aught else on earth, his Integrity and his Honour."

"'Tis a sad case," here rejoined Mr. Betterton, for her Ladyship had paused once more. "But, by your leave, I do not see in what way it concerns me."

"Nay! but I think you do, Sir Actor," Lady Barbara riposted harshly. "Love and Hate, remember, see clearly where mere Friendship and Indifference are blind. Love tells me that the Earl of Stour's Integrity is Unstained, his Honour unsullied. But the Hatred which you bear him," added her Ladyship almost fiercely, "makes me look to You for the cause of his Disgrace."

No one, however, could have looked more utterly astonished, more bland and uncomprehending, as Mr. Betterton did at that moment. He put up his hand and regarded the Lady with an indulgent smile, such as one would bestow on a hot-headed Child.

"Nay, your Ladyship!" he said courteously. "I fear that you are attributing to an humble Mountebank a power he doth not possess. To disgrace a noble Gentleman?" he exclaimed with well-feigned horror. "I?—a miserable Varlet—an insolent cur whom one thrashes if he dares to bark!"

"Ah!" she broke in, with a swift exclamation. "Then I have guessed the truth! This is your Revenge!"

"Revenge?" he queried blandly. "For what?"

"You hate the Earl of Stour," she retorted.

Once more his well-shaped hand went up, as if in gentle protest, and he uttered a kind and deprecating "Oh!"

"You look upon the Earl of Stour as your enemy!" she insisted.

"I have so many, your Ladyship," he riposted with a smile.

"'Twas you who obtained his Pardon from my Lady Castlemaine."

"The inference is scarcely logical," he retorted. "A man does not as a rule sue for pardon for his Enemy."

"I think," she rejoined slowly, "that in this case Mr. Betterton did the illogical thing."

"Then I do entreat your Ladyship," he protested with mock terror, "not to repeat this calumny. I, accused of a noble action! Tom Betterton pardoning his Enemies! Why, my friends might believe it, and it is so difficult these days to live down a good Reputation."

"You choose to sharpen your wit at my expense, Sir Actor," the lady rejoined with her former haughtiness, "and to evade the point."

"What is the point, your Ladyship?" he queried blandly.

"That you set an end to all these Calumnies which are levelled against the Earl of Stour."

"How can we stay the Sun in his orbit?" he retorted; "or the Stars in their course?"

"You mean that your Campaign of Slander has already gone too far? But remember this, Mr. Betterton: that poisoned darts sometimes wound the hand that throws them. You may pursue the Earl of Stour with your Hatred and your Calumnies, but God will never allow an innocent Man to suffer unjustly."

Just for a few seconds Mr. Betterton was silent. He was still regarding the Lady with that same indulgent smile which appeared to irritate her nerves. To me, the very air around seemed to ring as if with a clash of ghostly arms—the mighty clash of two Wills and two Temperaments, each fighting for what it holds most dear: she for the Man whom she loved, he for his Dignity which had been so cruelly outraged.

"God will never allow," she reiterated with slow emphasis, "an innocent Man to suffer at the hands of a Slanderer."

"Ah!" riposted Mr. Betterton suavely. "Is your Ladyship not reckoning over-confidently on Divine interference?"

"I also reckon," she retorted, "on His Majesty's sense of justice—and on the Countess of Castlemaine, who must know the truth of the affair."

"His Majesty's senses are very elusive," he rejoined drily, "and are apt to play him some wayward tricks when under the influence of the Countess of Castlemaine. The Earl of Stour, it seems, disdained the favours which that Lady was willing to bestow on him. He preferred the superior charms and intellect of the Lady Barbara Wychwoode. A very natural preference, of course," he added, with elaborate gallantry. "But I can assure your Ladyship that, as Helpmeets to heavenly Interference, neither His Majesty nor the Countess of Castlemaine are to be reckoned with."

She bit her lip and cast her eyes to the ground. I could see that her lovely face expressed acute disappointment and that she was on the verge of tears. I am not versed in the ways of gentle Folk nor yet in those of Artists, but I could have told the Lady Barbara Wychwoode that if she wanted to obtain Sympathy or Leniency from Mr. Betterton, she had gone quite the wrong way to work.

Even now, I think if she had started to plead ... but the thought of humbling herself before a Man whom she affected to despise was as far from this proud Woman's heart, as are thoughts of self-glorification from mine.

A second or two later she had succeeded in forcing back the tears which had welled to her eyes, and she was able once more to look her Adversary straight in the face.

"And will you tell me, Sir Actor," she queried with cold aloofness, "how far you intend to carry on this Infamy?"

And Mr. Betterton replied, equally coldly and deliberately:

"To the uttermost limits of the Kingdom, Madam."

"What do you mean?" she riposted.

He drew a step or two nearer to her. His face too was pale by now, his lips trembling, his eyes aglow with Passion masterfully kept under control. His perfect voice rose and fell in those modulated Cadences which we have all learned to appreciate.

"Only this, your Ladyship," he began quite slowly. "For the present, the History of the Earl of Stour's treachery is only guessed at by a few. It is a breath of Scandal, born as you say somewhat mysteriously, wafted through Palaces and noble Mansions to-day—dead, mayhap, to-morrow. But I have had many opportunities for thought of late," he continued—and it seemed to me as if in his quivering voice I could detect a tone of Threat as well as of Passion—"and have employed my leisure moments in writing an Epilogue which I propose to speak to-morrow, after the Play, His Majesty and all the Court being present, and many Gentlemen and Ladies of high degree, as well as Burgesses and Merchants of the City, and sundry Clerks and other humbler Folk. A comprehensive Assembly, what? and an attentive one; for that low-born Mountebank, Tom Betterton, will be appearing in a new play and the Playhouse will be filled to the roof in order to do him honour. May I hope that the Lady Barbara Wychwoode herself——"

"A truce on this foolery, Sir," she broke in harshly. "I pray you come to the point."

She tried to look brave and still haughty, but I knew that she was afraid—knew it by the almost unearthly pallor of her skin, and the weird glitter in her eyes as she regarded him, like a Bird fascinated by a Snake.

"The point is the Epilogue, my Lady," Mr. Betterton replied blandly. "And after I have spoken it to-morrow, I shall speak it again and yet again, until its purport is known throughout the length and breadth of the Land. The subject of that Epilogue, Madam, will be the secret History of a certain aborted Conspiracy, and how it was betrayed in exchange for a free Pardon by one of our noblest Gentlemen in England. Then, I pray your Ladyship to mark what will happen," he continued, and his melodious voice became as hard and trenchant as the clang of metal striking metal. "After that Epilogue has been spoken from the Stage half a dozen times after His Majesty has heard it and shrugged his shoulders, after my Lady Castlemaine has laughed over it and my Lord of Rochester aped it in one of his Pasquinades, there will be a man whose Name will be a by-word for everything that is most infamous and most false—a Name that will be bandied about in Taverns and in drinking Booths, quipped, decried, sneered at, anathematized; a Name that will be the subject of every lampoon and every scurrilous rhyme that finds over-ready purchasers—a Name, in fact, that will for ever be whispered with bated breath or bandied about in a drunken brawl, whene'er there is talk of treachery and of dishonour!"

At this, she—great Lady to her finger tips—threw up her head proudly, still defying him, still striving to hide her Fears and unwilling to acknowledge Defeat.

"It will be your Word against his," she said with a disdainful curl of her perfect lips. "No one would listen to such calumnies."

And he—the world-famed Artist—at least as proud as any high born Gentleman in the Land, retorted, equally haughtily:

"When Tom Betterton speaks upon the Stage, my Lady, England holds her breath and listens spellbound."

I would I could render the noble Accent of his magnificent Voice as he said this. There was no self-glorification in it, no idle boasting; it was the accent of transcendent Worth conscious of its Power.

And it had its effect upon the Lady Barbara Wychwoode. She lowered her Eyes, but not before I had perceived that they were full of Tears; her Lips were trembling still, but no longer with Disdain, and her hands suddenly dropped to her side with a pathetic gesture of Discouragement and of Anguish.

The next moment, however, she was again looking the great Actor fully in the face. A change had come over her, quite suddenly methought—a great Change, which had softened her Mood and to a certain extent lowered her Pride. Whether this was the result of Mr. Betterton's forceful Eloquence or of her own Will-power, I could not guess; but I myself marvelled at the Tone of Entreaty which had crept into her Voice.

"You will not speak such Falsehoods in Public, Sir," she said with unwonted softness. "You will not thus demean your Art—the Art which you love and hold in respect. Oh, there must be some Nobility in You! else you were not so talented. Your Soul must in truth be filled with Sentiments which are neither ignoble nor base."

"Nay!" he exclaimed, and this time did not strive to conceal the intense Bitterness which, as I knew well enough, had eaten into his very Soul; "but your Ladyship is pleased to forget. I am ignoble and base! There cannot be Nobility in me. I am only the low-born Lout! Ask my Lord of Stour; ask your Brother! They will tell you that I have no Feelings, no Pride, no Manhood—that I am only a despicable Varlet, whom every Gentleman may mock and insult and whip like a dog. To You and to your Caste alone belong Nobility, Pride and Honour. Honour!!!"—and he broke into a prolonged laugh, which would have rent your Heart to hear—"Honour! Your false Fetish! Your counterfeit God!! Very well, then so be it!! That very Honour which he hath denied me, I will wrench from him. And since he denied me Satisfaction by the Sword, I turn to my own weapon—my Art—and with it I will exact from him to the uttermost fraction, Outrage for Outrage—Infamy for Infamy."

His wonderful Voice shook, broke almost into a sob at last. I felt a choking sensation in my Throat and my Eyes waxed hot with unshed Tears. As if through a mist, I could see the exquisite Lady Barbara Wychwoode before me, could see that she, too, was moved, her Pride crushed, her Disdain yielding to involuntary Sympathy.

"But he is innocent!" she pleaded, with an accent verging on Despair.

"And so was I!" was his calm retort.

"He——" she entreated, "he loves me——"

"And so do I!" he exclaimed, with a depth of Passion which brought the hot Blood to her pale Cheeks. "I would have given my Life for one Smile from your Lips."

Whereupon, womanlike, she shifted her ground, looked him straight between the Eyes, and, oh! I could have blushed to see the Wiles she used in order to weaken his Resolve.

135

"You love me?" she queried softly, and there was now a tone of almost tender Reproach in her Voice. "You love me! yet you would drag the Man who is dearer to me than Life to Dishonour and to Shame. You trap him, like a Fowler does a Bird, then crush him with Falsehoods and Calumnies! No, no!" she exclaimed—came a step or two nearer to him and clasped her delicate Hands together in a Gesture that was akin to Prayer. "I'll not believe it! You will tell the Truth, Mr. Betterton, publicly, and clear him.... You will.... You will! For my sake—since You say You love me."

But the more eager, the more appealing she grew, the calmer and more calculating did he seem. Now it was his turn to draw away from Her, to measure Her, as it were, with a cold, appraising Look.

"For Your sake?" he said with perfect quietude, almost as if the matter had become outside himself. I cannot quite explain the air of detachment which he assumed—for it was an assumption, on that I would have staked my Life at the moment. I, who know him so well, felt that deep down within his noble Heart there still burned the fierce flames of an ardent Passion, but whether of Love or Hate, I could not then have told You.

She had recoiled at the coolness of his Tone; and he went on, still speaking with that strange, abnormal Calm:

"Yes!" he said slowly, "for Your love I would do what You ask ... I would forego that Feast of Satisfaction, the Thought of which hath alone kept me sane these past few months.... Yes! for the Love of Lady Barbara Wychwoode I could bring myself to forgive even his Lordship of Stour for the irreparable wrong which he hath done to Me. I would restore to him his Honour, which now lies, a Forfeit, in my Hands: for I shall then have taken Something from him which he holds well-nigh as dear."

He paused, and met with the same calm relentlessness the look of Horror and of Scorn wherewith she regarded him.

"For my Love?" she exclaimed, and once more the warm Blood rushed up to her face, flooding her wan Cheeks, her pale Forehead, even her delicate Throat with crimson. "You mean that I? ... Oh! ... what Infamy! ... So, Mr. Actor, that was your reckoning!" she went on with supreme Disdain. "It was not the desire for Vengeance that prompted You to slander the Earl of Stour, but the wish to entrap me into becoming your Wife. You are not content with Your Laurels. You want a Coat of Arms ... and hoped to barter one against Your Calumnies!"

"Nay, your Ladyship!" he rejoined simply, "in effect, I was actually laying a Name famed throughout the cultured world humbly at your feet. You made an appeal to my Love for You—and I laid a test for your Sincerity. Mine I have placed beyond question, seeing that I am prepared to drag my Genius in the dust before Your Pride and the Arrogance of Your Caste. An Artist is a Slave of his Sensibilities, and I feel that if, in the near Future, I could see a Vision of your perfect hand resting content in mine, if, when You pleaded again for my Lord Stour, You did so as my promised Wife— not his—I would do all that You asked."

She drew herself up to her full height and glanced at him with all the Pride which awhile ago had seemed crushed beyond recall.

"Sir Actor," she said coldly, "shame had gripped me by the throat, or I should not have listened so long to such an Outrage. The Bargain You propose is an Infamy and an Insult."

And she gathered up her Skirts around her, as if their very contact with the Soil on which he trod were a pollution. Then she half turned as if ready to go, cast a rapid glance at the Shrubberies close by, no doubt in search of her Attendant. Why it was that she did not actually go, I could not say, but guessed that, mayhap, she would not vacate the Field of Contention until quite sure that there was not a final Chance to soften the Heart of the Enemy. She had thrown down yet another Challenge when she spoke of his proposed Bargain as an Infamy; but he took up the Gage with the same measured Calm as before.

"As you will," he said. "It was in Your Ladyship's name that the Earl of Stour put upon Me the deadliest Insult which any Man hath ever put on Man before. Since then, every Fibre within Me has clamoured for Satisfaction. My Work hath been irksome to me ... I scarce could think ... My Genius lay writhing in an agony of Shame. But now the hour is mine—for it I have schemed and lied—aye, lied—like the low-born cur You say I am. A thousand Devils of Hate and of Rage are unchained within me. I cannot grapple with them alone. They would only yield—to your kiss."

"Oh!" she cried in uttermost despair, "this is horrible!"

"Then let the Man you love," he rejoined coldly, "look to himself."

"Conscious of his Innocence, my Lord Stour and I defy you!"

"Ah, well!" he said imperturbably, "the Choice is still with Your Ladyship. Remember that I do not speak my Epilogue until to-morrow. When I do, it will be too late. I have called my Phantasy 'The Comedie of Traitors.'"

Whereupon he bowed low before her, in the most approved Fashion. But already she was fleeing up the path in the direction of Westminster. Soon her graceful Figure was lost to our sight behind an intervening clump of Laurels. Here no doubt her Ladyship's Attendant was waiting for her Mistress, for anon I spied two figures hurrying out of the Park.

For a long time Mr. Betterton remained standing just where he was, one hand still clutching the knob of his Stick, the other thrust in the pocket of his capacious Coat. I could not see his Face, since his Back was turned towards me, and I did not dare move lest I should be interrupting his Meditations. But to Me, even that Back was expressive. There was a listlessness, hardly a stoop, about it, so unlike my Friend's usual firm and upright Carriage. How could this be otherwise, seeing what he had just gone through—Emotions that would have swept most Men off their mental balance. Yet he kept his, had never once lost control of himself. He had met Disdain with Disdain in the end, had kept sufficient control over his Voice to discuss with absolute calm, that Bargain which the Lady Barbara had termed infamous. There had been a detachment about his final Ultimatum, a "take it or leave it" air, which must have been bitterly galling to the proud Lady who had stooped to entreat. He was holding the winning Hand and did not choose to yield.

And it was from his attitude on that Day that I, dear Mistress, drew an unerring inference. Mr. Betterton had no Love for the Lady Barbara, no genuine, lasting Affection such as, I maintain, he has never ceased to feel for You. Passion swayed him, because he has, above all, that unexplainable artistic Temperament which cannot be measured by everyday Standards. Pride, Bitterness, Vengefulness— call it what you will; but there was not a particle of Love in it all. I verily believe that his chief Desire, whilst he stood pondering there at the bridgehead, was to humiliate the Lady Barbara Wychwoode by forcing her into a Marriage which she had affected to despise. He was not waiting for her with open, loving Arms, ready to take her to his Heart, there to teach her to forget the Past in the safe haven of his Love. He was not waiting to lay his Service at her feet, and to render her happy as the cherished Wife and Helpmate of the great Artist whom all England delighted to honour. He was only waiting to make her feel that She had been subjected to his Will and her former Lover brought down to Humiliation, through the Power of the miserable Mountebank whom they had both deemed less than a Man.

Thus meditating, I stood close to my Friend, until Chance or a fleeting Thought brought him back to the realities of Life. He sighed and looked about him, as a Man will who hath just wakened from a Dream. Then he spied me, and gave me his wonted kindly smile and glance.

"Good old John!" he said, with a self-deprecating shrug of the shoulders. "'Twas not an edifying Scene You have witnessed, eh?"

"'Twas a heartrending one," I riposted almost involuntarily.

"Heartrending?" he queried, in a tone of intense bitterness, "to watch a Fool crushing every Noble Instinct within him for the sake of getting even with a Man whom he neither honours nor esteems?"

He sighed again, and beckoned to me to follow him.

"Let us home, good Honeywood," he said. "I am weary of all this wrangle, and pine to find solace among the Poets."

Nor did he mention the name of the Lady Barbara again to me, and I was left to ponder what was going on in his Mind and whether his cruelly vengeful Scheme for the final undoing of my Lord Stour would indeed come to maturity on the following day. I knew that a great and brilliant Representation of the late Mr. William Shakespeare's play, "Twelfth Night," was to be given at the Duke's Theatre, with some of the new Scenery and realistic scenic Effects brought over last Autumn from Paris by Mr. Betterton. His Majesty had definitely promised that he would be present and so had the Countess of Castlemaine, and there would doubtless be a goodly and gorgeous Company present to applaud the great Actor, whose Performance of Sir Toby Belch was one of the Marvels of histrionic Art, proclaiming as it did his wonderful versatility, by contrast with his equally remarkable exposition of the melancholy Hamlett, Prince of Denmark.

That I now awaited that Day with Sorrow in my Heart and with measureless Anxiety, You, dear Mistress, will readily imagine. Until this morning I had no idea of the terrible Thunderbolt which my Friend had in preparation for those who had so shamefully wronged him; and I still marvelled whether in his talk with the Lady Barbara there had not lurked some idle Threats rather than a serious Warning. How could I think of the Man whom I had learned to love and to reverence as one who would nurture such cruel Schemes? And yet, did not the late Mr. Shakespeare warn us that "Pleasure and Revenge have ears more deaf than Adders to the voice of any true decision"? Ah, me! but I was sick at heart.

CHAPTER XIV

THE RULING PASSION

1

And now, dear Mistress, I come to that memorable Evening wherein happened that which causes You so much heart-ache at this Hour.

I know that the Occurrences of that Night have been brought to your Notice in a garbled Version, and that Mr. Betterton's Enemies have placed the Matter before You in a manner calculated to blacken his Integrity. But, as there is a living Judge above Us all, I swear to You, beloved Mistress, that what I am now purposing to relate is nothing but the Truth. Remember that, in this miserable Era of Scandal and Backbiting, of loose Living and Senseless Quarrels, Mr. Betterton's Character has always stood unblemished, even though the evil Tongue of Malice hath repeatedly tried to attack his untarnished Reputation. Remember also that the great Actor's few but virulent Enemies are all Men who have made Failures of their Lives, who are Idlers, Sycophants or Profligates, and therefore envious of the Fame and Splendour of one who is thought worthy to be the Friend of Kings.

2

We spoke but little together that day on our way home from the Park. Mr. Betterton was moody, and I silent. We took our dinner in quietude. There being no Performance at the Theatre that day, Mr. Betterton settled down to his Desk in the afternoon, telling me that he had some writing to do.

I, too, had some of his Correspondence to attend to, and presently repaired to my room, my Heart still aching with Sorrow. Did I not guess what Work was even now engrossing the Attention of my Friend? He was deep in the Composition of that cruel Lampoon which he meant to speak on the Stage to-morrow, in the presence of His Majesty and of a large and brilliant Assembly. Strive as I might, I could not to myself minimize the probable Effect of the

Lampoon upon the Mind of the Public. It is not for me, dear Mistress, to remind You of the amazing Popularity of Mr. Betterton—a Popularity which hath never been equalled ere this by any Actor, Artist or Poet in England. Whatever he spoke from the Stage would be treasured and reiterated and commented upon, until every Citizen of London and Westminster became himself a storehouse of Mud that would be slung at the unfortunate Earl of Stour. And the latter, by refusing to fight Mr. Betterton when the Latter had been the injured Party, had wilfully cast aside any Weapon of Redress which he might after this have called to his Aid.

Well! we all know the Effect of scurrilous Quips spoken from the Stage; even the great Mr. Dryden or the famous Mr. Wycherley have not been above interpolating some in their Plays, for the Confusion of their Enemies; and many a Gentleman's or a Lady's Reputation has been made to suffer through the Vindictiveness of a noted Actor or Playwright. But, as you know, Mr. Betterton had never hitherto lent himself to such Scandal-monging; he stood far above those petty Quarrels betwixt Gentlemen and Poets that could be settled by wordy Warfare across the Footlights. All the more Weight, therefore, would the Public attach to an Epilogue specially written and spoken by him on so great an occasion. And, alas! the Mud-slinging was to be of a very peculiar and very clinging Nature.

"Then let the Man you love look to himself!" the outraged Artist had said coldly, when confronted for the last time by the Lady Barbara's Disdain. And in my Mind I had no doubt that, for Good or for Evil, if Tom Betterton set out to do a Thing, he would carry it through to its bitter End.

3

When, having finished my work, I went into Mr. Betterton's study, I found him sitting beside his Desk, though no longer writing. He was leaning back against the cushions of his chair with eyes closed, his face set and hard. Some loose papers, covered with his neat, careful Caligraphy, lay in an orderly heap upon the Desk.

His Work was evidently finished. Steeped in Bitterness and in Vengeance, his Pen had laboured and was now at rest. The Eloquence of the incomparable Actor would now do the rest.

As I entered the Room, the tower clock of Westminster was just striking seven. The deep bay Window which gave on a solitary corner of St. James's Park, was wide open, and through it there came from afar, wafted upon the evening breeze, the strains of a masculine Voice, warm and mellow, singing to the accompaniment of one of those stringed Instruments which have been imported of late from Italy.

The Voice rose and fell in pleasing Cadences, and some of the Words of the Song reached mine Ear.

> "You are my Life. You ask me why?
> Because my hope is in your love."

Whether Mr. Betterton heard them or not, I could not say. He sat there so still, his slender Hands—white and tapering, the veritable Hands of an Artist—rested listlessly upon the arms of his chair.

> "Through gloomy Clouds to sunlit Skies,
> To rest in Faith and your dear Eyes."

So sang the sweet Minstrel out there in the fast gathering Gloom. I went up to the window and gazed out into the open Vista before me. Far away I could see the twinkling lights from the windows of St. James's Palace, and on my right those of White Hall. The Singer I could not see. He appeared to be some distance away. But despite the lateness of the hour, the Park was still alive with people. And indeed as I leaned my Head further out of the Window, I was struck by the animated spectacle which it presented.

No doubt that the unwonted mildness of this early spring evening had induced young Maids and Gallants, as well as more sober Folk and Gentlemen, to linger out in the open. The charm of the Minstrel and his Song, too, must have served as an additional Attraction, for as I watched the People passing to and fro, I heard snatches of Conversation, mostly in praise of the Singer or of the Weather.

Anon I espied Sir William Davenant walking with Mr. Killigrew, and my Lord of Rochester dallying with a pretty Damsel; one or two more Gentlemen did I recognize as I gazed on the moving Sight, until suddenly I saw that which caused me to draw my Head back quickly from the Window and to gaze with added Anxiety on the listless Figure of my Friend.

What I had seen down below had indeed filled my Heart with Dread. It was the Figure of my Lord Stour. I could have sworn to it, even though his Lordship was wrapped in a mantle from Head to Foot and wore a broad-rimmed Hat, both of which would indeed have disguised his Person completely before all Eyes save those of Love, of Hate, or of an abiding Friendship.

What was my Lord Stour doing at this Hour, and in disguise, beneath the Window of his bitterest Foe? My Anxiety was further quickened by the Certainty which I had that neither he nor the Lady Barbara would allow Mr. Betterton's Schemes to mature without another Struggle. Even as I once more thrust my Head out of the Window, in order to catch another glimpse of the moody and solitary Figure which I had guessed to be Lord Stour, methought that close by the nearest Shrubbery I espied the Figure of the Lady Barbara, in close conversation with her Attendant. Both Women were wrapped in dark Mantles and wore thick veils to cover their Hair.

A dark presentiment of Evil now took possession of my Soul. I felt like a Watch-dog scenting Danger from afar. The Man whom I loved better than any other on Earth was in peril of his Life, at the hands of an Enemy driven mad by an impending Doom—of that I felt suddenly absolutely convinced. And somehow, I felt equally convinced at the moment that we—I, the poor, insignificant Clerk, as well as my illustrious Friend—were standing on the Brink of an overwhelming Catastrophe.

I had thought to warn him then and there, yet dared not do so in so many words. Men in the prime of Life and the plentitude of their mental Powers are wont to turn contemptuous and obstinate if told to be on their guard against a lurking Enemy. And I feared that, in his utter contempt for his Foe, Mr. Betterton might be tempted to do something that was both unconsidered and perilous.

So I contented myself for the nonce with turning to my Friend, seeing that he had wakened from his reverie and was regarding me with that look of Confidence and Kindliness which always warmed my heart when I was conscious of it, I merely remarked quite casually:

"The Park is still gay with Ladies and Gallants. 'Tis strange at this late hour. But a Minstrel is discoursing sweet Music somewhere in the distance. Mayhap people have assembled in order to listen to him."

And, as if to confirm my Supposition, a merry peal of laughter came ringing right across the Park, and we heard as it were the hum and murmur of Pedestrians moving about. And through it all the echo of the amorous Ditty still lingering upon the evening air:

"For you are Love—and I am yours!"

"Close that window, John," Mr. Betterton said, with an impatient little sigh. "I am in no mood for sentimental Ballads."

I did as he desired, and whilst in the act of closing the Window, I said guardedly:

"I caught sight of my Lord Stour just now, pacing the open Ground just beneath this Window. He appeared moody and solitary, and was wrapped from head to foot in a big Mantle, as if he wished to avoid Recognition."

"I too am moody and solitary, good Honeywood," was Mr. Betterton's sole comment on my remark. Then he added, with a slight shiver of his whole body: "I prithee, see to the Fire. I am perished with the cold."

I went up to the Hearth and kicked the dying embers into a Blaze; then found some logs and threw them on the Fire.

"The evening is warm, Sir," I said; "and you complained of the Heat awhile ago."

"Yes," he rejoined wearily. "My head is on fire and my Spine feels like ice."

It was quite dark in the Room now, save for the flickering and ruddy firelight. So I went out and bade the Servant give me the candles. I came back with them myself and set them on the Desk. As I did so, I glanced at Mr. Betterton. He had once more taken up his listless Attitude; his Head was leaning against the back of his Chair, and I could not fail to note how pallid his Face looked and how drawn, and there was a frown between his Brows which denoted wearying and absorbing Thoughts. Wishing to distract him from his brooding Melancholy, I thought of reminding him of certain artistic and social Duties which were awaiting his Attention.

"Will you send an Answer, Sir," I asked him with well-assumed indifference, "to the Chancellor? It is on the Subject of the Benefit Performance in aid of the Indigent Poor of the City of Westminster. His Lordship again sent a messenger this afternoon."

"Yes!" Mr. Betterton replied readily enough, and sought amongst his Papers for a Letter which he had apparently written some time during the Day. "If His Lordship's Messenger calls again, let him have this Note. I must arrange for the Benefit Performance, of course. But I doubt if many members of the Company will care to give their Services."

"I think that Mr. Robert Noakes would be willing," I suggested. "Also Mr. Lilleston."

"Perhaps, perhaps!" he broke in listlessly. "But we must have Actresses too, and they——"

He shrugged his shoulders, and I rejoined with great alacrity:

"Oh! I feel sure that Mistress Saunderson would be ready to join in any benevolent Scheme for the betterment of the Poor."

"Ah! but she is an Angel!" Mr. Betterton exclaimed. And,

believe me, dear Mistress, that those words came as if involuntarily to his Lips, out of the Fulness of his Heart. And even when he had spoken, a Look of infinite Sadness swept over his Face and he rested his Head against his Hand, shading his Eyes from the light of the Candles, lest I should read the Thoughts that were mirrored therein.

"There came a messenger, too, this afternoon," I reminded him, "from Paris, with an autograph Letter from His Majesty the King of France."

"Yes!" he replied, and nodded his Head, I thought, uncomprehendingly.

"Also a letter from the University of Stockholm. They propose that You should visit the City in the course of the Summer and——"

"Yes, yes! I know!" he rejoined impatiently. "I will attend to it all another time ... But not to-night, good Honeywood," he went on almost appealingly, like a Man wearied with many Tasks. "My mind is like a squeezed Orange to-night."

Then he held out his Hand to me—that beautiful, slender Hand of his, which I had so often kissed in the excess of my Gratitude—and added with gentle Indulgence:

"Let me be to-night, good Friend. Leave me to myself. I am such poor Company and am best alone."

I took his hand. It was burning hot, as if with inward Fever. All my Friendship for him, all my Love, was at once on the alert, dreading the ravages of some inward Disease, brought on mayhap by so much Soul-worry.

"I do not relish leaving You alone to-night," I said, with more gruffness than I am wont to display. "This room is easy of Access from the Park."

He smiled, a trifle sadly.

"Dost think," he asked, with a slight shrug of the shoulders, "that a poor Mountebank would tempt a midnight Robber?"

"No!" I replied firmly. "But my Lord Stour, wrapped to the eyes in his Mantle, hath prowled beneath these Windows for an hour." Then, as he made no comment, I continued with some Fervour: "A determined Man, who hates Another, can easily climb up to a first floor Window——"

"Tush, friend!" he broke in sharply. "I am not afraid of his Lordship ... I am afraid of nothing to-night, my good Honeywood," he added softly, "except of myself."

You certainly will not wonder, dear Mistress, that after that I did not obey his Commands to leave him to himself. I am nothing of an Eavesdropper, God knows, nor yet would I pry into the Secrets of the Soul of the one Man whom I reverence above all others. But, even as I turned reluctantly away from him in order to go back to my Room, I resolved that, unless he actually shut the Door in my Face, I would circumvent him and would remain on the watch, like a faithful Dog who scents Danger for his Master. In this I did not feel that I was doing any Wrong. God saw in my Heart and knew that my Purpose was innocent. I thank Him on my Knees in that He strengthened me in my Resolve. But for that Resolve, I should not have been cognizant of all the details of those Events which culminated in such a dramatic Climax that night, and I would not have been able to speak with Authority when placing all the Facts before You. Let me tell You at once that I was there, in Mr. Betterton's Room, during the whole of the time that the Incident occurred which I am now about to relate.

He had remained sitting at his Desk, and I went across the Room in the direction of the communicating Door which gave on my own Study. But I did not go through that Door. I just opened and shut it noisily, and then slipped stealthily behind the tall oaken Dresser, which stands in a dark Angle of the Room. From this point of Vantage I could watch closely and ceaselessly, and at the slightest Suspicion of immediate Danger to my Friend I would be free to slip out of my Hiding-place and to render him what Assistance he required. I had to squat there in a cramped Position, and I felt half suffocated with the closeness of the Atmosphere behind so heavy a Piece of Furniture; but this I did not mind. From where I was I could command a view of Mr. Betterton at his Desk, and of the Window, which I wished now that I had taken the Precaution to bar and bolt ere I retired to my Corner behind the Dresser.

For awhile, everything was silent in the Room; only the great Clock ticked loudly in its case, and now and again the blazing logs gave an intermittent Crackle. I just could see the outline of Mr. Betterton's Shoulder and Arm silhouetted against the candle light. He sat forward, his elbow resting upon the Desk, his Head leaning against his Hand, and so still that presently I fell to thinking that he must have dropped to sleep.

But suddenly he gave that quick, impatient Sigh of his, which I had learned to know so well, pushed back his chair, and rose to his

Feet. Whereupon, he began pacing up and down the Room, in truth like some poor, perturbed Spirit that is denied the Solace of Rest.

Then he began to murmur to himself. I know that mood of his and believe it to be peculiar to the artistic Temperament, which, when it feels itself untrammelled by the Presence of Others, gives vent to its innermost Thoughts in mumbled Words.

From time to time I caught Snatches of what he said—wild Words for the most part, which showed the Perturbation of his Spirit. He, whose Mind was always well-ordered, whose noble Calling had taught him to co-ordinate his Thoughts and to subdue them to his Will, was now murmuring incoherent Phrases, disjointed Sentences that would have puzzled me had I not known the real Trend of his Mood.

"Barbara!..." he said at one time. "Beautiful, exquisite, innocent Lady Babs; the one pure Crystal in that Laboratory of moral Decomposition, the Court of White Hall...." Then he paused, struck his Forehead with his Hand, and added with a certain fierce Contempt: "But she will yield ... she is ready now to yield. She will cast aside her Pride, and throw herself into the arms of a Man whom she hates, all for the sake of that young Coxcomb, who is not worthy to kiss the Sole of her Shoe!"

Again he paused, flung himself back into his Chair, and once more buried his Face in his Hands.

"Oh, Woman, Woman!" I could hear him murmuring. "What an Enigma! How can the mere Man attempt to understand thee?"

Then he laughed. Oh! I could not bear the sound of that laugh: there was naught but Bitterness in it. And he said slowly muttering between his Teeth:

"The Philosopher alone knows that Women are like Melons: it is only after having tasted them that one knows if they are good."

Of course, he said a great deal more during the course of that dreary, restless hour, which seemed to me like a Slice out of Eternity. His Restlessness was intense. Every now and then he would jump up and walk up and down, up and down, until his every Footstep had its counterpart in the violent beatings of my Heart. Then he would fling himself into a Chair and rest his Head against the Cushions, closing his Eyes as if he were in bodily Pain, or else beat his Forehead with his Fists.

Of course he thought himself unobserved, for Mr. Betterton is, as You know, a Man of great mental Reserve. Not even before me— his faithful and devoted Friend—would he wittingly have displayed such overmastering Emotion. To say that an equally overwhelming Sorrow filled my Heart would be but to give You, dear Mistress, a feeble Statement of what I really felt. To see a Man of Mr.

Betterton's mental and physical Powers so utterly crushed by an insane Passion was indeed heartrending. Had he not everything at his Feet that any Man could wish for?—Fame, Honours, the Respect and Admiration of all those who mattered in the World. Women adored him, Men vied with one another to render him the sincerest Flattery by striving to imitate his Gestures, his Mode of Speech, the very Cut of his Clothes. And, above all—aye, I dare assert it, and You, beloved Mistress will, I know, forgive me—above all, he had the Love of a pure and good Woman, of a talented Artist—yours, dear Lady—an inestimable Boon, for which many a Man would thank his Maker on his Knees.

Ah! he was blind then, had been blind since that fatal Hour when the Lady Barbara Wychwoode crossed his Path. I could endorse the wild Words which he had spoken to her this forenoon. A thousand devils were indeed unchained within him; but 'tis not to her Kiss that they would yield, but rather to the gentle Ministration of exquisite Mistress Saunderson.

CHAPTER XV

MORE DEAF THAN ADDERS

1

I felt so cramped and numb in my narrow hiding-place that I verily believe I must have fallen into a kind of trance-like Slumber.

From this I was suddenly awakened by the loud Clang of our front-door Bell, followed immediately by the Footsteps of the Serving Man upon the Landing, and then by a brief Colloquy between him and the belated Visitor.

Seriously, at the moment I had no Conception of who this might be, until I glanced at Mr. Betterton. And then I guessed. Guessed, just as he had already done. Every line of his tense and expectant Attitude betrayed the Fact that he had recognized the Voice upon the Landing, and that its sound had thrilled his very Soul and brought him back from the Land of Dreams and Nightmare, where he had been wandering this past hour.

You remember, dear Lady, the last time Mr. Betterton played in a Tragedy called "Hamlett," wherein there is a Play within a Play, and the melancholy Prince of Denmark sets a troupe of Actors to enact a Representation of the terrible Crime whereof he accuses both his Uncle and his Mother? It is a Scene which, when played by Mr. Betterton, is wont to hold the Audience enthralled. He plays his Part in it by lying full length on the Ground, his Body propped up by his Elbow and his Chin supported in his Hand. His Eyes—those wonderful, expressive Eyes of his—he keeps fixed upon the guilty Pair: his Mother and his Uncle. He watches the play of every Emotion upon their faces—Fear, Anger, and then the slowly creeping, enveloping Remorse; and his rigid, stern Features express an Intensity of Alertness and of Expectancy, which is so poignant as to be almost painful.

Just such an Expression did my dear Friend's Face wear at this Moment. He had pushed his Chair back slightly, so that I had a fuller view of him, and the flickering light of the wax Candles illumined his clear-cut Features and his Eyes, fixed tensely upon the door.

2

The next moment the serving Man threw open the door and the Lady Barbara walked in. I could not see her until she had advanced further into the middle of the Room. Then I beheld her in all her Loveliness. Nay! I'll not deny it. She was still incomparably beautiful, with, in addition, that marvellous air of Breeding and of Delicacy, which rendered her peerless amongst her kind. I hated her for the infinite wrong which she had done to my Friend, but I could not fail to admire her. Her Mantle was thrown back from her Shoulders and a dark, filmy Veil, resembling a Cloud, enveloped her fair Hair. Beneath her Mantle she wore a Dress of something grey that shimmered like Steel in the Candlelight. A few tendrils of her ardent Hair had escaped from beneath her Veil, and they made a kind of golden Halo around her Face. She was very pale, but of that transparent, delicate Pallor that betokens Emotion rather than ill-health, and her Eyes looked to me to be as dark as Sloes, even though I knew them to be blue.

For the space of one long Minute, which seemed like Eternity, these two remained absolutely still, just looking at one another.

Methought that I could hear the very heart-beats within my breast. Then the Lady said, with a queer little catch in her Throat and somewhat hesitatingly:

"You are surprised to see me, Sir, no doubt ... but ..."

She was obviously at a loss how to begin. And Mr. Betterton, aroused no doubt by her Voice from his absorption, rose quickly to his Feet and made her a deep and respectful Obeisance.

"The Angels from Heaven sometimes descend to Earth," he said slowly; "yet the Earth is more worthy of their Visit than is the humble Artist of the Presence of his Muse." Then he added more artlessly: "Will You deign to sit?"

He drew a Chair forward for her, but She did not take it, continued to speak with a strange, obviously forced Gaiety and in a halting Manner.

"I thank you, Sir," she said. "That is ... no ... not yet ... I like to look about me."

She went close up to the Desk and began to finger idly the Books and Papers which lay scattered pell-mell upon it, he still gazing on her as if he had not yet realized the Actuality of her Presence. Anon she looked inquiringly about her.

"What a charming room!" she said, with a little cry of wonder. "So new to me! I have never seen an Artist's room before."

"For weeks and months," Mr. Betterton rejoined simply, "this one has been a temple, hallowed by thoughts of You. Your Presence now, has henceforth made it a Sanctuary."

She turned full, inquiring Eyes upon him and riposted with childlike Ingenuousness:

"Yet must You wonder, Sir, at my Presence here ... alone ... and at this hour."

"In my heart," he replied, "there is such an Infinity of Happiness that there is no Room for Wonder."

"An Infinity of Happiness?" she said with a quaint little sigh. "That is what we are all striving for, is it not? The Scriptures tell us that this Earth is a Vale of Tears. No wonder!" she added naïvely, "since we are so apt to allow Happiness to pass us by."

Oh! how I wished I had the Courage then and there to reveal myself to these Twain, to rush out of my Hiding-place and seize that wily Temptress who, I felt sure, was here only for the undoing of a Man whom she hated with unexampled Bitterness. Oh, why hath grudging Nature made me weak and cowardly and diffident, when my whole Soul yearns at times to be resourceful and bold? Believe me, dear Mistress, that my Mind and my Will-power were absolutely torn between two Impulses—the one prompting me to put a stop to this dangerous and purposeless Interview, this obvious

150

Trap set to catch a great and unsuspecting Artist unawares; and the other urging me not to interfere, but rather to allow Destiny, Fate or the Will of God alone to straighten out the Web of my Friend's Life, which had been embroiled by such Passions as were foreign to his noble Nature.

And now I am thankful that I allowed this latter Counsel to prevail. The Will of God did indeed shape the Destinies of Men this night for their Betterment and ultimate Happiness. But, for the moment, the Threads of many a Life did appear to be most hopelessly tangled: the Lady Barbara Wychwoode, daughter of the Marquis of Sidbury, the fiancée of the Earl of Stour, was in the house of Tom Betterton, His Majesty's Well-Beloved Servant, and he was passionately enamoured of her and had vowed Vengeance against the Man she loved. As he gazed on her now there was no Hatred in his Glance, no evil Passion disturbed the Look of Adoration wherewith he regarded her.

"Barbara," he pleaded humbly, "be merciful to me.... For pity's sake, do not mock me with your smile! My dear, do you not see that I scarce can believe that I live ... and that you are here? ... You! ... You!" he went on, with passionate Earnestness. "My Divinity, whom I only dare approach on bended Knees, whose Garment I scarce dare touch with my trembling Lips!"

He bent the Knee and raised the long, floating End of her cloudlike Veil to his Lips. I could have sworn at that Moment that she recoiled from him and that she made a Gesture to snatch away the Veil, as if his very Touch on it had been Pollution. That Gesture and the Recoil were, however, quite momentary. The next second, even whilst he rose once more to his Feet, she had already recovered herself.

"Hush!" she said gently, and drew herself artlessly away from his Nearness. "I want to listen.... People say that Angels wait upon Mr. Betterton when he studies his Part ... and I want to hear the flutter of their Wings."

"The Air vibrates with the Echo of your sweet Name," he rejoined, and his exquisite Voice sounded mellow and vibrant as a sensitive Instrument touched by a Master's Hand. "Your name, which with mad longing I have breathed morning, noon and eve. And now ... now ... I am not dreaming ... You are near me! ... You, the perfect Lady Barbara ... my Lady Babs.... And you look—almost happy!"

She gave him a Look—the true Look of a Siren set to enchain the Will of Man.

"Happy?" she queried demurely. "Nay, Sir ... puzzled, perhaps."

151

"Puzzled?" he echoed. "Why?"

"Wondering," she replied, "what magic is in the air that could make a Woman's Heart ... forsake one Love ... for ... for Another."

Yes! She said this, and looked on him straight between the Eyes as she spoke. Yet I knew that she lied, could have screamed the Accusation at her, so convinced was I that she was playing some subtle and treacherous Game, designed to entrap him and to deliver him helpless and broken into her Power. But he, alas! was blinded by his Passion. He saw no Siren in her, no Falsehood in her Smile. At her Words, I saw a great Light of Happiness illumine his Face.

"Barbara!" he pleaded. "Have pity on me, for my Reason wanders. I dare not call it back, lest this magic hour should prove to be a Dream."

He tried to take her in his Arms, but she evaded him, ran to the other side of the Desk, laughing merrily like a Child. Once again her delicate Fingers started to toy with the Papers scattered there.

"Oh, ho!" she exclaimed, with well-feigned astonishment. "Your desk! Why, this," she said, placing her Hand upon the neat pile before her, "must be that very Thunderbolt wherewith to-morrow you mean to crush an arrogant Enemy!"

"Barbara!" he rejoined with ever growing passion, and strove to take her Hand. "Will you not let me tell You——"

"Yes, yes!" she replied archly, and quietly withdrew her Hand from his grasp. "You shall speak to me anon some of those Speeches of our great Poets, which your Genius hath helped to immortalize. To hear Mr. Betterton recite will be an inestimable Privilege ... which your many Admirers, Sir, will envy me."

"The whole world would envy me to-night," he retorted, and gazed on her with such Ardour that she was forced to lower her Eyes and to hide their Expression behind the delicate Curtain of her Lashes.

I, who was the dumb Spectator of this cruel Game, saw that the Lady Barbara was feeling her way towards her Goal. There was so much Excitement in her, such palpitating Vitality, that her very Heart-beats seemed to find their Echo in my breast. Of course, I did not know yet what Game it was that she was playing. All that I knew was that it was both deadly and treacherous. Even now, when Mr. Betterton once more tried to approach her and she as instinctively as before recoiled before him, she contrived to put strange softness into her Voice, and a subtle, insidious Promise which helped to confuse his Brain.

"No—no!" she said. "Not just yet ... I pray you have pity on my Blushes. I—I still am affianced to my Lord Stour ... although..."

"You are right, my beloved," he rejoined simply. "I will be

patient, even though I am standing on the Threshold of Paradise. But will You not be merciful? I cannot see you well. Will you not take off that Veil? ... It casts a dark shadow over your Brow."

This time she allowed him to come near her, and, quite slowly, she unwound the Veil from round her Head. He took it from her as if it were some hallowed Relic, too sacred to be polluted by earthly Touch. And, as her back was turned towards him, he crushed the Gossamer between his Hands and pressed its Fragrance to his Lips.

"There!" she said coolly. "'Tis done. Your magic, Sir Actor, has conquered again."

It seemed to me that she was more self-possessed now than she had been when first she entered the Room. Indeed, her Serenity appeared to grow as his waned perceptibly. She still was a little restless, wandering aimlessly about the Room, fingering the Books, the Papers, the Works of Art that lay everywhere about; but it seemed like the restlessness of Curiosity rather than of Excitement. In her own Mind she felt that she held the Winning Hand—of this I was convinced—and that she could afford to toy with and to befool the Man who had dared to measure his Power against hers.

After awhile, she sat down in her Chair which he had brought forward for her, and which stood close to the Desk.

"And now, Sir," she said with cool composure, "'tis You who must humour me. I have a fancy ... now, at this moment ... and my Desire is to be thoroughly spoiled."

"Every Whim of yours," he rejoined, "is a Command to your humble Slave."

"Truly?" she queried.

"Truly."

"Then will You let me see you ... sitting at your Desk ... Pen in hand ... writing something just for me?"

"All my work of late," he replied, "has been done because of You ... but I am no Poet. What I speak may have some Merit. What I write hath none."

"Oh!" she protested with well-simulated Coquetry, "what I desire You to write for me, Sir Actor, will have boundless Merit. It is just a couple of Lines designed to ... to ... prove your Love for me— Oh!" she added quickly, "I scarce dare believe in it, Sir ... I scare understood ... You remember, this morning in the Park, I was so excited, yet you asked me—to be—your Wife!"

"My Wife!" he cried, his Voice ringing with triumphant Passion. "And you would consent?——"

"And so I came," she riposted, evading a direct Answer, "to see if I had been dreaming ... if, indeed, the great and illustrious Mr.

153

Betterton had stooped to love a Woman ... and for the sake of that Love would do a little Thing for Her."

Lies! Lies! I knew that every Word which she spoke was nothing but a Lie. My God! if only I could have unriddled her Purpose! If only I could have guessed what went on behind those marvellous Eyes of hers, deep and unfathomable as the Sea! All I knew—and this I did in the very Innermost of my Soul—was that the Lady Barbara Wychwoode had come here to-night in order to trick Mr. Betterton, and to turn his Love for her to Advantage for my Lord Stour. How carefully she had thought out the Part which she meant to play; how completely she meant to have him at her Mercy, only in order to mock and deride him in the End, I had yet to learn.

Even now she completed his Undoing, the Addling of his noble Mind, by casting Looks of shy Coquetry upon him. What Man is there who could have resisted them? What Man, who was himself so deeply infatuated as was Mr. Betterton, could believe that there was Trickery in those Glances? He sat down at his Desk, as she had desired him to do, and drew Pen, Ink and Paper closer to his Hand.

"An you asked my Life," he said simply, "I would gladly give it to prove my Love for You." Then, as she remained silent and meditative, he added: "What is your Ladyship's wish?"

"Oh!" she replied, "'tis a small matter ... It concerns the Earl of Stour ... We were Friends ... once ... Playmates when we were Children ... That Friendship ripened into a—a—Semblance of Love. No! No!" she went on rapidly, seeing that at her Words he had made a swift Movement, leaning towards her. "I pray you, listen. That Semblance of Love may have gone ... but Friendship still abides. My Lord Stour, the Playmate of my Childhood, is in sore trouble ... I, his Friend, would wish to help him, and cannot do this without your Aid. Will You—will You grant me this Aid, Sir," she queried shyly, "if I beg it of You?"

"Your Ladyship has but to command," he answered vaguely, for, in truth, his whole Mind was absorbed in the contemplation of her Loveliness.

"'Twas You," she asserted boldly, "who begged for his Lordship's pardon from the Countess of Castlemaine ... 'Twas not he who betrayed his Friends. That is a Fact, is it not?"

"A Fact. Yes," he replied.

"Then I pray you, Sir, write that down," she pleaded, with an ingenuous, childish Gesture, "and sign it with your Name ... just to please me."

She looked like a lovely Child begging for a Toy. To think of Guile in connection with those Eyes, with that Smile, seemed almost a Sacrilege. And my poor Friend was so desperately infatuated just then! Has any Man ever realized that Woman is fooling him, when she really sets her Wiles to entrap him? Surely not a Man of Mr. Betterton's keen, artistic and hot-blooded Temperament. I saw it all now, yet I dared not move. For one thing, the time had gone by when I might have done it with good Effect. Now it was too late. Any interference on my part would only have led to Ignominy for myself and the severance of a Friendship that I valued more than Life itself. Betwixt a Friend's warning and a Woman's Cajolery, what Man would hesitate? What could I, in any event, have done now, save to hold up the inevitable Catastrophe for a few Moments—a few Seconds, perhaps? Truly, my hour was past. I could but wait now in Silence and Misery until the End.

There she sat, pleading, speaking that eternal Phrase, which since the beginning of primeval times hath been used by wily Woman for the undoing of a generous-minded Man.

"Will You do this, Sir—just to please me?"

"I swear to You that it shall be done," he rejoined with passionate fervour. "But will you not let me tell you first——"

"No!—No!" she said quickly, clasping her delicate hands. "I pray You—not just yet. I—I so long to see You write ... there ... at this Desk, where lie piled letters from every illustrious Person and every crowned Head in Europe. And now You will write," she entreated, in the tone of an indulged and wayward Child. "You will? Just one little Document for me, because ... because You say You love me, and ... because ... I..."

"Barbara!" he cried in an Ecstasy of Happiness. "My Beloved!"

He was on the point of falling on his Knees, but once more a demure Gesture, a drawing back of her whole Figure, restrained him.

"No! No!" she reiterated firmly. "When you have written, I will listen——"—another Glance, and he was vanquished. Then she completed her Phrase—"to all you have to say."

He drew back with a sigh, and took up his Pen.

"As you command," he said simply, and made ready to write.

3

Even now, whene'er I close mine Eyes, I can see those twain as a vivid Picture before me. The Massive Desk, littered with papers, the Candles flickering in their Sconces, illumining with their elusive Light the Figure of the great Actor, sitting with shoulders slightly

155

bent forward, one Arm resting upon the Desk, half buried in the filmy folds of her Ladyship's Veil, his Face upturned towards the Enchantress, who held him at this Hour an absolute Slave to her Will. She had risen from her Chair and stood immediately behind him; her Face I could not see, for her back was towards me, but the light caught the loose Tendrils of her fair Hair, and from where I stood watching, this looked just like a golden Aureole around her small Head, bent slightly towards him. She too was leaning forward, over him, with her Hand extended, giving him Directions as to what he should write.

"Oh, I pray You," she said with an impatient little Sigh, "do not delay! I will watch You as You write. I pray You write it as a Message addressed to the Court of White Hall. Not in Poetry," she added, with a nervous little Laugh; "but in Prose, so that all may understand."

He bent to his task and began to write, and she straightened out her elegant Figure and murmured, as if oppressed: "How hot this room is!"

Slowly, as if in Absence of Mind, She wandered towards the Window.

"I have heard it said," she remarked, "that Mr. Betterton's worst enemy is the cold. But a fire! ... on such a glorious Evening. The first Kiss of awakening Spring."

She had reached the Window now, and stood for awhile in the Bay, leaning against the Mullion; and I could not help but admire her Duplicity and her Pluck. For, indeed, She had risked Everything that Woman holds most dear, for the sake of the Man she loved. And She could not help but know that She herself and her fair Name would anon be at the mercy of a Man whom her Cajoleries and her Trickery would have rendered desperate.

Anon, as if quite overcome by the Heat, she threw open the Casement, and then leaned out, peering into the Darkness beyond. Ensconced in my Corner at some distance from the Window, I was conscious of the Movement and subdued Noise which came up from the still crowded Park. A number of People appeared to be moving out there, and even as I strained my Ears to listen, I caught the sweet sound of the selfsame Song of awhile ago, wafted hither on the cool night Air:

"You are my Life! You ask me why?
Because my Hope is in Your Love."

I caught myself marvelling if the Ladies and Gallants of the Court had strolled out into the Park at this hour, drawn thither by

156

the amorous Melodies sung by the unknown Minstrel; or by the balmy Air of Spring; or merely by the passing Whim of some new Fashion or Fancy. I even strained my Ears so that I might recognise the sound of Voices that were familiar to me. I heard my Lord of Rochester's characteristic Laugh, Sir William Davenant's dictatorial tones and the high-pitched Cackle of Mr. Killigrew.

So doth our Mind oft dwell on trivial Thoughts at times of gravest Stress. Her Ladyship had sat down on a low Stool beside the Window. I could only see the vague outline of her—the Expression of her Face, the very Poise of her Head, were wrapt in the surrounding Gloom.

For awhile there was perfect Silence in the Room, save for the monotonous ticking of the old Clock and the scratching of Mr. Betterton's Pen as he wrote with a rapid and unhesitating Hand.

The Minutes sped on, and anon he had completed his Task. I saw him lay down his Pen, then raise the Paper and read through very carefully all that he had written, and finally strew Sand upon the momentous Document. For awhile after that he remained perfectly still, and I observed his clear-cut Face, with Eyes fixed as it were inwards into his own Soul, and sensitive Lips pressed tightly one against the other. The Hand which held the Document was perfectly steady, an obedient slave to his Will. And yet that Sign-manual, as directed by her Ladyship, was a direct Avowal of a dastardly Deed, of the gratuitous Slandering of an innocent Man's Honour, without Provocation or Justification, seeing that no mention was made in the Confession of the abominable Outrage which had brought about this grim Retaliation, or of the Refusal on the part of his Lordship to grant the Satisfaction that is customary between Gentlemen. It was, in fact, his own Integrity and his own Honour that the eminent Actor was even now bartering for a Woman's Love. This will prove to You, dear Mistress, that Mr. Betterton's Love for the Lady Barbara Wychwoode did not at any time resemble true Affection, which, of all the Passions to which the human Heart is apt to become Slave, is the one that leads the Mind to the highest and noblest Thoughts; whereas an Infatuation can only be compared to a Fever. Man hath no more control over the one than he hath over the other, and cannot curb its Violence or the Duration of its Attack.

The next thing that I remember most clearly is seeing Mr. Betterton put the fateful Paper down again, take up her Ladyship's Veil and bury his Face in its cloudy Folds. I heard him murmur faintly, after awhile:

"Now, if I dared, I would believe myself almost happy!"

Then he rose, picked up the Paper, and with it went up to the Lady Barbara.

"'Tis done, as you did command," he said quite quietly, and placed the Document in her Hand. She took it from him and rose to her Feet.

"A Light, I pray You," she said coldly.

He brought one of the Candles across and stood beside her, holding it aloft. She read the Paper through with great Deliberation, nodding Approval from time to time as she did so. Then she folded it into a very small Compass, while she thanked him coldly and guardedly. He then went back to the Desk with the Candle and put it down. During these few Seconds, whilst his back was turned to her, I noticed that the Lady Barbara took a heavy, jewelled Brooch from her Gown and fastened it by its pin to the Document. Her movements were methodical but very quick, and my own Mind worked too slowly to guess at her Intention.

The next moment, Mr. Betterton was once more by her side. Eager, alert, and with the glow of Triumph in his Eyes, he flung himself at her Feet. She was his now!—his by Right of Conquest! He had won her by measureless Self-Sacrifice, and now he meant to hold the Guerdon for which he had paid so heavy a Price.

"Because you deigned to cross this humble Threshold," he said, and his arms encircled her Waist with the masterful and passionate Gesture of a Victor, "the poor Actor places his Name and Fame, his Pride and baffled Revenge, at your feet."

"At the World's Feet, Sir Mountebank!" she cried exultantly, and with a swift movement she flung the weighted Paper far out through the Window. Then, leaning out into the Darkness, she called at the top of her Voice: "To me, Adela! Here is the Message from Mr. Betterton. Take it to my Lord Sidbury at once!"

But Mr. Betterton was no longer in a mental State to care what happened after this; I doubt if he realized just what was impending. He was still on his Knees, holding on to her with both Arms.

"Nay!" he said wildly. "That is as You please. Let the whole

World think me base and abject. What care I for Honour, Fame or Integrity now that You are here, and that You will be my Wife?"

Ah! the poor, deluded Fool! How could he be so blind? Already the Lady Barbara had turned on him with flashing Eyes, and a loud, hysterical Laugh of measureless Contempt broke from her Lips.

"Your Wife!" she exclaimed, and that harsh laugh echoed through the Silence of the House. "So, Mr. Actor, you thought to entrap the Daughter of the Marquis of Sidbury into becoming your Wife! ... Nay! you miserable Fool! 'Twas I entrapped and cheated you.... Your Wife! Ye Saints in Heaven, hear him! His Wife! The Wife of Thomas Betterton, the Mountebank!! I!!!"

Her Words, her Laughter, the Bitterness of her Contempt, stung him like a Whip-lash. In an instant, he was on his Feet, staggered back till he came in contact with the Desk, to which he clung with both hands, while he faced her, his Cheeks pale as Ashes, his Eyes glowing with a Light that appeared almost maniacal.

"You cheated me?" he murmured inarticulately. "You lied to me? ... You ... I'll not believe it ... I'll not believe it...."

She appeared not to heed him, was gazing out of the Window, shouting directions to some one—her waiting-maid, no doubt, or other Confidante—who was searching for the Paper down below.

"There, Adela!" she called out eagerly. "Dost see ... just by those bushes ... something white ... my brooch.... Dost see?"

Suddenly she gave a Cry of Triumph, and then turned back exultantly to her baffled Foe.

"My maid," she said, somewhat wildly, and panting as if she were exhausted with fast running. "We had planned it all ... She is devoted to me ... She has been on the Watch ... She has the paper now ... There!" she added, and with outstretched arm pointed out into the Gloom beyond. "There; Do you see?"

Can You wonder that her Trickery, her Contempt had made him mad? Indeed, even I felt that at that moment I could have held her slender throat between my two Hands and crushed the Life out of her. To a Man of Mr. Betterton's temperament, the Provocation was obviously beyond his Powers of Endurance. Even in the dim Light, I could see a positive Fury of Passion akin to Hate literally distorting his Face. The next second he was once more by her side, and whilst she still cried wildly: "Do you see? Do you see? Run, Adela, run!" he seized her in his arms and retorted roughly:

"I see nothing now but your Beauty, and that has made me mad."

"Run, Adela! Run!" she cried again. "That message from Mr. Betterton is for the whole World to see!"

But he held her tightly round the Shoulders now, and she, probably realizing her Danger for the first time, strove to struggle against his Embrace.

"Let me go!" she commanded. "Let me go! or I swear by God in Heaven that I will find the Strength to kill myself and You."

"I love You," was his only reply to her Threat. "Nay!" he added, speaking in rapid, jerky Phrases, the while she continued to struggle with ever growing loss of Power. "You shall kill me later if You will, but not till I have lived. My Dear, my Love, my Saint! Have I not worshipped you for days and months? Have I not held You in Dream in my Arms? You are my Muse, my Divinity, my Hope! Mine! Mine! Exquisite, adorable Lady Barbara! No! No! You cannot escape, struggle how You might. This is my hour! 'Tis you who gave it me, and I defy Heaven itself to rob me of a single instant!"

My God! what could I do? More and more did I curse the Folly and Cowardice which had kept me riveted to this Spot all this while. Now there was nothing for it but to reveal my Presence, to draw upon my foolish Head the Contempt and Anger of a Man for whom I would gladly have laid down my Life. My Brain became confused. I ceased to see clearly. A ruddy Mist was gathering before my Eyes. I was on the Verge of losing Consciousness and was struggling pitifully to retain Command over my Senses. Through this fast approaching Swoon I could hear, as through an intervening Veil, the hoarse and broken Accents of the Voice that I loved so well:

"You are here alone with me. The last shred of my Reason is scattered to the Winds. England, Fame, the World, are empty Words to me. Do you not see that now I am ready to die an hundred Deaths, for at last I shall have lived ... I shall have held You in my Arms."

And one great and pitiful Appeal from her Lips: "Oh, God! If there is Justice in Heaven—defend me now——"

And, even half conscious as I was, I saw her—yes, saw her quite distinctly give a sudden wrench which freed her right Arm. She plunged her Hand into the bosom of her Gown, and the next instant the flickering light of the Candle flashed a vivid gleam upon the narrow steel blade of a dagger which she held. This, with the swiftness of lightning, brought me back to the Consciousness of the present, grim Reality. With a loud and sudden Cry, I darted out of my Hiding Place and stood there before them both, pale no doubt with a well-nigh unearthly Pallor, which must have given me the Appearance of a Ghost.

It was now the Lady Barbara who was nigh to Swooning. But, with that coolness which comes at times to the Helpless and the Weak, I had already snatched her Veil from the Desk, and whilst she tottered and almost fell into my Arms, I wrapped it around her Head.

"Quick! The Door!" I said. "You are quite safe!"

I dared not look at Mr. Betterton. Indeed, I could not even now tell You in what Attitude or with what Expression of Face he watched me whilst I seemed thus to take Command of the Situation. The Lady Barbara was trembling so violently that some few moments elapsed before she was able to walk across the Room. When she finally did so, her Foot kicked against the Dagger which had dropped from her Hand when I so suddenly appeared before her. She gave a faint Cry of Horror, and I stooped and picked up the Dagger and placed it back in her Hand without looking at her.

5

Her Ladyship then went on towards the door. But suddenly she came to a halt, and I, who was close to her heels, paused likewise, for I felt that every drop of Blood within me had turned to Ice. From the Hall below there had come the sound of angry Altercation and a Man's voice was raised loudly and peremptorily, saying:

"Let me pass, man! I will speak with Mr. Betterton."

The voice was that of my Lord Stour.

The Lady Barbara stood quite still for a moment, rigid as a carved Statue. Then a low, inexpressibly pathetic Moan rose to her Lips.

"Oh! for the Earth to open!" she cried pitiably, "and bury me and this Shame——"

She was overwrought and weak with Emotion, but in any Event it was a terrible Position for any Lady of Rank to be found in, at this late hour, and alone. Overcome no doubt with the superabundance of harrowing Sensations, she tottered as if about to swoon. Mr. Betterton caught her as she fell.

"My Divinity! My Queen!" he murmured quickly. "No one shall harm you, I swear it! No one shall!" Then he added under his breath: "Heaven above me, help me to protect her!"

Whereupon he lifted her up in his Arms as if she were a Child, and carried her as far as the Embrasure of the Window. Then, with one of those quick movements which were so characteristic of him, he drew the Curtains together, which shut off the Bay from the rest of the Room and screened its fair Occupant completely from view.

He was a different Man now to the Passion-racked Creature of awhile ago; absolutely calm; the Man I had known and loved and respected all these years. Though my whole Being was still convulsed in an Agony of Apprehension, I felt that from him now would come moral Comfort for me and Protection for the unfortunate Lady, whose Burden of Sorrow had at last touched his Heart. And I do verily believe, dear Lady, that in that Instant of supreme Danger for us all, his Passion fell from him like a Curtain from before his Eyes. It had gone through its culminating Anguish when he discovered that she whom he loved had lied to him and cheated him. Now, when she stood here before him, utterly helpless and utterly crushed, his Infatuation appeared to writhe for one Moment in the Crucible of his own Manliness and Chivalry, and then to emerge therefrom hallowed and purified.

6

In the meanwhile, less than a minute had elapsed. My Lord Stour had ascended the Stairs, undeterred by the Protestations of Mr. Betterton's Servant. The next moment he had violently wrenched the Door open and now stood before us, pale, trembling with Rage or Excitement, hatless, his Mantle thrown back from his Shoulders. His right Hand clutched his naked Sword, and in his Left he had a crushed ball of paper, held together by her Ladyship's brooch. His entire Attitude was one of firm and deadly Menace.

"I heard a Voice!" he exclaimed, staring wildly around him. "I saw a Face—a Form.... This Paper was flung out from yonder Window ... was picked up by a serving Wench.... What does it mean?" he queried harshly, and advanced threateningly towards Mr. Betterton, who was standing midway between him and the curtained Bay.

"How can I tell?" riposted the great Actor blandly, with a careless Shrug of his Shoulders. "I was not moon-gazing, as your Lordship appears to have done. A paper, did You say?"

"You are not alone," retorted my Lord roughly. "I heard a voice ... just now...."

"We are all apt to hear voices in the moonlight, my Lord," Mr. Betterton rejoined simply. "The Artist hears his Muse, the Lover his Mistress, the Criminal his Conscience."

162

His unruffled calm seemed to exasperate his Lordship's fury, for he now appeared even more menacing than before.

"And did You perchance hear a Voice to-night, Sir Actor," he queried, his voice hoarse with Passion, "warning You of Death?"

"Nay!" replied Mr. Betterton. "That Voice whispers to Us all, and always, my Lord, even in our Cradles."

"Then hear it for the last time now, and from my Lips, you abominable Mountebank!" my Lord cried, beside himself in truth. "For unless You draw aside that Curtain, I am going to kill You."

"That is as you please," retorted Mr. Betterton simply.

"Stand aside!" commanded his Lordship.

But Mr. Betterton looked him calmly up and down and did not move one inch.

"This is a most unwarrantable Interference," he said quietly, "with the Freedom of His Majesty's well-beloved Servant. Your Lordship seems to forget that every inch of this Floor is mine, and that I stand on it where I please. I pray you, take that Paper—that Message—elsewhere. An it came down from Heaven, read it—but leave me in Peace."

"I'll not go," asserted my Lord harshly, "till you have drawn aside that Curtain."

"Then we'll see whose Legs will weary first, my Lord, yours or mine," was Mr. Betterton's unruffled rejoinder.

"Draw then and defend yourself!" cried my Lord, who before his Enemy's unbroken Calm, had lost what Semblance of Self-Control he still possessed.

"I am unarmed," riposted Mr. Betterton simply.

"Then let Satan have his due," exclaimed the young Hothead, and raised his Sword ready to strike, "for your Soul shall go down to Hell at last!"

In a moment, of course, I was on him. But he had the vigour of a trained Soldier, enhanced by an overwhelming Passion of Enmity and of Rage; and though I seized him unawares—I doubt if he had realized that I was in the Room—he shook me off in an instant, as a Dog might shake off an importunate Rat. Before I had time to recover my breath from his quick and furious Defence, he had turned on me and dealt me such a vigorous Blow with his Fist between the Eyes, that the whole Room began to gyrate around me and the Atmosphere became peopled with Stars. I staggered and half fell against the Dresser that had sheltered me awhile ago. For the space of half a dozen seconds mine Eyes were closed.

When I opened them again, the Scene had indeed changed. Her Ladyship had pushed the Curtains aside and stood there in the window Embrasure, revealed to her irate Lover. And he, though he must have known that she was there all the Time, appeared so staggered by her Apparition that his Arm dropped by his side and his Sword fell with a clatter to the Ground, while he murmured as if in the last Throes of mental Suffering:

"Barbara ... my Barbara .. here—alone—at night ... with this Man!..."

Her Ladyship, however, appeared perfectly composed. The light of the Candles revealed her exquisite Face, pale but serene, and her small Head crowned with the Aureole of her golden Hair, held up proudly as one who hath naught to fear, naught for which she need be ashamed. She pointed with perfect steadiness to the Paper which my Lord still held tightly clasped in his left Hand.

"That paper!" she said, and only a slight veiling of her Voice betrayed the Emotion which she felt. "I sent it. 'Tis for you, my Lord. It will clear your Honour, and proclaim your Innocence."

But his Lordship did not appear to hear her. He continued to murmur to himself mechanically, and in tones of the deepest Despair:

"Barbara ... alone ... with him!"

"Read that Paper, my dear Lord," her Ladyship insisted with calm dignity, "ere with another Thought you further dare to wrong me!"

These simple Words, however, so full of conscious Worth and of Innocence, let loose the Floodgates of my Lord's pent-up, insensate jealousy.

"Wrong you!" he cried, and a harsh, almost maniacal laugh broke from his choking Throat. "Wrong you! Nay! I suppose I must be grateful and thank Heaven on my Knees that You, my promised Bride, deigned to purchase mine Honour at the Price of your Kisses!"

At this gross Insult her Ladyship uttered a pitiful Moan; but ere she could give Reply, Mr. Betterton, who hitherto had not interfered between the Twain, now did so, and in no measured Tone.

"Silence, Madman!" he commanded, "ere You blaspheme."

But my Lord had apparently lost his last Shred of Reason. Jealousy was torturing him in a manner that even Hatred had failed to do.

"God!" he exclaimed repeatedly, calling to the Almighty to witness his Soul-Misery. "I saw her at that Window.... Who else saw her?... How many Varlets and jabbering Coxcombs know at the present moment that the Lady Barbara Wychwoode spends the night alone with a Mountebank?" In an excess of ungoverned Rage he tore the Paper to shreds and threw the Scraps almost into her Ladyship's Face. "Take back your Proofs!" he cried. "I'll not take mine Honour from Your hands! Ah!" he added, and now turned once more toward Mr. Betterton, who, I could see, was calmly making up his Mind what next to do. "Whoever you are—Man or Devil—are you satisfied with your Revenge? Was it not enough to cover me with Infamy; what need had You to brand Her with Dishonour?"

Overcome with Emotion, his Soul on the Rack, his Heart wounded and bleeding, he appeared like a lost Spirit crying out from an Abyss of Torment. But these last Ravings of his, these final, abominable Insults, levelled against the Woman who had done so much for him, and whom he should have been the first to protect, lashed Mr. Betterton's ire and contempt into holy Fury.

"Ye gods in Heaven, hear him!" he cried, with an outburst of Rage at least as great as that of the other Man. "He loves her, and talks of Dishonour, whilst I love her and only breathe of Worship! By all the Devils in Hell, my Lord Stour, I tell you that you lie!"

And before any of us there realized what he meant to do, he ran to the Window, threw open all the Casements with such violence that the glass broke and fell clattering down upon the gravelled place below.

"Hallo!" he called in a stentorian Voice. "Hallo, there!"

My Lord Stour, bewildered, un-understanding, tried to bluster.

"What are you doing, man?" he queried roughly. "Silence! Silence, I say!"

But Mr. Betterton only shouted the louder.

"Hallo, there! Friends! Enemies! England! Here!"

I could hear the Tumult outside. People were running hither from several directions, thinking, no doubt, that a Fire had broken out or that Murder was being done. I could hear them assembling beneath the window, which was not many feet from the Ground. "Why! it's Tom Betterton!" some of them said. And others added: "Hath he gone raving mad?"

"Is any one there who knows me?" queried Mr. Betterton loudly.

"Yes! Yes!" was the ready response.

"Who is it?" he asked, peering into the darkness below.

I heard Sir William Davenant's voice give reply.

"Killigrew and I are down here, Tom. What in the Name of — — is the matter?"

"Come round to my rooms, Davenant," Mr. Betterton replied; "and bring as many friends with you as you can."

He was standing in the Bay of the Window, and his Figure, silhouetted against the Light in the Room, must have been plainly visible to the crowd outside. That a number of People had assembled by now was apparent by the Hum and Hubbub which came to us from below. Unable to restrain my Curiosity, I too approached the open Casements and peered out into the Gloom. Just as I thought, quite a Crowd had collected down there, some of whom were making ready to climb up to the Window by way of the Gutter-pipes or the solid stems of the Ivy, whilst others were trooping down the narrow little Alley which connects Tothill Street with the Park at the base of Mr. Betterton's house. There was a deal of talking, laughing and shouting. "Tom Betterton is up to some Prank," I heard more than one Person say.

8

Perhaps You will wonder what was my Lord's Attitude during the few minutes—it was less than five—which elapsed between the Instant when Mr. Betterton first threw open the Casements, and that when the Crowd, headed by Sir William Davenant and Mr. Killigrew, trooped down the Alley on their Way to this House. To me he seemed at first wholly uncomprehending, like a Man who has received a Blow on the Head—just as I did from his Fist a moment ago—and before whose Eyes the Walls of the Room, the Furniture, the People, are all swimming in an Ocean of Stars. I imagine that at one time the Thought flashed as Lightning through his Mind that this was but the culminating Outrage, wherewith his Enemy meant to pillory him and his Bride before a jeering Public. That was the moment when he turned to her Ladyship and, uttering a hoarse Cry, called to her by Name. She was, just then, leaning in semi-consciousness against the Angle of the Bay. She did not respond to his Call, and Mr. Betterton, quick in his Movements, alert now like some Feline on the prowl, stepped immediately in front of Her, facing my Lord and screening Her against his Approach.

"Stand back, Man," he commanded. "Stand back, I tell You!

You shall not come nigh Her save on bended Knees, with Head bowed in the Dust, suing for Pardon in that you dared to Insult her."

Everything occurred so quickly, Movements, Events, High Words, threatening Gestures from both sides, followed one another in such rapid Succession, that I, overcome with Agitation and the Effect of the stunning Blow which I had received, was hardly able to take it all in. Much less is it in my Power to give You a faithful Account of it all. Those five Minutes were the most spirit-stirring ones I have ever experienced throughout my Life—every Second appeared surcharged with an exciting Fluid which transported Me to supernal Regions, to Lands of Unrealities akin to vivid Dreams.

At one Moment, I remember seeing my Lord Stour make a rapid and furtive movement in the direction of his Sword, which lay some little Distance from him on the Ground, but Mr. Betterton was quicker even than his Foe, more alert, and with one bound he had reached the Weapon, ere my Lord's Hand was nigh it, had picked it up and, with a terrific Jerk, broke it in half across his Knee. Then he threw the mangled Hilt in one direction, the Point in another, and my Lord raised his Fists, ready, methinks, to fly at his Throat.

But, as I have already told You, dear Mistress, the whole Episode stands but as a confused Mirage before my Mind; and through it all I seemed to see a mere Vision of her Ladyship, pale and ethereal, leaning against the Angle of the Bay; one delicate Hand was clutching the heavy Curtain, drawing it around her as it were, as if in a pathetic and futile Desire to shield herself from view.

CHAPTER XVI

THE GAME OF LOVE

1

In the meanwhile, the Crowd all round the House had visibly swelled. Some People were still standing immediately beneath the Bow-window, whilst Others swarmed into Tothill Street; the foremost amongst the Latter had given a vigorous Tug at the Bell-pull, and the front Door being opened for them by the bewildered

Servant, they had made a noisy Irruption into the House. We could hear them clattering up the Stairs, to the Accompaniment of much Laughing and Talking, and the oft-reiterated Refrain: "Tom Betterton is up to some Prank! Hurrah!"

Some few again, more venturesome and certainly more Impudent than most, had indeed succeeded in scrambling up to the Window, and, one after another, Heads and Shoulders began to appear in the Framework of the open Casements.

Her Ladyship had no doubt realized from the first that Escape became impossible, within two Minutes of Mr. Betterton's first Summons to the Public. Just at first, perhaps, if my Lord had preserved his entire Presence of Mind, he might have taken her by the Hand and fled with Her out of the House, before the unruly Crowd had reached Tothill Street. But my Lord, blinded by jealous Rage, had not thought of Her quickly enough, and now the Time was past, and he remained impotent, gasping with Fury, hardly conscious of his Actions. He had been literally swept off his Feet by Mr. Betterton's eagle-winged coup de main, which left him puzzled and the prey to a nameless Terror as to what was about to follow.

Now, when he saw a number of Gentlemen trooping in by the Door, he could but stare at them in utter Bewilderment. Most of these Gallants were personally known to him: Sir William Davenant was in the forefront with Mr. Thomas Killigrew of the King's Theatre, and the Earl of Rochester was with them, as well as Mr. Wycherley. I also recognized Sir Charles Sedley and old Sir John Denham, as well as my Lord Roscommon, among the crowd.

They had all rushed in through the Door, laughing and jesting, as was the wont of all these gay and courtly Sparks; but at sight of the Lady Barbara, they halted. Gibes and unseemly Jokes broke upon their Lips, and for the most part their Hands went up to their Hats, and they made her Ladyship a deep obeisance. Indeed, just then she looked more like a Wraith than a living Woman, and the Light of the Candles, which flickered wildly in the Draught, accentuated the Weirdness of her Appearance.

"What is it, Tom? What is amiss?" Sir William Davenant was thus the first to speak.

"We thought You were playing some Prank."

"You did call from that Window, did You not, Tom?" my Lord Rochester insisted.

And one or two of the Gentlemen nodded somewhat coldly to my Lord Stour.

"Yes. I did call," Mr. Betterton replied, quite firmly. "But 'twas no Whim on my Part thus to drag You into my House. It was not so much my Voice that you heard as the Trumpet blast of Truth."

At this, my Lord Stour broke into one of those harsh, mirthless Fits of Laughter which betokened the perturbation of his Spirit.

"The Truth!" he exclaimed with a cutting Sneer. "From You?"

"Aye! the Truth!" Mr. Betterton rejoined with perfect calm, even whilst his Friends glanced, puzzled and inquiring, from my Lord Stour to him, and thence to her Ladyship's pale face, and even to Me. "The Truth," he added with a deep Sigh as of intense Relief; "The Truth, at Last!"

He stood in the centre of the Room, with one Hand resting upon the Desk, his Eyes fixed fearlessly upon the Sea of Faces before him. Not the slightest Tremor marred the perfect Harmony of his Voice, or the firm poise of his manly Figure. You know as well as I do, dear Mistress, the marvellous Magnetism of Mr. Betterton's Personality, the Way he hath of commanding the Attention of a Crowd, whenever he chooseth to speak. Think of him then, dear Lady, with Head thrown back, his exquisite Voice rising and falling in those subtle and impressive Cadences wherewith he is wont to hold an Audience enthralled. Of a truth, no experienced Manager in Stage-Craft could have devised so thrilling an Effect, as the Picture which Mr. Betterton—the greatest Actor of this or of any Time— presented at that Moment, standing alone, facing the Crowd which was thrilled into deadly Silence, and with the wraith-like Figure of that exquisitely beautiful Woman as a Foil to his own self-possessed, virile Appearance.

"Gentlemen," he began, with slow, even Emphasis, "I pray you bear with me; for what I have to say will take some time in telling. Awhile ago his Lordship of Stour put upon me such an Insult as the Mind of Man can hardly conceive. Then, on the Pretence that I was not a born Gentleman as he was, he refused me Satisfaction by the Sword. For this I hated him and swore that I would be even with him, that I would exact from his Arrogance, Outrage for Outrage, and Infamy for Infamy." He then turned to my Lord Stour and spoke to him directly. "You asked me just now, my Lord, if my Revenge was satisfied. My answer to that is: not yet! Not until I see You on Your bended Knees here, before these Gentlemen—my Friends and Yours—receiving from the miserable Mountebank whom you mocked, the pitiful cur whom You thrashed, that which you hold—or should hold—more precious than all the Treasures of this earth: your Honour and the good Name of the Lady who honours You with her Love! Gentlemen!" he went on, and once more faced the Crowd. "You know the Aspersions which have been cast on my Lord Stour's Loyalty. Rumours have been current that the late aborted Conspiracy was betrayed by him to the Countess of

Castlemaine, and that She obtained his Pardon, whilst all or most of his Associates were driven into Exile or perished on the Scaffold. Well, Gentlemen, 'twas I who begged for my Lord's pardon from the Countess of Castlemaine. His Degradation, his Obloquy, was the Revenge which I had studiously planned. Nay! I pray you, hear me unto the End," he continued, as a loud Murmur of Horror and of Indignation followed on this Self-Accusation. "My Lord Stour is no Traitor, save to Her whom he loves and whom in his Thoughts he hath dared to outrage. The Lady Barbara Wychwoode deigned to plead with me for the Man whom she honoured with her Love. She pleaded with me this afternoon, in the Park, in sight of many Passers-by; but I in my Obstinacy and Arrogance would not, God forgive me, listen to her."

He paused, and I could see the beads of Perspiration glittering upon his Forehead, white now like Italian Alabaster. They all stood before him, subdued and silent. Think of Sir William Davenant, dear Mistress, and his affection for Mr. Betterton; think of my Lord Roscommon and of Sir Charles Sedley and his Lordship of Rochester, whose Admiration for Mr. Betterton's Talent was only equalled by their Appreciation for His Worth! It was before them all, before all these fastidious Gentlemen, that the great and sensitive Artist had elected to humble his Pride to the dust.

But you shall judge.

"Gentlemen," Mr. Betterton went on after a brief while; "We all know that Love is a Game at which one always cheats. I loved the Lady Barbara Wychwoode. I had the presumption to dream of her as my future Wife. Angered at her Scorn of my Suit, I cheated her into coming here to-night, luring her with the Hope that I would consent to right the Man for whose sake she was willing to risk so much, for whom she was ready to sacrifice even her fair Name. Now I have learned to my hurt that Love, the stern little god, will not be trifled with. When we try to cheat him, he cheats us worse at the last; and if he makes Kings of us, he leaves us Beggars in the End. When my Lord Stour, burning with sacrilegious jealousy, made irruption into my Room, the Lady Barbara had just succeeded in wringing from me an Avowal which proclaimed his Integrity and my Shame. She was about to leave me, humbled and crushed in my Pride, she herself pure and spotless as the Lilies, unapproachable as the Stars."

Mr. Betterton had ceased speaking for some time; nevertheless, Silence profound reigned in the dark, wainscotted Room for many seconds after the final echo of that perfect Voice had ceased to reverberate. Indeed, dear Mistress, I can assure You that, though there were at least fifty Persons present in the Room, including those unknown to Me who were swarming around the Framework of the Casements, you might have heard the proverbial Pin drop just then. A tense Expression rested on every Face. Can You wonder that I scanned them all with the Eagerness born of my Love for the great Artist, who had thus besmirched his own fair Name in order to vindicate that of his bitterest Foe? That I read Condemnation of my Friend in many a Glance, I'll not deny, and this cut me to the Quick.

True! Mr. Betterton's Scheme of Vengeance had been reprehensible if measured by the high Standards of Christian Forbearance. But remember how he had been wronged, not once, but repeatedly; and even when I saw the Frown on my Lord Roscommon's brow, the Look of Stern Reproof in Sir Charles Sedley's Face, there arose before mine Eyes the Vision of the great and sensitive Artist, of the high-souled Gentleman, staggering beneath the Blows dealt by a band of hired Ruffians at the Bidding of this young Coxcomb, whose very Existence was as naught in the Eyes of the cultured World beside the Genius of the inimitable Mr. Betterton.

I said that the Silence was tense. Meseemed that no one dared to break it. Even those idly Curious who had swarmed up the Rainpipes of this House in order to witness one of Tom Betterton's Pranks, felt awed by the Revelation of this Drama of a great Man's Soul. Indeed, the Silence became presently oppressive. I, for one, felt a great Buzzing in mine Ears. The Lights from the Candles assumed weird and phantasmagoric Proportions till they seared my aching Eyes.

Then slowly my Lord Stour approached her Ladyship, sank on his Knees before Her and raised the Hem of her Robe to his Lips. A sob broke from her Throat; she tried to smother it by pressing her Handkerchief into her Mouth. It took Her a second or two to regain her Composure. But Breeding and Pride came to her Aid. I saw the stiffening of her Figure, the studied and deliberate Movement wherewith She readjusted her Mantle and her Veil.

My Lord Stour was still on his Knees. At a sign from her

Ladyship he rose. He held out his left Arm and she placed her right Hand on it, then together they went out of the Room. The Crowd of Gentlemen parted in order to make way for the Twain, then when they had gone through, some of the Gentlemen followed them immediately; others lingered for awhile, hesitating. Sir William Davenant, Mr. Killigrew, my Lord Rochester, all of Mr. Betterton's Friends, appeared at first inclined to remain in order to speak with him. They even did me the Honour of consulting me with a Look, asking of my Experience of the great Actor whether they should stay. I slowly shook my Head, and they wisely acted on my Advice. I knew that my Friend would wish to be alone. He, so reserved, so proud, had laid his Soul bare before the Public, who was wont to belaud and to applaud him. The Humiliation and the Effort must have been a terrible Strain, which only Time and Solitude could effectually cure.

He had scarce moved from his Position beside the Desk, still stood there with one slender Hand resting upon it, his Gaze fixed vaguely upon the Door through which his Friends were slowly filing out.

Within two minutes or less after the Departure of my Lord Stour and her Ladyship, the last of the Crowd of Gentlemen and of Idlers had gone. Anon I went across the Room and closed the Door behind them. When I turned again, I saw that the knot of quidnuncs no longer filled the Casements, and a protracted hum of Voices, a crackling of Ivy twigs and general sound of Scrimmage and of Scrambling outside the Window, proclaimed the Fact that even they had had the Sense and the Discretion to retire quietly from this Spot, hallowed by the Martyrdom of a great Man's Soul.

3

Thus I was left alone with my Friend.

He had drawn his habitual Chair up to the Desk and sat down. Just for a few Moments he rested both his Elbows on the Desk and buried his Face in his Hands. Then, with that familiar, quick little Sigh of His, He drew the Candles closer to him and, taking up a Book, he began to read.

I knew what it was that he was reading, or, rather, studying. He had been absorbed in the Work many a time before now, and had expressed his ardent Desire to give public Readings of it one

172

day when it was completed. It was the opening Canto of a great Epic Poem, the manuscript of which had been entrusted to Mr. Betterton for Perusal by the author, Mr. John Milton, who had but lately been liberated from prison through the untiring Efforts of Sir William Davenant on his behalf. Mr. Milton hoped to complete the Epic in the next half-dozen years. Its Title is "Paradise Lost."

I remained standing beside the open Window, loath to close it as the Air was peculiarly soft and refreshing. Below me, in the Park, the idle, chattering Crowd had already dispersed. From far away, I still could hear the sweet, sad Strains of the amorous Song, and through the Stillness of the Evening, the Words came to mine Ear, wafted on the Breeze:

> "You are my Faith, my Hope, my All!
> What e'er the Future may unfold,
> No trial too great—no Thing too small.
> Your whispered Words shall make me bold
> To win at last for Your dear Sake
> A worthy Place in Future's World."

I felt my Soul enwrapt in a not unpleasant reverie; an exquisite Peace seemed to have descended on my Mind, lately so agitated by Thoughts of my dear, dear Friend.

Suddenly a stealthy Sound behind Me caused me to turn; and, in truth, I am not sure even now if what I saw was Reality, or the Creation of mine own Dreams.

The Lady Barbara had softly and surreptitiously re-entered the Room. She walked across it on tip-toe, her silken Skirts making just the softest possible frou-frou as she walked. Her cloud-like Veil wrapped her Head entirely, concealing her fair Hair, and casting a grey Shadow over her Eyes. Mr. Betterton did not hear her, or, if he did, he did not choose to look up. When her Ladyship was quite close to the Desk, I noticed that she had a Bunch of white Roses in her Hand such as are grown in the Hot-houses of rich Noblemen.

For a few Seconds she stood quite still. Then she raised the Roses slowly to her Lips, and laid them down without a word upon the Desk.

After which, she glided out of the Room as silently, as furtively, as she came.

And thus, dear Mistress, have I come to the end of my long Narrative. I swear to You by the living God that everything which I have herein related is the Truth and Naught but the Truth.

There were many People present in Mr. Betterton's room during that memorable Scene, when he sacrificed his Pride and his Revenge in order to right the Innocent. Amongst these Witnesses there were some, whom Malice and Envy would blind to the Sublimity of so noble an Act. Do not listen to them, honoured Mistress, but rather to the promptings of your own Heart and to that unerring Judgment of Men and of Events which is the Attribute of good and pure Women.

Mr. Betterton hath never forfeited your Esteem by any Act or Thought. The Infatuation which momentarily dulled his Vision to all save to the Beauty of the Lady Barbara, hath ceased to exist. Its course was ephemeral and hath gone without a Trace of Regret or Bitterness in its wake. The eminent Actor, the high-souled Artist, whom all cultured Europe doth reverence and admire, stands as high to-day in that same World's Estimation as he did, before a young and arrogant Coxcomb dared to measure his own Worth against that of a Man as infinitely above him as are the Stars. But, dear Mistress, Mr. Betterton now is lonely and sad. He is like a Man who hath been sick and weary, and is still groping after Health and Strength. Take pity on his Loneliness, I do conjure You. Give him back the inestimable Boon of your Goodwill and of your Friendship, which alone could restore to him that Peace of Mind so necessary for the furtherance of his Art.

And if, during the Course of my Narrative, I have seemed to you over-presumptuous, then I do entreat your Forgiveness. Love for my Friend and Reverence for your Worth have dictated every Word which I have written. If, through my Labours, I have succeeded in turning away some of the just Anger which had possessed your Soul against the Man whom, I dare aver, you still honour with your Love, then, indeed, I shall feel that even so insignificant a Life as mine hath not been wholly wasted.

I do conclude, dear and honoured Mistress, with a Prayer to Almighty God for your Welfare and that of the Man whom I love best in all the World. I am convinced that my Prayer will find Favour before the Throne of Him who is the Father of us All. And He who reads the innermost Secrets of every Heart, knows that your

Welfare is coincident with that of my Friend. Thus am I content to leave the Future in His Hands.

And I myself do remain, dear Mistress,
Your humble and obedient Servant,
JOHN HONEYWOOD

EPILOGUE

Ring down the Curtain. The Play is ended. The Actors have made their final Bow before You and thanked You for your Plaudits. The chief Player—a sad and lonely Man—has for the nonce spoken his last upon the Stage.

All is Silence and Mystery now. The Lights are out. And yet the Audience lingers on, loath to bid Farewell to the great Artist and to his minor Satellites who have helped to wile away a few pleasant Hours. You, dear Public, knowing so much about them, would wish to know more. You wish to know—an I am not mistaken—whether the Labour of Love wrought by good Master Honeywood did in due course bear its Fruitfulness. You wish to know—or am I unduly self-flattered—whether the Play of Passion, of Love and of Revenge, set by the worthy Clerk before You, had an Epilogue—one that would satisfy your Sense of Justice and of Mercy.

Then, I pray You, turn to the Pages of History, of which Master Honeywood's Narrative forms an integral and pathetic Part. One of these Pages will reveal to You that which You wish to know. Thereon You will see recorded the Fact that, after a brief and distinguished Visit during that Summer to the City and University of Stockholm, where Honours without number were showered upon the great English Actor, Mr. Betterton came back to England, to the delight of an admiring Public, for he was then in the very Plenitude of his Powers.

Having read of the Artist's triumph, I pray You then to turn over the Page of the faithful Chronicle of his Career, and here You will find a brief Chapter which deals with his private Life and with his Happiness. You will see that at the End of this self-same year 1662, the Register of St. Giles', Cripplegate, contains the Record of a Marriage between Thomas Betterton, Actor, of the parish of St.

Margaret's, Westminster, and Mary Joyce Saunderson, of the aforesaid parish of St. Giles'.

That this Marriage was an exceptionally happy one we know from innumerable Data, Minutes and Memoranda supplied by Downes and others; that Master John Honeywood was present at the Ceremony itself we may be allowed to guess. Those of us who understand and appreciate the artistic Temperament, will readily agree with the worthy Clerk when he said that it cannot be judged by ordinary Standards. The long and successful Careers of Thomas Betterton and of Mistress Saunderson his Wife testify to the Fact that their Art in no way suffered, while their Souls passed through the fiery Ordeal of Passion and of Sorrow; but rather that it became ennobled and purified, until they themselves took their place in the Heart and Memory of the cultured World, among the Immortals.

THE END